Voices of Fear

by

Sherie L. Howard

To Donna –
my friend, my sister,
and
my *only* reason to question science

Chapter 1

I learned at an early age that everything could be taken away with the push of a button. The U-Haul parked on Lorman Street in Motor City was just a symbol, just a reminder that nothing was sacred – not kindergarten friends, not a German shepherd that had slept with me since I was two, and not being able to choose which toys got to go and which toys were left behind – unless you were my little sister, then favorite toys would be boxed, and laps would be shared. She was almost two when we moved; I was six. And, being allowed to exist was the biggest gift I received in my childhood. My namesake had left a trail of rubble and debris and carried with it the guilt of destroying everything it came in contact with. And the images of destruction, instantaneous death, and historical references would follow me into my adult years.

My name is Enola May Fears. My mom chose not to name me before or after my birth, still recovering from childbirth and too bitter about the fact that I existed. My dad thought it was appropriate to name me after a story on the front page of the *Detroit Press,* which lay crinkled next to the hospital bed, which recapped events that had happened in previous years on that same day – the sixth day of August – which in turn defined who I was. Everything about me was discarded and vaporized into nothingness from the moment I filled the hospital delivery room with my very first cry. My world felt hollow from my earliest memory. The U-Haul landed in Asheville, North Carolina, where sharing the history of my name reminded me that I was an unwanted child born into a damaged world.

"My name is Enola May Fears," my then six-year-old voice said, as I adjusted my weight from one leg to the other. After each sentence, I searched the other six and seven-year-old eyes for any sign of judgment, something I had become good at recognizing by that point in my life, something I was so used to receiving. But instead, the young eyes in the first-grade classroom listened openly. "My parents didn't plan to have me; I was an accident." I could see the eyes become more interested as I stumbled for words. "I was born on the sixth of August in 1961." I stopped to catch my breath, to make sure I wasn't crying, at least not on the outside. "My dad said that was exactly sixteen years after the first atomic bomb was dropped." Several of the boys in the class were already raising their hands. "I was named after the plane that dropped that bomb." I had heard my dad tell the story hundreds, maybe thousands of times.

You're lucky we didn't name you Enola Gay, exactly like the plane. I can still hear him in my thoughts, laughing every time he told the story. *You're lucky your mom let me use the M from her first name in your middle name.* He'd always finish the story with more laughter. Then he'd look in my mother's direction searching for a smile that was never there. Never.

When my mother's mom died, unexpectedly, the U-Haul appeared, ripping up and tearing apart everything in its path: friends, pets, schools, and then mountains as it effortlessly made its way to Asheville. That's where Alma had lived, the grandmother I had only met once, when she visited Detroit, the one whose middle name I would never learn. What I had learned, was that my mother, Melantha Lou Fears was only twenty when she had me, and my father Dacey Sherman Fears hadn't reached twenty-two. I also knew my mom left home when she was a teenager, moving from Asheville to Detroit; she never shared why. She had a lot of secrets underneath the pain and suffering on her face, and I just made it worse. A baby in Motor City wasn't easy for any couple in 1961. They constantly reminded me I was an accident – an explosive device that had radiated their world like Little Boy had done to Hiroshima when it dropped from the belly of the Enola Gay. By the time I was six years old, I had studied my name forward and backward. Enola was *alone* spelled backward. I didn't discover that by myself. That was another announcement Dacey Sherman Fears would routinely make in front of strangers, so I would feel abandoned, so I would remember I was a genetic hazard, unlike my baby sister. She had a beautiful name, one that reminded people of spring and flowers, April Lynn Fears. She was planned. Wanted. Maybe she's the reason God killed Alma, so my parents would move from Detroit to Asheville. My sister was too perfect to be in a city where black people killed white people, and white people killed black people. She deserved to feel safe. I'm sure that's why God killed Alma.

I still remember the feeling of thick black smoke, engulfing me as I stood in front of my new first-grade classroom. "The plane's name was Enola Gay, but I was named Enola May because of my mother's M." There were a few chuckles, as young minds pondered how funny it would have been to be named Gay instead of May. Polite laughter.

I often wondered who God would kill for me. Sometimes I hated God. I tried not to because I knew it wasn't nice to hate someone you had never met, but he seemed to take care of bad people and let good people take care of themselves, so I hated him.

April Lynn, who I sometimes thought was bad, and sometimes thought was good, would get phone calls from Dacey's mom in Motor City. That grandmother's name was Easter Lynn Humphreys. I'm sure she loved April because they shared the same middle name, completely – *all* the letters. L-Y-N-N.

"Gvgeyui." I'd hear Easter say it loudly from her Motor City living room, like a bullhorn from Detroit to Asheville, to make sure April heard it before passing the hard-plastic phone receiver back to Dacey with her small hand.

"Ga-gay-u-ee." April would try to say it back. It was a Cherokee Indian word for *I love you,* something Easter Lynn Humphreys never said to me. Besides sharing the same middle name, April had Easter's milk chocolate Cherokee-eyes and dark hair. My eyes were a run of the mill blue, and my hair was a light brown, both like those of my mother. Looking like her didn't help though; she hated me all the same. I felt like I reminded her of someone that made her sad. I still remember begging for the phone, begging for a chance to say *gvgeyui* into the receiver. I could say it perfectly, but no one wanted to hear it. Not then.

Luckily, Ms. Norton helped me with the big words during my presentation about my name. I liked the way she encouraged me to keep going. No one had ever done that. That's the day I met Dixie. She was named after something to do with the South. Everyone liked her name. Dixie Louise Nault. She was six years old just like me but would be turning seven soon.

Asheville felt safe in 1967. That was the first time I had ever felt safe, standing in Ms. Norton's classroom, even with the few chuckles in the back of the room. Ms. Norton used my presentation to talk about the atomic bomb that was dropped from the Boeing B-29 in 1945. She used a map to show the wide-eyed students where Hiroshima was located.

Kids looked at me like I was important. I'm glad she let me sit down before she started talking about the 80,000 people who were killed and about the other 60,000 who would die because of the bomb's radiation. I didn't want to be compared to a bomb. I wanted to sit down while I was still important, before devastation surrounded me. I sat by Dixie Louise Nault. I thought about how her middle name had all three of my mom's letters, and I thought about how my mom and dad were at a funeral that I wasn't allowed to attend – my own grandmother's. April was only two, but she got to go. Dad said it was because I needed to start school right away. I knew better than to ask again. So, I went to school where I explained my name and met Dixie Louise. It was still in my head. *LOU.*

#

Melantha Lou Fears' world was consumed by voices. Repeating the same thing over and over. *He killed me Mellie.* The voice was that of a little girl, an unspeakable memory, but one she often compared to her oldest daughter. Enola felt judged, the way her mother would seldom make eye contact, and when she did, it was an evil look, apprehensive and cold. *He should have died,* the tender voice continued, as Melantha walked quickly past April who was saying *gvgeyui* into the phone, past Dacey who had just reached for another shot of whiskey, and past Enola, with no eye contact, making her way to the new 1967 Toyota Corona Sedan, leaving Dacey and the kids to fend for themselves, in a house Dacey's mother had arranged the down payment on.

The sun showed the time around three o'clock, if she hurried, she would make it back to the empty farmhouse before Abner or Delmer. A chance to rummage through her mother's private belongings. A silent place in which she could grieve the sudden death of her mother. She hit the gas and sped, turning onto the dirt road. Fast. *Slow down girl. You're going to kill yourself.* She heard a voice say. This time it was older, probably late twenties, probably black. Female. She wiped her tears as she braked silently beside her mother's old farmhouse, remembering the call from Alma Paine's doctor, just one hour before ordering Dacey to get a U-Haul and fill it. She glanced at the lawnmower as she walked toward the front door of the farmhouse. *He should have been the one to die.* She heard the black voice again. *It was his Goddamned lawnmower anyway.* Her mind was racing with noise. Sometimes the voices were crystal clear; sometimes she could only hear noise. She reached for the door, opening it, and all the time, wishing he had been the one to accidentally hit the giant wasp nest with the mower, wishing he had been the one to suffer the pain of over ninety stings, wishing he had been the one whose body went into anaphylactic shock, wishing he had been the one she hadn't had time to say goodbye to. *Ernie, you've got to help me kill him.* Melantha liked to talk back to the black voice. She never talked back to the young voice.

She hated her stepfather. She hated his excuses every time her mother confronted him about his drinking: *Alma, it helps me relax. Alma, I can quit whenever I want. Alma, all men drink.* She wondered what it would have been like to have a better childhood and not be sent away from home at sixteen years old. There had been years of abuse – years of forced oral sex, years of touching, years of groping, years of threats to keep silent, and somewhere in there, years of forced penetration. *It will help you become a woman. Why are you crying?* The last voice was her stepfather's, although he wasn't there. Not yet. Her eyes started to tear as she thought about him. She needed her mother more than ever. Now.

"Mel, is that you?" She knew the words were real this time. Her blue eyes looked toward the unexpected voice coming from the kitchen. She had been just sixteen years old the last time she laid those blue eyes on him, ten years back. She had never seen the seven-year-old boy standing beside him, only knew his name – Delmer – her half-brother she had never met. He was a product of her mother's weakness – men. Melantha stared at the faces before her. The face of her step-father triggered the smell of whiskey and unwanted depredation. She hated him. She hated strong odors. She hated whiskey on Dacey's breath. Hell, she hated her life. She hated the look of the cold linoleum-laid kitchen, as she stared at her step-father in disgust, wondering how her life could have been without him, then stopped promptly to look him straight in the face. She wasn't afraid of him anymore. *That must be Delmer.* She couldn't stop her thoughts. *Why did you let him fuck you Mom? Especially, after he fucked me.*

"What the hell are you doing here?" Melantha's words were as cold as the linoleum.

"This is my house too, Mel." He didn't get too close to her, noticing her anger filling the room, filling those twenty-six-year-old eyes he still recognized.

"This is my mother's house! You're a low-life! You're a drunk!" She paused before answering the black voice's demand out loud, leaving Abner confused. "He can only lay claim to what he has earned, and he has never earned a damn thing."

"Mel." Abner Paine held on to the white gas stove, trying to get his feet in order, making sure he didn't fall. "I miss her too." Delmer glared up at the sister he had never met with his seven-year-old eyes. They were Alma's eyes. *He looks like my mother.* Then she stopped her thoughts again, giving a hateful stare to the drunk before her, the same man who had forced her to perform like a whore. She picked up the kitchen phone, without asking, instructing Dacey to rent another U-Haul, instructing him to leave six-year-old Enola in charge of April, and instructing him to hurry. She would take a whore's payment, filling the same U-Haul that had just been emptied days before, with pieces of Alma Paine's life, her dead mother, and leave.

Chapter 2

I was ten years old before I ever met Abner Paine or saw the stucco-sided farmhouse. My dad, Dacey as I prefer to call him now, was always working, too busy, usually controlled by the endless demands that Melantha kept waiting for him, and Melantha had no desire to return to the farmhouse – at least not then. I never understood my parents' relationship, only that my mom, I mean Melantha, was the controller and Dacey was the enforcer. *I'll let your father deal with you when he gets home. He'll make you into more of a woman.* The words were constantly going through my head, as I had heard them enough, as I wondered what she meant, and as I wondered why April had never been sent to her room. She was six years old at the time, old enough, at least based on my own past experiences.

My father, or whatever his name was, who had usually spent the last hour on the phone with an angry customer, who always had sores on his feet from standing for ten hours in cheap white patent leather shoes, would take off his matching white leather belt in anger so he could teach me a lesson. Lessons that had been beaten into me since I could remember, leaving me with bruises and cuts that I would hide under long sleeves at Johnston Elementary School from Dixie and my teachers. For the longest time, it was difficult to decide if my father's uncontrollable rage was from my mother's prodding or if his rage was a result of his many failures in life, and his eventual need to fulfill his perverse behavior. Desires, that I used to wonder, were in place to capture a cheaply earned hard-on? There had been several times that I noticed his pants bulging, the material trying to hold back the monster inside of him. I had seen it pointing in my direction when he kicked, hit, and thrust me around like a ragdoll, had seen it pointing at full attention whenever a sexy teenage girl was on television and had seen it pointing in full salute whenever a black man suffered an injury on the news. He reeked of perversions and prejudices and was made up of layers of evil. Hidden beneath his skin, like a volcano, his anger would explode at me and the black men he came across in his life. I hate the other word he used. *Niggers.*

Next time I'll break your Goddamned arm, turn over. I could still hear him even when I was at school, and I could feel him each time I tried to make eye contact with my mom's emotionless blue eyes. He would rip off his belt in anger, hitting me with all 210 pounds, leaving black and blue marks that would soon swell and last for weeks. Sometimes he needed more, a need to teach me more. That's when he'd make me take off my school jeans, down to my panties. It wasn't a punishment anymore. It was something I didn't recognize at the time, just like my first time to the farmhouse, just like my first time seeing Abner Paine, just like my first time meeting an uncle that I didn't even know existed, only one year older than me. I could never get over how weird that was. One-year difference. Delmer Paine. I never knew his middle name either, only that he was a gift my dead grandma left behind, an accident, a pre-menopause baby, rarely talked about, the latter just like me. I wanted desperately

to be my dad's little girl, but I knew the position was taken by April.

Besides, my father was considered God-like by those who still kept

in touch with him from Detroit, an admiration he had earned by

being the fill-in preacher at a downtown church for about six

months, so I always knew he wasn't someone who could love

someone like me. I wasn't God-like. And, he appeared to be a loyal

husband, and a perfect father of two little girls, by those who didn't

know about the beatings and perverse urges. *Maybe all fathers did*

that once in a while, I would try to reason time and time again. *After*

all, it's not like we had sex. He just wanted to teach me a lesson. He

wanted to beat me while my little girl panties fought to get off the

bed. I saw how Melantha manipulated him, how she forced him to

do things he didn't want to do, how she controlled everything that

went on. That's when I decided I could control Delmer with my

body. He was eleven years old when I was ten. I looked in the mirror

one day after a beating, studying my bruises, studying my cuts that

Dacey sometimes made with his big silver buckle, wondering if,

Delmer would pretend to love me, pretend to be a doctor, or at least

pretend to make things better. There were a few years that the grandfather I didn't really know, would drop Delmer off, on his way into town, for a few hours. No one missed us, when the two of us would play in the basement, at the house on Cedar Hill Road, sometimes as husband and wife, sometimes as doctor and patient. We role-played through most of middle school, until we were caught by April, who was then eight at the time. Melantha made sure I knew I was a whore at twelve years old when I finally got caught. She screamed it in my face over and over for hours, until Dacey got home, feet sore, belt off. I don't remember too much about the beating, except that I would tell people for years about how I busted my left kneecap on the cement basement floor trying to do a handstand, when in reality, Dacey Sherman Fears, used it for baseball practice until the bone cracked. Loud. They said I was an embarrassment when I limped, so I didn't. I put the pain away, just like I did when Melantha thought I should go to Florida to live with her real father and his new wife. I had just turned fifteen years old when I went to Florida. *Alone*, my name spelled backward. They kept the perfect child. April was eleven years old the day I left. I would only see my sister one or two more times in my life. *Alone.*

#

Enola May Fears was fifteen years old when she moved into the small, two-bedroom, concrete house in North Fort Myers, Florida with Homer and Barbara Parrish. Strangers. Homer, a retired pipefitter, had recently spent over a year doing on-site consultation work, in Alaska, on the Trans-Alaska Pipeline, and had only been home to his wife for a few months. Barbara Parrish supported him, by loving him in his absence, by remaining faithful, and by welcoming his estranged granddaughter into their home. Enola wanted her parents to be like them, wanted her mom to support her father's dreams, living out west and having his own tire business. But she knew her mom could never change. An ordinary life, a husband with a dead-end job at a small tire company, a woman who held the reins to "a lesson to remember" and "when your father gets home." Still only fifteen years old, Enola was tired of excuses and beatings, and desperately wanted more from life. She wanted to be someone strong, in control of her own life, her own destiny. She was free to start liking boys now, without Melantha staring over her shoulder, free to get her learner's permit, and free to dream about her future. Enola spent every minute just trying to enjoy life, trying to succeed, doubling up on classes at her high school to graduate early, riding the Fort Myers city-bus to the beach on the weekends to anxiously swallow up a sunset, looking for someone that could bring some peace and happiness into her life.

#

Kelsey's brown eyes captured my soul the first time I ever laid eyes on them. He had these deep brown eyes, like my sister, like Dacey, but his were trusting – a shade I'd never seen before. He stood up when I got on the city bus, offering me his seat and his smile. I imagined he was a couple years older, but he was warm and looked at me in a way I wasn't used to. He offered an escape from men in white patent leather shoes. It didn't take long before we were like one soul instead of two, but we progressed slowly, both still virgins, swallowing weekend sunsets together, laughing, talking, and simply holding each other as the sun would dip down for the night, until Melantha called late one night, and thirty minutes later, as I stood in the Key West style Florida home, she was threatening to have me return to Asheville, where I would get the worst beating of my life. Her words. I still remember saying good-bye to Kelsey the next day on the phone, saying goodbye to our last shared sunset, agreeing we would save ourselves for each other. I would just focus on graduating, then I could be with Kelsey, and then I could permanently rid myself of Melantha's words that haunted me, and surround myself with his gentleness. *Next time, I will fly down there Enola May. Do you understand? You can't keep being a slut and a whore!* I tried to erase the words from my memory. I tried for years not to let my mom's words eat at me. *A slut? A whore? Sleeping around? Intercourse? Sex? Who did I have sex with? Kelsey had never tried. We just kissed – a lot. Dacey? Was she worried about Dacey?* And then there were my middle school years spent with Delmer. *Touching each other's private areas isn't sex, is it? Looking at them?* I spent years trying to determine if my mother was right. Was I a slut? A whore? I had lost everything. Kelsey. My sister. My parents. Dixie. Myself.

Chapter 3

The sins of a man can eat the souls of his children. Abner Paine had

committed many sins in his lifetime. He died at the farmhouse in the

middle of the night. Delmer had just turned seventeen years old

when he found his father's body – cold, stiff, and stretched lifeless in

a bed he used to share with Alma, a messy mixture of linen, a white

piece of which seemed permanently glued to his right hand.

Melantha had gotten the call from a neighbor. She didn't cry.

She didn't tell anyone that she had been out the evening before, just her, an unexpected visit, a treasured family heirloom delivered in secret. She didn't give a damn about Abner or anyone else. Not at that moment. The look she had when the phone call came was one of sadness, but it wasn't for Abner, it wasn't for the seventeen-year-old that would have to figure out his own life, no, it was for herself and the fact that she wouldn't be able to watch him suffer. Again.

Even though she did love April, then twelve years old, she didn't show it. She was emotionless always and bitter about the fact that she had spent thirty-six years of her life wishing she was somewhere else, with someone else. She thought back about the first time she walked into the small Detroit Baptist Church and saw Dacey Fears for the very first time. It was early December in 1960. Cold. The years of civil unrest and bitter winters had left the small Detroit church with faded red shutters, an exterior that begged for paint, and a doorway that welcomed *white* people, as the blacks were asked to find a church that served their own *kind* if they attempted to enter.

"Welcome to my church…" He was only twenty-one at the time, aspiring to be a man of God, serving and loyal, but when he first met Melantha, he changed completely. When he saw her, a delicate nineteen-year-old woman with a confused beautiful face, he was no longer a servant to God but a servant to her. She had a certain style of manipulation and a way of controlling him like he was putty. He looked into her eyes as he preached, a look that penetrated her see-through, blue chiffon blouse, which matched her eyes. Not a blouse to be worn in the winter in Detroit. And he was careful not to call attention to his interest in her, at least not then. He too was confused; he too had lost his direction in life at such an early age; he too had been branded by his dysfunctional childhood. *They're not the same as us boy. Don't help 'em. Don't try and save 'em. Save your own kind. Save God's children.* His own father's voice could still be heard whenever he closed his eyes to pray. Melantha would become the one person he could talk to about those memories. Together they were able to talk about things that had been sealed away. She told him about her stepfather, how she became his sex slave, losing her soul to the devil himself. He became her counselor, a job he felt qualified to do, since he had been in the church counseling others, freeing them from their sinful existence. He counseled Melantha after church sermons, for the next few weeks, privately. She found out she was pregnant by year's end, so they decided it was best to get married; the wedding was an inexpensive formality, catered by the justice of the peace in a dusty downtown courtroom, away from the whispers and spreading rumors, about the young preacher that had unexpectedly left the small Detroit Baptist Church. It didn't take long for Melantha to realize that she had gotten herself stuck in a mundane life. She had married a dreamer, a pushover, nothing but a puppet. A mannequin. He was a lost ship. He had lost everything somewhere behind a shed when his father beat him repeatedly with a brightly colored green weeping willow limb, that he was always instructed to select himself before the beating would begin. *This will make you into more of a man boy. Someday you'll thank me for this.* Dacey could still feel the sting of the willow hitting his naked flesh. *I don't want to hear of you helping anymore of them niggers. I don't care what the reason is. You let their God help them.* Melantha couldn't handle feeling his pain; she couldn't handle feeling her own. She felt best when she directed the fate of his soul-less body, when she pulled and twisted the strings from which he hung. A puppet. And she would make him pay and his bastard child, but for now, at least then, he was her only chance at survival.

She loved him for a little while – around the time they tried to have another baby – this one planned. "I'll miss you; be careful on your trip," she'd say as she pulled her pregnant belly away from his new white convertible. That was Detroit 1965. But, the voices still fought her emotions. *He doesn't care anymore about me than I care about him. Maybe I should kill him first. Maybe I should kill Enola while he's at work today. I could say it was an accident. Four-year-old kids drown all the time. Maybe she'll fall down the stairs. Maybe she'll run out in front of a car chasing that damn German shepherd. Maybe she'll just die.*

Now, twelve years later, she stood emotionless, Abner is dead, like her mom, her daughters are twelve and sixteen, one stood before her, and the other almost 1000 miles away, and Dacey, the trustworthy husband of almost sixteen years, turned out to be her biggest deception. Nights away from home were excuses to try and fill the emptiness that had been inside him since he was a child – a quick screw. It would be cheap and meaningless. It was part of the thrill. He was trying to feed his crumbled soul, one that God had left, since meeting Melantha, so it seemed. He wanted to believe he was perfect. The perfect father, husband, man. He wasn't. He was nothing; he was a liar, a cheat, and a child-beater. A poor excuse for

a human being. And he showed no guilt, only an empty heart with

the inability to be sincere and loving. His God had left him when he

left the church. In a short time, his only true friend was the devil.

Dacey would bring home meaningless trinkets for April and

Melantha from his business trips. He spent days away at a time, but

he was always home for the weekends, lying about meetings and

bonuses. The cheap one-night stands continued, and weekends home

evaporated into weekend-days home. Weekend-nights were spent

carousing neighborhood bars with his buddies from the tire store.

Once more he couldn't turn away from a dare, a challenge. This time

he would pay the price. The quick screw-to-be was a girl, barely

older than Enola, with an innocent smile and hard-to-read blue eyes

just like what he was used to, a confused child of seventeen years old

looking for a good time, anxious to show off her new Trans-am to a

passing Asheville tire salesman driving a thirteen-year-old car.

Dacey was quick to accept any invitation she offered: a key to her

motel room which stood next to the bar, an invitation to put his

almost thirty-seven-year old penis inside her seventeen-year-old

vagina, an offer to speed recklessly through the night with a promise of unconditional love, no, just lust. And so, they traveled at a rate of seventy mph down the dark curvy road, leaving the only signs of life behind, the bar's flashing neon and the dirty motel. Fast. Out of control.

Unaware of the lone deer standing alert and ready to greet the bright red Trans-am: too late. The girl's ruby lips gasped for breath, as her weak hands clenched the steering wheel, which had become part of her. She needed Dacey to loosen her with his free hands. But she was his last concern. His marriage was his second. Getting caught was his first. She would die at seventeen years of age; she would bleed to death as she lay pinned, impaled by the car's steering wheel. Helpless. *Alone*, just like Enola. Dacey felt no regret or sadness but made his way quickly on foot to his only friend, Jack Daniels, hiding beneath the flashing red neon, which after a few drinks would dim to a burnt orange. Dacey, eyes bloodshot from the night air and Jack, watched the orange turn to a final color of ash gray from the rearview mirror of his weathered convertible that, like an old dog, had so patiently waited for his return, waited while he left it parked in the bar parking lot, waited while he fucked a seventeen-year-old girl, and waited while he left her to bleed to

death. *Alone.*

#

I remember hearing Homer and Barbara Parrish whispering about it

in on the back screened-in North Fort Myers porch like it was almost

yesterday, unaware that I had just gotten home from North Fort

Myers High School, unaware that I was within clear range. I

remember gasping for air as they talked about Dacey, how he would

probably try to use Melantha as his alibi, how he would play the

puppet to whatever tune she sang, how he needed her, how the cops

knocked on the door early the next morning, and how Dacey's jacket

was found in the crushed red Trans-Am with a stack of his business

cards for Sultan Tires, neatly tucked away in an inside pocket and a

room key to the motel in the outer.

"Why did Melantha even call you Homer?" The question was

extra inquisitive, as Barbara knew Melantha never involved Homer

in her life unless she wanted something.

"She needed my help getting a good attorney for Dacey." He

knew his money was the only reason he had any idea what was

going on. "The cops suspect that he left the girl to die after the motel together. I'm not sure my money can get him out of this mess."

"I'm glad Enola is with us." Barbara looked around to make sure neighbors weren't in the adjoining backyard before adding on. "I can't believe he was with a seventeen-year-old girl."

"He's always been a loose cannon." My grandfather replied. And that's when I knew, when I pieced it all together, beating me in my underwear, noticing he had a hard-on the last time two times, at least, and remembering how he looked at teenage girls on television and in magazines. I knew Melantha was no one to mess with. She might get him an attorney, but it was only so she would have more control. I suspected she knew where he had been: a cheap run-down motel, fucking a girl one year older than me.

#

Melantha retained an attorney but made it clear that he wasn't to be released for at least forty-eight hours. She wanted him to feel afraid. She wanted him to feel empty. And, she needed the time to drive to the farmhouse which had recently been put up for sale, which still had the smell of her mother on linen and clothes, which she knew sat empty since she had heard Delmer had a girlfriend in town that he was staying with. Drive.

She walked past the white stove without noticing Abner's stained coffee cup sitting on the counter, a mold incubator representing his life, still a third of the way full of coffee, and one or two spoons of whiskey, Abner's preferred creamer. The electric had been shut off for lack of payment, but Melantha remembered how a light would glisten off the oak dresser as the sound of the floor creaked beneath her feet, entering her mom's world, and placing a piece of her past on the bed's linen sheets, unmade, waiting for the unshaven drunk to return. She displayed the item she had brought with her near the pillow, where it wouldn't be missed, then turned her body and attention to the dresser across the room.

Her fingers searched the small wooden drawers, nothing special, most were cheap pieces, few things of value, except for the cold feel of metal, a solid gold cross, far from costume jewelry, about an inch and a half long, with the body of Jesus Christ woven into the shiny finish. *Fuck Jesus Christ. He ain't never did anything for us Mel.* Melantha knew it was Tiger – the white voice. *Where was Jesus when that bastard was holding your head still and jerking off into your mouth?* Melantha's eyes glistened as she held the gold

cross close to her face. She had lost her mother but was able to keep

one small part of her. She slipped the chain over her neck and tucked

the cross inside her black high-cut dress, making sure it would be

concealed from the world, the cold feel of gold pressing against her

breast. Today would be the last day she would ever come to the

farmhouse, today would be a new beginning, and *today* – as she

thought about the word – she was glad Dacey was locked behind

bars. It was a good day to start over, to make amends to Enola. This

would be the day she would call her, inviting her home for a visit.

This would be the beginning of her plan on how to make Dacey

suffer. He was, after all, a murderer, and in her opinion, he deserved

to be where he was – in jail. He had left a young girl to die. It was an

act of murder as far as Melantha was concerned, an inexcusable act.

His God, if he still had one, would have to be pretty forgiving. And

he would have a price he'd have to pay – Melantha's price. She had

taken enough from him and had now stopped – today. He would

become a real puppet, and she would run the entire show. He would

pay for what he had done. Step one: call Enola. Step two: get her to fly home for a visit. Step three: ruin whatever was left of Dacey

Fears.

#

Staying with Homer and Barbara Parrish was like a vacation to me.

It was a place where I didn't have to watch my back, a place where

my lacy underwear didn't have to fight for cover from the white

leather belt, a safe place, except for one day – with Ricky Sagner. I

smiled as I looked into my mother's eyes – they seemed a darker

blue when she greeted me at the airport. I knew she was up to

something, but then again, she sounded so empty on the phone, like

she needed me, maybe for the first time.

"We need this chance to be together, before you graduate

from high school." It still sounded unbelievable to me too. I would

still only be sixteen years old when I graduated in just a few more

weeks. I had been attending both sessions at North Fort Myers High

School, taking advantage of the fact that they were over-crowded

and offered two sessions, taking advantage of the fact that I was

ready to graduate and get on with my life, taking advantage of the

fact that no matter how hard I tried I couldn't get Kelsey out of my

mind. "We can try, right?" There was a feeling of tension between us that she was trying to cover up. "Your father is in jail, and my mother is dead."

I thought about when she died – *ten years ago*, and then, *let it go now Mom.*

"And - Abner." Her voice sounded almost sickened when she mentioned her stepfather's name. I watched as she put her arms back at her side and looked helplessly at me, waiting for a hug or some sign of emotion, besides confusion, besides looking like I was waiting for the other shoe to drop.

I always wanted my mother's love. *Did she love me now? Or was she just in need of someone to use in her game?* I wanted one last try to know the woman that stood before me. I hugged her like I meant it, like we loved each other. I wanted a mother to love me – help me with the Ricky's in my life. I chose my words carefully, keeping the pieces of the puzzle hidden until she was ready to reveal them. I could play the game too.

"Why is Dad in jail? What did he do? Is he hurt? Did he hurt someone else?" I rattled off the questions quickly. I had always wanted my father's love, no matter how abusive he was, no matter how many times he had beat me, no matter how many bruises and scars, both inside and outside, he had left. "Mom, is Dad okay?" I could see she was still thinking about something else, maybe the gold cross hanging from a chain around her neck, the shiny pendant fighting for a hidden spot within the palm of her hand that I watched clutch it. "Please answer me. Is Dad okay?"

My mother's tricky blue eyes searched my face and met her twin blue eyes in a sudden lock. I could tell she was planning something, what I did not know. But she answered despite her mind being elsewhere, "I miss my mother Enola. She didn't deserve to die so young. She was only forty-seven." I thought about grandma Alma. I had met her once when I was four, when she visited Detroit for a week. That's it. I barely remembered anything about her, other than the fact that she often spoke French, like Mom did sometimes when she seemed confused, or angry.

"I miss Grandma Alma too." *She died ten years ago*, I thought again. "But I'm worried about Dad. Is he in trouble? Why did you want me here?" *Time to let her go Mom.* Again.

"He's going to be released from jail later today." I watched her hand open, tucking the gold cross just inside her dress. "He was arrested for not paying several speeding tickets."

"Should we go to the jail with money?" I knew she was lying. I had heard enough of Barbara and Homer's conversation to know what had happened. I just wanted to make her feel in charge. Like always.

"I have a lawyer there now. He's taking care of everything." I knew it was Homer Parrish's years of hard work that had paid for those services.

"Oh, good." I let my face relax a little, trying to show that I was buying into her nonsense. She didn't care about my father at all. He had cheated on her so many times when I was growing up I suspected, from the way his eyes would wander, from the way he'd smell when he came home late, whiskey and pussy. She knew the kind of person he was. The problem was, she was no better.

"Enola?" I hated hearing my mother use my first name, almost always pausing after it to give it time to be *Alone*. "How's school?" She looked into my eyes again. Something I wasn't used to. "Do you have a boyfriend?"

"School is fine. And I'm fine." I didn't want to talk to her about boys, about how she had messed up things for me with Kelsey, or about anything for that matter. And, I certainly didn't want to tell her about Ricky, about what he tried to do to me.

"Rein ne se passé? Nothing is happening?" She always put her arms out when she spoke French. She lived in a boarding school around nuns who spoke nothing but French.

"No, just studying and trying to get through school." I thought about Ricky Sagner. I thought about how Barbara Parrish looked at me when I came home that day. I went out with him two times, after Kelsey, after feeling alone. Melantha would have no sympathy for me, after learning I had been alone with yet another boy, after learning I had skipped a day of school with him to hang out at the beach, after being unable to shake the loneliness I felt from missing Kelsey, and after learning Ricky had pinned me between his car's front bucket seats, lifted my skirt, and put his fingers inside of me without permission, all the while, trying to put more. She wouldn't praise me for fighting back, hard, my body a collector for bruises it was used to receiving, just another hidden secret.

"Graduation will be here before you know it." The sound of losing control over me could be heard in her voice.

And so, it went, our conversation became full of short and meaningless questions; the answers were not responded to: and once again we were drifting our separate ways. Apart.

Chapter 4

Melantha had a hard time putting her mother's death out of her

mind. She expected her to be around longer, expected she would

always be a part of her life, and expected that the move from Detroit

would be at a later time, a time when Alma and she could spend

more time together. She looked old, the blackened sky reflected in

the window behind her at the Asheville jail, but most people would

who had lived Melantha's life. It was the result of a bad childhood,

the years of physical and sexual abuse, the nights of performing with her stepfather like a cheap prostitute on Merrimon Avenue in downtown Asheville. Years later, the pain and mental anguish, the cheating husband, and the inability to love or need anyone – even one of her daughters – made her that much older.

She heard Dacey's voice follow her as she walked away from the woman that had announced his release. It was a begging, pleading, yet thankful voice. Did he think she'd ever forgive him? Doubtful. She would punish him for the rest of his life. She would milk the situation for all it was worth, ordering him around to meet her every need, whatever it was.

"Mel...I'm..."

"I'll let you know when I'm ready to talk to you." The nasty-sounding voice came from the back of her head, already ten steps ahead of him, nothing but hair. "Don't speak to me until I ask you to. I mean it." She felt the coldness in her voice, like the gold cross that lay hidden between her breasts. "You don't have the right to address me Dacey."

"I'm sorry, Mel." Dacey should have known better, should have known to remain silent, and definitely should have known not to call her Mel. Abner did that, and he was dead, something she'd make sure Dacey was if he kept it up.

"Don't fucking call me Mel! I said to be quiet." The nasty voice belonged to a woman who had reached her breaking point. Within seconds, Melantha Fears stopped and glared at his lying brown eyes, her blue ones filled with hatred, and planted her feet squarely in front of his careless ones.

"I'm sorry Melantha." Dacey's voice was weak, like his character, begging for a chance to make things right. Melantha couldn't help but stare through him, into his soul, or into the lack of one. She was capable of bringing a full-grown man to his knees with just one look, a look that would haunt him for the rest of his life. She wasn't going to give him an ounce of dignity, not now, not ever. But she didn't want to dismiss his presence all together either. Melantha was good at turning people into toys, and Dacey was going to be her favorite toy.

"We're not going to discuss how you fucked a seventeen-year-old." The sound of insistence vibrated the walkway leading to the car, where Enola sat with April, too young to enter a jailhouse in Melantha's opinion. "Don't bring this up around the kids!" Melantha wasn't kidding.

She was ready to lunge forward when she noticed the four

eyes, two blue and two brown watching from the car. The first two

belonged to Enola and the second set to April. The sisters would

share just a few more minutes together, before car doors would open,

then close, and silence would begin. The sky was completely black

now, finally filled with rain, covering all traces of the muddy skid

marks that had marked the death of a seventeen-year-old girl in a red

Trans-Am and masking the silence that filled the car ride home.

#

I thought about the silence. *Let it be. It's not my problem.* When the

car pulled down the drive on Cedar Hill Road I could feel my

stomach turn. There weren't a lot of good memories in that house for

me. Most I tried to forget, but I can still remember my mom's, I

mean Melantha's, phone conversation as I listened through the

closed bedroom door, both parents neatly tucked inside, and April in

her room, leaving me free to spy, free to put more pieces together.

"Thanks Grover." I could hear Melantha whisper, probably

glaring at Dacey as he sat on the edge of the master bed, waiting for

his set of instructions. "The bartender wasn't a problem?" I heard silence for a while, wondering what that meant. Then, "Good, Dacey gave his jacket to the homeless man because it was cold." I imagined her eyes were dark blue at the time. "Good, no prints in the car." And, "Yes, I'll call you, if he breaks our agreement." Her phone call ended, the tone changing, and then became directed at Dacey.

I don't know what was said word for word, but I do know that Dacey wasn't allowed to talk to his mother anymore. No more *gvgeyuis* would be pronounced carefully into the phone. It was a word that I didn't hear again for many years. I remember hearing Melantha's voice one last time before the bedroom door opened.

"You'll become the answer to some unsolved case. Worth at least ten to fifteen years behind bars." It was said with the assurance of a woman who knew how to get even.

"I understand, Melantha." He knew better than to shorten her name by that point, as he reached for a hug, the bedroom door opened just enough for me to catch a glance, to watch him be rejected. She was just getting started. Losing his mother wouldn't be the last thing she'd take away from him. She looked at me, as she exited the room in front of the man I had for a father. She knew he wanted family, even me. I was his mistake. His daughter…the one he'd take his anger out on when instructed to, the child who begged

for months to go fishing with him, the child who wanted so badly to

please him and wanted him to just love me in return. He was my

only chance to be loved when I was growing up. My mother wasn't

capable. She never said the words. Never.

I didn't know that my smile toward the man who was

standing behind her wasn't about to be reciprocated. I had missed

that part of the behind-the-door conversation. I had missed

Melantha's instructions to Dacey about me. I loved my dad, despite

his bad temper, despite how he had made me strip down to my lacy

underwear for the last couple of beatings, okay many beatings,

despite how he had been only in his underwear the last time he beat

me, despite the fact that he didn't control the protruding organ in his

tight white briefs, and despite the fact that he had left me with

bruises and cuts more times than I could remember.

"Hi, Dad. Sorry you had to go to jail." I still remember his

reply to this day. Nothing. He barely made eye contact with me, but I

could tell by my mother's expression that she had instructed him not

to. He looked sad and preoccupied. He seemed to lose ten years off

his life when I mentioned Grandma Easter. I know it was a mean thing bringing her up, but I wanted him to hurt, wanted him to feel alone, like he was making me feel.

"Enola, I don't mind if you get some rest." Melantha's voice was emotionless. "I know you have to catch a flight back in the morning." I didn't react. *One day was long enough with her.* I thought. "You've been such a help with your sister. But I don't want…"

"You're right Mom. It's time for me to turn in." Now, I understood why April had removed herself from the living room the moment we had entered the house. Best to stay locked away. Best to be hidden.

"Good night." Melantha echoed the words to the side of my face, not turning quickly enough for her liking.

It was over. The parents I kept hoping would work out, were shells of themselves, and I was a casualty of war, like my namesake, dropping a bomb that exploded around me, swallowing me whole. I couldn't reply to her anymore. My voice wouldn't be able to hide the sadness or emptiness I felt. I wanted to tell her that I knew she had a shitty childhood, but that I loved her anyway, but I couldn't let my emotions be seen around her. I exited the room. I would fly out tomorrow – back to what life I had, alone, with an empty belly like the Enola Gay.

#

There were few words exchanged the next morning at the airport. Melantha turned away when Enola looked in her direction. She had used her daughter in a game. What good was she anymore? Why should she look at her? Was the cost of never seeing her again too much for Melantha to handle, letting her go forever, ignoring the eyes that matched her own? She wasn't sorry for using Enola, and they both knew that's exactly what she did. Melantha had masterminded a game, making sure Dacey felt the pain of losing everything, losing his oldest daughter permanently, leaving her with nothing but memories of bruises and a busted knee-cap, one which still hurt when the Florida rain came down. He had earned his pain. He had driven God out of his soul, filling it with hatred, each time he beat Enola with uncontrollable rage, each time he cheated on Melantha, and finally, when he had sex with a girl nearly his own daughter's age and left her to die.

Melantha watched Dacey's stare, emotionless, empty, before speaking to him. "You've lost your oldest daughter Dacey. I hope you're proud of yourself."

He chose his words slowly and carefully. "I'm sorry Melantha. I will make it up to you. I promise."

"Do you think I want you to?" She nearly laughed when she asked the question, thinking about the attorney she had hired, thinking about how he had done exactly what she wanted him to, with money, the right amount, and with a little persuasion. Okay, a lot of persuasion. Dacey wasn't the only one who was capable of fucking someone else. "You'll never be able to make things right."

"I love you, Mel…Melantha." He corrected his nearly fatal mistake.

"You smell of pussy and prison." She knew he hadn't showered since being released, and she imagined he hadn't showered since sticking his dick in a seventeen-year-old.

"It wasn't prison Melantha, just jail." He knew the words shouldn't have left him. He remembered she had driven the car to the airport, and he hadn't paid attention to where she had parked and was unable to keep up with the woman whose back was now steps ahead of him. Maybe time alone would be good for him or at least

good for her, so she could cool off. But he didn't look forward to

calling a buddy from work to pick him up. *Had the guys at his job*

heard about the accident? He wondered. *No, they hadn't seen the*

girl he left the bar with. "Mel…" Luckily, she was out of earshot.

Shortening her name again would be the end of his life.

He watched her disappear, like his mother and oldest

daughter. He wondered what would disappear next. His eyes were

cold and no longer sparkled. He sat down for a moment in the

middle of the crowded airport, thinking about everything he had

done to Enola, to the daughter that was somewhere over Georgia by

now: how he dropped her German shepherd off in the middle of

Detroit, lanes of traffic, crisp leaves scattered on the ground, leaving

him to fend for himself, how he sentenced her to her room for two

days, no food, very little water, allowing her out only for the

bathroom, because she wanted a black girl from Johnston

Elementary School to come to a sleep over, how he reared back the

elastic strap on her birthday hat, snapping her in the nose, leaving a

trail of blood that turned into a scab a few days later, and how he

asked her to go hiking, because April was too young, and Melantha hated hiking, only to come across a black man, probably in his thirties, lying in the woods, unable to move, moaning, obviously in severe pain, begging for help, covered with large open cuts that looked like they had been made from being beaten with a chain. Enola had pleaded with him to get the man help, but instead, he grabbed her by the hair, hard, pulling her away, deeper into the sea of trees, further away from the bleeding negro, their trail writhing throughout rarely trampled woods. Pulling hard, threatening without taking a breath, insisting she not look back. Ignore. Let him bleed to death. Dacey put his face in his hands and wept uncontrollably. It was the first time he had talked to God in years. *I'm sorry God for all I've done.* But there was no answer. Only thoughts.

The thoughts of Enola kept coming. *Busted kneecap. Beatings. Lacy panties. Beatings. Lacy panties. Beatings. Lacy panties. Beatings. Lacy panties. Beatings. Hard-on. Lacy panties. Hard-on. She's gone. Forever.*

Chapter 5

"We missed you Nola. Don't worry about anything, just focus on graduating." It seemed to me like Homer and Barbara Parrish had rehearsed the lines together, as they were said together when they picked me up at the Fort Myers Airport.

I responded to their plea, which couldn't be covered with the volume of two voices. "I'm glad to be back." I knew that's what they needed to hear. I knew Homer had witnessed Melantha's manipulative behavior throughout the years, and he knew, as well as

I did, that I had just traveled almost 1000 miles each way to be a pawn in my mother's game. "I'm looking forward to getting back to school." I could see that my grandfather looked relieved, happy I wasn't suffering. Actually, I was, but I had learned to hide it early in my childhood. I thought about everything I had lost, everyone I had lost, and everyone I had never had. *Just stay focused.* I pulled myself back to the here and now. "Hopefully I can make up all the final exams."

"No need Enola. I spoke with your principal yesterday; I told him it was a family emergency. You're excused from the exams; the teachers already agreed." Homer was a take-charge type of man. He looked proud when he saw my blue eyes relax for the first time since seeing Melantha. Satisfied. Then they both hugged me. I felt loved by two *almost* strangers, grandparents that I had known mostly through hit-and-miss birthday and Christmas cards, since moving from Detroit to Asheville. Before that, they didn't exist in my life, weren't part of my world, but now they felt like they were my world.

#

You are destroying Dacey, Mel. The voice was Tiger's. Melantha didn't care that her hooker friends shortened her name. She felt comfortable around Tiger and Ernie. She had her hands full with Dacey, and her hands full with keeping her only other daughter at a distance. April was scheduled to go to cheerleading camp. Good. Thirty days alone with Dacey. A lot more damage could be done in thirty days.

Dacey didn't answer the phone, a sound, which brought Melantha away from the voice in her head. Ring. Dacey was near the unanswered phone but wouldn't make a move without Melantha's approval. Melantha walked to the annoying sound slowly, deliberately, smiling when she thought about who it probably was. Easter Lynn Humphreys. Perfect timing. April had left just one hour earlier. No witness to what was about to happen.

"Hello." Melantha waited to see if the voice was Dacey's mom. Yes, it was – a deep earthy reply.

"How come my son hasn't called me in a few days?" Her Cherokee Indian tone was brief and direct. "Melantha?" Still silence

"Au revoir, Easter!" Melantha knew it would piss her off, one – not to answer her question, two – to hang up, and three – to say good-bye in French.

You've got your man by the shorthairs now, Mel. Melantha

could hear Tiger laugh. *Can't wait to see what you come up with next.*

#

"Hey Dixie! It's so great to talk to you." Enola couldn't stop smiling as she spoke into the phone. Homer Parrish had tracked Dixie Nault's contact information down. It had been months since Enola had spoken with Dixie. Homer knew helping Enola connect with her best friend would lift her spirits. He knew how to play Melantha's game. If she wanted money for an attorney, an attorney that could be compromised, she'd give up Dixie's parents' names, and the rest, being the take-charge type of man, would be easy. He knew Enola would need the extra push to get over whatever damage Melantha had caused. A phone call to her old friend would help.

"I miss you Dixie." Dixie thought about all the laughter the two of them had shared throughout the years. Even though there were long periods of time when they hadn't seen each other, like now, Dixie and Enola were able to jump right back into a conversation, right back into each other's lives. "I wish you could come down for my high school graduation." *Would Dacey and Melantha Fears be there? Would April, the sister I barely knew?*

Enola thought the words but wouldn't say them aloud, carefully shifting the conversation in her head back to Dixie.

"I'll be there." Dixie Nault, turning seventeen soon, still had one more year of high school, because she hadn't doubled up on classes like Enola, because she still lived with both of her parents, because she still spoke with her sibling, a brother, and, so it seemed, because she was able to make decisions without getting permission from some controlling authority. She had light blue eyes, almost strawberry red hair, and she cherished the friendship that Enola and she had managed to hang on to throughout the last ten years. In between beatings, in between a broken knee-cap, and in between Melantha's games, Enola and Dixie had managed to have a few special moments together: taking all their stuffed animals out to eat at McDonald's when they were in the first part of high school, just before Enola moved to Florida, and having all-night talks about boys and life while snuggled in their sleeping bags, usually at Dixie's parents' house, where Enola felt safe to laugh. Hell, sometimes they'd laugh so hard they'd almost pee themselves.

Of course, there were the moments Dixie had witnessed some of Enola's pain too: Dixie always noticed the way Enola would tear up when she saw a black face at school, not out of fear, no, it was more tears of shame. *Was the bleeding black man that kid's uncle? That kid's dad?* Dixie couldn't hear the thoughts in Enola's mind but always knew her face was searching for answers. Dixie noticed the limp too, noticed the way Enola would turn her eyes away when explaining how she hurt her knee, how she must have fallen while doing a handstand in the basement at home, how she didn't realize she had hurt it so badly. And, she noticed how Enola wouldn't be in a room alone with Dacey, even with Dixie over, not like at Dixie's house where being in a room alone with her dad felt safe. Dixie noticed many things throughout the years: long shirts in summer, fearfulness in Enola's eyes, how she never wanted to go home from a sleepover, how her appetite always picked up at Dixie's house – her appetite for food, for family, for life.

"You're coming down?" Enola couldn't believe her ears. *Why did she answer so quickly? Why wasn't there a moment to ponder the cost of a plane flight? Whether or not her parents would approve?* "Dix, did you say you're coming to my graduation?" Enola waited for clarification but couldn't stop the tears that were already clouding her vision; she put her free hand up to her heart and started to cry. Homer walked up behind her and hugged her. He had arranged the trip down for Dixie, already had Dixie's parents' approval, and already purchased Dixie's flight with his own money. He kissed Enola on her wet cheek and wiped her face with his almost seventy-year-old hand.

"Yes! Your grandfather took care of everything." She was so excited to see Enola. It had been almost a year. "He bought my ticket and got permission from my parents." She caught her breath. "Do you think you can put up with me for a week?"

"Are you kidding?" Enola was still crying; they were happy tears. Not like the ones she was used to. "I can't believe it." *Will Melantha let this happen?* She couldn't help but wonder, but could tell by her grandfather's touch, that he had already taken care of that too.

Enola and Dixie talked for another forty-five minutes before hanging up the phone, which had been cleaned thoroughly with tears by that point, then Enola hurried to the arms of her grandfather, Homer Parrish, who was sitting on the screened-in porch with Barbara. He was smiling. *How did a man with such a giving heart have a daughter so evil?* Enola wondered.

Chapter 6

"Grandpa Homer, I don't know what to say. Do you want me to pay you back for Dixie's plane-flight?" I spoke through tears still coming down my face. "No one's ever done something so nice for me. I don't know what to say, Grandpa."

"Just tell me you're happy." He was smiling but lost in thought, probably wondering how kids make it to my age without having more people be nice to them, probably thinking about why his daughter, Melantha, had turned out the way she did, and probably imagining how life would have been different, had Alma not left for a man like Abner Paine.

"I'm so happy Grandpa. I can't believe Dixie is coming to my graduation."

"That's payment enough Nola." *I loved it when he called me that. It made me feel different than the plane that dropped the bomb. It made me feel like I had my own identity.* He hugged me for a long time, but I didn't fight to get away, and I didn't want it to end. "I always called or sent cards, since you were born, but Melantha always intercepted the calls, and I'm sure she intercepted most of the cards too." The information tore at my very insides, deeply seeded loneliness that I had always been forced to live in. I wondered how it would have been to be raised by a father like Homer Parrish and a mother like Barbara Parrish. He looked happy with me snuggled in his arms – a look of serenity, a look that said he could handle whatever life threw his way. He was the strongest man I had ever known by that point in my life.

"Okay you two, ready for some lemonade?" Barbara Parrish stepped out onto the porch, where Homer and I still sat looking at each other, a look of wonder on both of our faces, both of us probably questioning why things were the way they were. She sat down a tray with three empty glasses and a pitcher of freshly squeezed ice-cold lemonade, the lemons straight from her backyard. "All that happiness and talking on the phone must have worked up some thirst." Barbara didn't wait for an answer from either one of us, quickly pouring and handing each of us our own glass. Yum.

"Thanks Grandma. I love you." She knew I did. She was the only grandmother I had. Living or otherwise. By marriage or by blood.

"Thanks Barbie. I love you too." She smiled at the man's voice who had become her husband about ten years ago, when I was only six, when the U-Haul on Lorman Street was being stuffed with memories, most of which weren't mine.

"Okay, you two, don't let me stop you from talking." Barbara looked like she realized that she was about to witness a long night of conversation as she settled back into an empty wicker chair near the porch door, eyeing the sun as it settled down in between the lemon trees. "I just want to relax. You two don't mind me." Neither of us did; you could tell. I felt free as a bird to talk about anything I wanted to around the two of them. It was a peaceful evening, probably because I was in a home where I could let my guard down, relax, question, wonder, and in a place where no one would call me names or threaten me.

Barbara got up to reach for a photo album just inside the adjoining room, pulling it off the top shelf, behind a few displayed china pieces, covering its whereabouts from others, who would just walk on by without giving the dusty album so much as a glance. She dusted off the front of the album she was holding before handing it to Homer, who I had noticed, was searching the top of the shelves just moments earlier with his eyes, in sync with Barbara's, who recognized what he wanted. It had a photo showing through the display on the front: a little girl sitting on an unattended garden-wall, dried weeds and dead flowers at her back, separating her from the white stucco-sided house, a four-rung wooden ladder propped against its corner. She sat, her feet dipped in a set of white bobby-socks and neatly tucked into a pair of black Mary Jane shoes. Names that I had heard Melantha use when sorting through the cedar chest at the end of her bed, a ritual she did once or twice a year with April, but something she never wanted me too close for, still I recognized the bobby-socks and Mary Jane shoes. They looked the same as the ones I had caught glimpses of at the top of the cedar chest, when the lid was left open, and when Melantha wasn't guarding its contents.

I stared back at the photo. The little girl's dress looked too white for the dirt that surrounded her, but her face showed no sign of worry, her forehead a playground for light brown curls. She seemed to look at me. I froze, recognizing the pattern of the steps off to the small child's left – one large slab solid with the earth, just before two additional slabs of cement, only they were higher and shaped more like steps. I knew they were the same ones I had seen at the farmhouse when I met Abner Paine, and I had heard Melantha mumble about seeing a little girl in a white ruffle-fronted dress a couple of times in my lifetime, usually when she seemed overly stressed. *Who was the girl in the white dress? And better yet, where is she now?* And, then, *was that the same dress Melantha kept in the cedar chest?* I thought about how she never pulled it out, not even for April, and I thought about how I had noticed her shifting it from side to side in the cedar chest, when I'd walk behind her, her eyes focused on Memory Lane, and her hands coiling back from the item like it was a poisonous snake. I felt goosebumps go down the back of my neck and spine. I sat there looking at the picture, feeling like minutes were passing by, before it registered in my head that my grandfather was talking. Explaining.

"I called her Jo-Jo." He choked back tears. "This is the only photo I have of her," he spoke slowly, forcefully, and I noticed he was trying to show his strength at that very moment, trying not to cry. "She was my oldest daughter. Her name was Joanne Parrish." He stopped to look at me. "She was only five years old when she died. Melantha was only four." He stopped again. This time he let me speak.

"My mom had a sister?" *Why had no one ever mentioned this before?* Then I looked closer at the photo. She was a spitting image of me. *No wonder Grandpa Parrish accepted me like I was his daughter. I looked exactly like her. And, no wonder, Melantha hated me, I reminded her of someone she had lost. But how?* Then I asked it aloud. "How did Jo-Jo die?"

"Police said it was an accident…that she had fallen." Grandpa Homer could barely form the words in his throat. He was trying to focus on the conversation I could tell.

"You don't believe that do you Grandpa?" The question was prompted by his expression; the look on his face said it all. I thought about what I knew had happened in my mother's life when she was three, maybe four. I knew that's when the stepfather, Abner Paine, came into the picture. And, I knew that's when my mom and her mother had first started living at the farmhouse. I never knew about Jo-Jo. I never knew my mom had a sister. I was getting goosebumps thinking about it. *The farmhouse. Is that where it had happened?* "Did Jo-Jo die at the farmhouse?" The question was out before I thought about whether it was insensitive or not.

Homer Parrish couldn't talk at that point. He simply shook his head up and down. Slowly. He had lost his wife and two young girls to a drunk because he was always working. No wonder he appreciated Barbara. She stood by him even when he was away for over a year working on the Trans-Alaska Pipeline. Alma scooted into the arms of a man who…? My thoughts were running wild. *Did Abner have something to do with Jo-Jo's death? Did he hurt her? Did he kill her? Why?*

"I don't want you to talk about it if you don't want to Grandpa." I didn't want to see him break. He was the strongest person I knew. I wanted him to stay that way.

"I'm okay. I need to tell you, so that you know." He paused, gaining his composure, and looking down at the only photo he had of Jo-Jo. "Melantha was sent to boarding school before I knew." He stopped for a moment, looking me in the eyes. "He was sexually abusing your mom, and I later had a medical coroner review Jo-Jo's autopsy records. The coroner suspected that someone had broken Jo-Jo's neck on purpose – the damage to her eyes, internal bleeding – that it probably wasn't a fall, but deliberate, but there was no way to prove it beyond a shadow of a doubt." He took a long swallow of lemonade. "It had been over ten years by that point, too late to exhume Jo-Jo's body and do a full investigation." More lemonade. "I believe Abner Paine killed her because she refused to do what he wanted."

"Grandpa, I'm so sorry." I tried not to cry. I preferred to cry alone when they were sad tears. More pieces of my life were coming together. I thought about how I had heard Melantha talk about Abner. "You did everything you could do back then." I didn't know what else to say to the man that was hurting beside me.

#

Enola tried to focus on school. Her wavy, long brown hair outlined a face that was constantly somewhere else. She moved her five-foot-four frame through the congested hallways at North Fort Myers High School. She didn't pay attention to the guys who would pass her in the hall, glancing at her, desiring her. No, there was no time for that. She had the willpower to focus on one more week of school, and she acted like the faces didn't exist. She looked beautiful like her mom, but she didn't feel it most of the time and tried not to call much attention to herself. Today Enola wore a pair of no-name jeans with a baggy, button-down blouse, lace-trimmed to reflect how she liked being a young woman. She couldn't take the time to think about Melantha or the aunt who she never knew existed. No, today was the beginning of the last week of her senior year. Monday. Friday was graduation. And, Thursday was the day Homer was taking her to the airport to pick up Dixie. Enola smiled at the thought of Dixie coming to her graduation.

The week went by quickly, and Enola filled her days with marking things off her to-do list: Monday get a dress for graduation, Tuesday find a pair of simple black pumps, Wednesday pick up cap and gown, Thursday attend morning rehearsal to get tickets. Four tickets per family was the rule. *Grandpa Homer, Grandma Barbara, Dixie, and...maybe I should give the extra one away to a family that needed it.* Her thoughts were interrupted.

"Excuse me. Would you like an extra ticket?" Enola had just thought it, but it wasn't her voice asking the question. She looked at the chocolate brown eyes that demanded her attention as he spoke. She had never seen eyes so dark. "I'm Rex Narducci. I don't think we've met, but I thought you might need an extra graduation ticket for your family.

"Is that Spanish...your name I mean?" She thought for a second and corrected herself. "No, that's Italian." She studied his chocolate brown eyes. He had dark sparkling eyes, an olive-colored complexion, black-wavy hair, and a smile that was throwing her off schedule. She had to meet Grandpa Homer soon, to make it to the airport, to make it to Dixie. "Isn't it?"

"Yes – yes, it is. And Fears..." he stopped to think. She was thinking too. *How does he know my last name?* She stopped her thoughts to watch him. He couldn't tell her nationality from her fair colored skin, but he sensed she wasn't born in Florida. Her soft-spoken slightly southern voice had to be from somewhere different, perhaps Kentucky. "Probably, English. Where are you from?"

"From North Carolina." She thought about how one of the assistant principals had just addressed her as Ms. Fears when handing her the envelope with tickets inside. *Oh, that's how he knew.* "Well, I lived in Detroit until I was six and then North Carolina until the beginning of this school year." She watched him. He was looking at her lips as she spoke. "My father is English and Cherokee Indian, and my mother is French and Irish.

"What a mixture. No wonder you have such a pretty face." He was still staring at her. He admired her natural look, no make-up or weird haircut, only a clear glowing face highlighted by soft blue eyes, rosy-colored cheeks, and a beautiful smile.

"Thanks for the offer…but.. it looks like I have an extra one myself, because my parents aren't coming, because it's just my grandparents and my friend – a girlfriend I mean." She stumbled over her words, as she tried not to blush. She stopped herself and thought about his smile, his eyes, and his charm. "But maybe I'll see you there." She checked the school clock. Time to go. "I hope."

"Write your number down on my envelope…oh, and please tell me your first name." Enola wrote down the number for Grandpa and Grandma Parrish's house, her house, and the word *Nola.*

"I'll see you, graduation night I'm sure." She smiled at him as she handed back the envelope. He was already smiling back.

#

I was so happy to see Dixie get off the air tram and enter the main gateway area. She looked beautiful, her strawberry, almost red hair, made her stand out from the rest of the passengers that had de-boarded flight 173 from Asheville, North Carolina. We ran to each other and hugged. *Why were we such good friends? What was it she saw in me that she liked? What was it that kept our friendship going throughout the years?* I questioned myself. I sensed that she liked my strength. That's all I had – nothing else. I knew I liked how I could talk to her about anything or anyone. She always seemed to care about me.

My grandparents treated her like they had known her forever. She liked them, and I could tell Grandpa was happy he had brought her down for my graduation. Hours passed quickly. Before we took our first pause in conversation about parents and boys, we were in my bedroom curled up together on the bed. The last thing I remember was three a.m. and talking about Kelsey. Then Rex.

"So, tell me more about this Rex Narducci?" She wanted to know everything, wanted to know about his eyes, his smile, and his quick compliments. "And, what about Kelsey?" I had forgotten that I had sent her a letter, just to tell her I was in Florida, just to tell her about Kelsey. No one knew. Melantha wouldn't have been happy if she had known I was trying to make a pen-pal friend out of Dixie. She wanted me to feel alone. Abandoned. I think that's why she freaked out when she knew I was hanging out with Kelsey, someone to talk to, someone to lean on that was my age, and someone I might possibly find happiness with. But now, I had almost forgotten Kelsey. At least I did earlier in the day, when I was staring into Rex's chocolate brown eyes. I tried to remember Kelsey Albert Gwaltney's eyes, but I couldn't. *A light brown maybe?* I tried to picture them. I do remember they were always polite, always kind, but what was supposed to be the white part of his eyes, was usually red and his pupils usually dilated. Pot. His eyes were pot-colored. That's all I could remember as I answered Dixie.

"Kelsey's not for me." I thought about Grandpa Parrish. Take-charge. "I need a take-charge kind of guy." I laughed at how funny I sounded. My voice was sleepy, yet authoritative. Funny.

We didn't get up until late. Barbara Parrish had breakfast ready even though it was well after lunch. Grandpa Parrish was holding a small box and card that I could tell he was dying for me to open. I tore into the box before devouring my first pancake. Inside there was a gold watch with the date inscribed on the back – June 6, 1978, and my initials – NMF. I smiled. He never called me *Enola*. I was *Nola* even in solid gold. I opened the card in between chatting with Dixie, Homer and Barbara. It felt like I had a real family. It read:

To Nola,

Of all the stars in the sky, I would pick you

You light the way for others to see

You give hope to the darkness

Congratulations on your high school graduation

Love forever,

Grandpa Homer

"I love you so much." That's all I could say without crying in front of Dixie.

"We love you too." I smiled. Again, they had said it perfectly in stride.

#

Dixie had just zipped the solid white dress Enola was wearing. Polyester, low cut, with chiffon barely covering her shoulders. No room for error. It showed every curve. She slipped her legs into the black pumps and looked in the mirror. She smiled. This time it was because she realized the sixteen-year-old in the mirror was attractive. This time it was because she realized that Rex would be sitting somewhere right behind her, probably two or three rows back, just enough where he could study her neckline and picture-perfect shoulders. It was time to go. She slipped on her graduation robe and zipped it, hiding secrets underneath.

They smiled at each other as administrators and teachers lined them up to enter the gymnasium, looking into each other's eyes, walking within a few feet of each other at one point. Rex didn't take his eyes off Enola. *Why is his smile catching my attention and not letting go? What is he doing to me? Is he seriously that into me already?* She questioned herself privately. He was. He couldn't take his eyes off her. Her legs moved perfectly underneath the red graduation robe; her dress hugged her figure secretively and privately. He noticed how she walked gracefully in the black pumps, swaying from side to side as she walked to the row directly in front of his. The chances of him being directly behind her hadn't been calculated in her head.

"You don't have to turn around. I know you're smiling at me." He spoke loudly to the wavy long brown hair in front of him.

"I'm not smiling." Her voice said otherwise. "I'm trying not to laugh."

He was trying too, imagining her beautiful blue, no, heavenly blue eyes. "Nola, promise me a hug when this is all over."

She wished she could see his face, wanting to watch the plea in his chocolate brown eyes, begging for a hug, maybe more. "I promise." She wanted to hug him. There was something in the way his voice hit the back of her neck that made her tingle. And she wanted to kiss him badly. Was Kelsey Albert Gwaltney gone from her memory now?

"I'm holding you to that." He wanted to kiss her lips so badly, but he knew asking her to promise a kiss was being too pushy. He held back his thoughts, taking what he thought would be a safe approach, but he wanted her in more ways than he could imagine.

She turned her attention to the speaker, finishing up a speech about how the future is what you make of it, reminding her that she was at the beginning of a new part of her life.

"I want you to hold me, Rex." The words slipped out of her mouth, before she realized she had said them loud enough for him to hear.

She caught a glance of Homer, Barbara, and Dixie in the crowd, seven or eight rows up in the stands. Dixie had been watching her and was blushing for her, as she had figured out that Enola was chatting with the olive complexion sitting directly behind her.

The names were called quickly and the graduates' chairs began to empty one row at a time as diplomas were handed out in an orderly fashion on stage, and then would fill up again as they returned to their seats before the next row of graduates would stand. Enola noticed he watched her stand, his eyes glaring at the red graduation gown, wondering what was underneath. His smile widened when her name was announced, almost at the same time his row of graduates stood to wait their turn.

Enola May Fears.

Homer, Barbara, and Dixie could be heard cheering loudly, even eight rows up into the stands. He wondered why she had called herself Nola. *Was Enola too formal? It's beautiful.* He thought.

Rex made his way onto the stage just as Enola's row of chairs filled back up. He looked out at his mother and her boyfriend, who were ironically enough just two rows above Homer and Barbara Parrish. He wished his grandmother had been there, but she wasn't. He had known his grandfather wouldn't be, not since his mother had started dating a black man, but he had hoped his grandmother would at least show. She didn't. He caught a glance of Enola just as his name was being announced.

Rex Narducci.

No middle name. He saw that she was smiling directly at him.

The crowd of seniors erupted into a sea of tossing red caps about twenty minutes later. Rex reached for Enola the moment they were standing, pulling her gently over the back of her chair and into

his arms. He kissed her without permission. Long. Passionately. She

felt the strength in his arms as well as his kiss. It was that moment

that she had completely forgotten Kelsey Albert Gwaltney, and

forgotten she secretly saw him just one week earlier.

Did Rex want her as badly as she wanted him? She

wondered. She felt one arm leave her, as Dixie, Homer and Barbara

Parrish made their way through the crowd, voices calling her name.

Rex's mom and her boyfriend had made their way down too, just

long enough to hug his free arm and to tell him to be careful driving.

It was obvious that they were leaving him to his own devices. For a

moment, Enola forgot she was still holding Rex's other arm, smiling

at her grandfather, before letting go to hug Dixie with both.

"What about a nice dinner out?" It was the voice of Homer

Parrish. "Nola, ask your friend if he's available." That was one of

the things Enola liked about her grandfather. He noticed everything,

especially Enola's feelings.

"Thanks for the offer sir, but I don't want to intrude," Rex

spoke up as he reached to shake Homer's hand, a move that

impressed Homer Parrish.

"I would like you to dine out with us." Homer could tell by Enola's eyes that she wanted him to also.

Dixie had taken Enola by one arm and Barbara had taken the other, congratulating her on finishing high school at only sixteen years old, as they walked outside into the Florida June sky. Rex and Homer were walking side by side, talking about the Tampa Bay Buccaneers, and agreeing that Chili's would be the best place to go, at 9:15 at night, for graduation dinner, so that Rex would know where to drive the vehicle that waited outside for him in the lot. An AMC Gremlin. Powder blue. 1970. Eight years old.

Enola excused herself for a moment to chat with Rex at his car door. "Are you sure you don't mind hanging with all of us?" Her smile had faded, as she suddenly felt awkward that she hadn't formally introduced him to Barbara or Dixie, and as she realized he might not want to spend his graduation evening with strangers.

"I want to be wherever you are." He almost couldn't breathe as she reached for the zipper to her red graduation robe, unzipping it, peeling off a satin layer that attracted the moist Florida June heat, exposing the solid white dress that hugged her as he had earlier. He helped her slip it off her shoulders, noticing the roundness of them through the chiffon. "You look beautiful."

She smiled, a smile that said thank-you. "See you in a few minutes." He watched as she turned to walk away. The red graduation gown no longer blocked his view of her backside.

The five of them laughed, talked, and simply relaxed for almost two hours. Chili's was slammed with graduates from North Fort Myers High School and their families. Enola felt surrounded by people who loved her. She touched Rex's hand underneath the table. He was disappointed when Enola took hers away but recovered quickly when he realized where she had left his – on her thigh.

Chapter 7

I talked to Rex Narducci on the phone almost every day while Dixie

was in town, but I didn't see him again after graduation, not until

after Dixie had left to go home. I wanted to spend my time with her,

wanted to turn my learner's permit into a driver's license, wanted to

think about my life, and wanted to figure out why Melantha Fears

had called three times while Dixie and I were out, driving my

grandfather's car to the Edison Mall, and driving around the beach where Kelsey and I used to sit and watch the sunset, only this time I couldn't feel his presence anymore.

It was a Saturday, almost six p.m. when Rex picked me up at my grandparents' house. I joked with him about how I would drive, now that I had my license, but I wanted him to take charge of the whole evening. He said he had a special spot he wanted to take me, a forty-five-minute drive, long enough to talk about things we hadn't.

"Why did you have to finish high school down here, Nola? Not that I'm complaining." He smiled. I smiled back, noticing that he called me Nola.

"It's too complicated to explain." I still wondered why my mother had called a fourth time last night, when I drove Dixie to the airport, carefully, in my grandfather's car.

"I'm sorry." Rex was silent for a brief moment. "I didn't mean to pry." He looked embarrassed for making me feel uncomfortable. I could tell he didn't mean to bring up anything that made me uneasy.

"My father gets violent sometimes. My mother doesn't want me anywhere around, but she doesn't want to lose control over me either." I paused. No judgment. "It's a weird situation."

"I don't know my father." He looked at my face, trying to show me that he could relate to a world full of coldness and despair. "And my mother…well, she's young and makes a lot of mistakes. She was only fourteen when I was born." He talked about how she had used drugs most of her life, how she had been in and out of rehab. Nothing worked. I could tell he was hurting, just like I had hurt so much over the pain my parents had caused. For the last five minutes of the drive we just held hands, looking out the window toward the June gulf that glowed a burnt orange. He kissed me gently on my fingers when we stopped at a light, and I felt it reach up my arm and deep into my heart.

"I'm sorry." That was all I could say to his pain as we drove with the radio turned low – music filling the car, setting close to one another. The stretch of beach where he was headed was an area I hadn't been before. Good. Not that I would be thinking of Kelsey anyway. He pulled his car into the Sandpiper Inn parking-lot, the gulf a stone's throw away, a stretch of private beach in the background, the sand wet, and the waves cold for late June; maybe it was just because the sun was settling deep into the water. The houses lining the beach were glistening with lights, mostly white, on poles and lanterns that one would expect to see at a Polynesian Luau, not a North Carolina mountain in sight, but special in its own way. Refreshing. I didn't feel claustrophobic like I often felt when surrounded by mountains. And, it had a certain charm: traditional stone and ceramic pelicans lined the sandy Florida yards. A tall palm tree blew in the distance, full of coconuts that seemed to dance in the darkening sky, nothing like the old pine tree I used to hide in off Cedar Hill Road in Asheville. None of the beach houses had chimneys or stacks of firewood on the front porches like I remembered most of the houses having in Asheville. But the small houses celebrated the unusually cool June evening with curtains open, shades up, and the doors seldom closed. We walked miles down the beach, admiring the final glow from the bright orange sunset that met the ocean's skyline.

"Maybe we should head back." I looked at him desirably as we cut through a vacant lot, making our way to the two-lane road that lined the other side of the small houses. I wanted to hold him, wanted to stay with him the entire night, but didn't want it to be my suggestion. "What do you think?" I muttered the question, thinking about how Homer and Barbara Parrish weren't even home this evening, as they had traveled upstate to Gainesville to make their once or twice a year visit to see Barbara's sister, and I wanted to leave Rex the opportunity to suggest something else.

"Nola, would you like to check into the Sandpiper Inn for the evening?" There wasn't any pressure in his voice. I smiled as we crossed the two-lane road and walked into the motel office. Rex who would be turning nineteen soon, showed his ID, and collected the key to room 217, where he escorted me with his hand on my lower back, where there was a small oak table inside, where there was an oversized bed, and where he lay me down on the flowered bedspread just as the clock approached nine p.m. Few words were exchanged. No promises. No forever. Darkness overcame us as he gently entered me. He was the first one.

#

Enola turned seventeen on the sixth of August. After a birthday dinner with Enola's grandparents and Rex, a small velvet box appeared in front of Enola. She opened it. Fast. She knew it wasn't a ring, probably a necklace, as the box was rectangular.

"What is it, Rex?" Enola asked – her voice excited.

"Open it. You'll see." He watched her as she slowly peeked inside and was confused when she started to cry.

"It's similar to the one my mom wears." Rex knew recent phone calls with Melantha Fears weren't going well, and he regretted his choice of buying Enola a gold cross immediately.

"Nola, you can exchange it if you want to."

"Are you kidding? I love it!" Her tears glistened on her rose-colored cheeks. She thought about the last time she had watched her mother's hand clutch the gold cross she kept hidden underneath her clothing, thought about how her mom had called at least three or four times each week for the last two months trying to persuade Enola to come home for a reason Enola was sure involved manipulating and hurting someone, and thought about how she had told her mother that she couldn't, that she wanted to start community college in late August, and that she wanted to get her own apartment, and that she couldn't be in the middle of a war zone between Dacey and Melantha, especially after finding out that April Lynn Fears, the sister she felt she hardly knew, had been shipped back to Detroit to live with Dacey's mother. *Gvgeyui.* Enola thought about how Easter Lynn and April Lynn were probably saying it at that very moment. *Gvgeyui.* Then she thought about how Melantha only wanted her back because she was running out of people to torture, running out of people to torture Dacey with. Then she thought about how the cross would feel around her neck, a cold, welcome reminder that Melantha was several states away and needed to stay that way, a reminder that maybe God was real. Dixie thought he was.

"Good, I'm glad you like it." Rex could see she did. "Happy birthday, Nola, I love you." She looked at him without speaking – absorbing the fact that he had just said those three words for the first time. *I love you too.* Enola thought it too but did not answer; instead she turned allowing Rex to fasten the gold chain around her neck. It did look a lot like the one Melantha secretly wore beneath her silk blouse, over 900 miles away, where she was gleaming with a magical smile that only she understood. She had rid herself of April, soon to be thirteen, not because she wanted to, but because it would hurt Dacey to see her go, sent away to a mother he wasn't allowed to communicate with. Melantha was enjoying the pain and misery that Dacey was bathing in every day of his life. He had lost his God, his mother, and now, both daughters. She wasn't going to let Enola stay;

she only wanted to use her, to toy with Dacey, and then send her away again. She was happiest when she was ruining someone's life, controlling someone's destiny, and causing pain like the pain she was in.

Enola looked at the faces in the dining room where they were now enjoying pineapple upside-down cake for her birthday. It had been a perfect seventeenth birthday. No call from Melantha today.

"Grandpa Homer and Grandma Barbara, do you care if Rex and I go for a walk?" Enola looked at her grandparents, noticing they were laughing, talking, the way she wished her parents could be.

"No, enjoy yourselves." Homer Parrish had taken a liking to Rex. He liked the way he seemed to protect Enola.

Enola grabbed Rex's hand. "Come on, it's time for me to give you your present." She smiled, curling up the corners of her soft lips. Rex smiled back, making her hornier than she already was. She looked into his deep brown eyes, making sure no one else was watching, she slid her hand down toward his zipper, and began to pull.

"What do you have in mind?" He almost looked embarrassed, hoping Enola's grandparents hadn't seen his manhood jump to full attention. They raced outside and hurried back behind the vacant house next door where a wooden privacy fence blocked other neighbors from the view, secure and private. They were alone. Enola began to undress herself. First her cut-off shorts followed by her mauve-colored tank top, size 34B bra, and pink lace panties. She stood before him, completely naked, except for the gold cross, which hung between her breasts. "Do you like the present I got you for *my* birthday?" She was wet with excitement. He mopped her up with his mouth first before plunging deep inside of her.

Chapter 8

"Stop the car." I barely got the words out, opened the passenger car

door to Rex's AMC Gremlin, and heaved, forming a small puddle on

the side of the road. "I think I caught my Grandpa Homer's flu."

Then I settled back into the bucket car seat, thinking about how

Melantha was calling more, almost daily, trying to persuade me to

come back to North Carolina, just for a visit. "Or, I'm stressed from

my mother leaving phone messages for me all the time."

"Nola, maybe I should take you to see a doctor. My mom's new boyfriend is a doctor. He'll see you without an appointment."

"Okay." I wiped the residue off my lips. "I'm sick." Then thinking: *Why now? I start at Edison Community College in just two days, the twenty-eighth of August.*

"I'll take you now before the office closes for lunch." Rex turned his Gremlin south, towards a man his mother had known for only a few weeks, towards his mother's recent lover and friend. Within twenty minutes, Rex pulled the car into the Cypress Lake Medical Center in south Fort Myers. "I'll get your door." Rex hurried around the right side of the car, and I grabbed his extended hand when I tried to stand up. I felt light-headed and dizzy, probably from throwing up, probably from not eating.

"Hi Suzzi. Can Dr. Farri take a look at my girlfriend?" I could tell the woman at the desk in the small medical office knew Rex by face. "She's got a touch of the flu and starts community college on Monday." He paused. "We both do."

"I'm sure we can fit her in, Rex. How's your mother?" She asked the question while handing me a patient intake form. He hated talking about his mother, if he could have ignored the question all together he would have, but he didn't want to be rude. Suzzi had fit Rex in for a free head to toe physical just last week. No appointment necessary.

"Enola Fears." A young nurse called my name before I could even sit down, leaving Rex at the counter still chatting with Suzzi. She was filling him with details about her recent trip to Salamanca, Spain and her intermediate Spanish class at the University of Salamanca. I signaled for him to keep chatting, as I followed the nurse into the patient exam room. They were still chatting when I came out, almost forty minutes later. I heard Suzzi talk about her husband's favorite part of the trip. Costa Del Sol, Spain. It wasn't until after he said good-bye to Suzzi, and we had reached the car, that I finally spoke. Slowly.

"I'm pregnant, Rex." I spit out the words, almost hoping he wouldn't hear them, then realizing the man who had just pulled up beside us in the gray van was listening, windows down, as he peered over the top of Rex's car, for Rex's reaction.

Rex's head turned quickly. He smiled with that same sexy, Italian grin I had noticed almost eleven weeks earlier, and he ran around the car to kiss me. "We're going to have a baby!"

"No, I'm going to have a baby!" I realized I sounded paltry. "It's just bad timing, I mean."

"Yeah, but we do love each other. Nola, will you marry me? Will you be my wife?"

I started crying, hard, and wishing he had asked me before – before he knew I was just over two months pregnant with his baby. "I can't, I can't marry you just because …I'm pregnant. I want to get married for the right reason, not like my parents."

"Love is the right reason." He looked at me. I could tell he did love me. We had been saying it to each other all the time. I felt it too.

"Would you want to marry me now, even if I wasn't pregnant?" I watched his eyes. His brown eyes were dark, but not dark enough to hide the truth. He didn't have to answer, but he did.

"Not until after college, I guess." I watched him stare at the red light, now in the poor part of town, east Fort Myers. I wondered why he had said that, as I opened my door and stepped out at the curb, the light turning green, a black man behind Rex's Gremlin laying on the horn, waiting for Rex to move. Evans Street. I looked back at him. I knew my way around. Kelsey had taken me down this road several times to buy his weekly pot stash. I could see he didn't mean to hurt my feelings, so I turned to say goodbye before I walked away.

"I need the weekend alone, okay? I just need to think."

"Nola, please, this is not the best part of town. Get in. I'll take you to your grandparents. The light is green. Will you get in?" He sounded angry. "Get in Enola," he was shouting now and using my full first name, "I'll take you home."

I couldn't look at him. Not now – especially after calling me Enola. My mind was racing. *My mother was in this exact situation,* I thought. I knew she had felt forced to get married, when she was pregnant, and now she's miserable. Crazy. I watched him drive away.

I walked down Evans Street, looking at mothers, some pushing strollers, and wondering what they would have become without their children. I couldn't treat another human being the way I had been treated as a child. Unloved. Unwanted. I stopped walking when I came to the free health clinic on the right-hand side of the road. I noticed a gray van pulling up just as I reached for the clinic door. I realized I wasn't alone.

#

Saturday, the twenty-seventh of August, 6:00 A.M.

Melantha Fears walked into the police station in downtown

Asheville, North Carolina off Merrimon Avenue. She was wearing

an outfit that was unusually revealing, a red silk blouse that was

extremely low cut, and a black leather mini-skirt. Her calls to Enola

had been ignored, her marriage was empty, and both daughters were

gone. She wanted attention. She waved to Desk-Sergeant Wayne

Zubbel, as she walked past him, her only concern to meet a couple of

women who were being released from overnight custody. When she

rounded the corner, she met her imaginary friends. They were

dressed the same, lots of makeup, high heels, and revealing,

somewhat slutty, attire.

"Meg, we over here. You da bomb posting for us, honey."

She smiled at Ernie's voice inside her head, a tall black woman with

a warm, friendly smile and eyes you couldn't trust, the other, a white

woman with an unsightly overbite, but a body that would stop

traffic, and had on many occasions. Melantha, known as Meg by the

two women she was collecting, not Mel, looked around like she had

never been there before and then collected her friends and left. To them she had no last name. But if asked, it was Fleming. Meg

Fleming, twenty-six years old, a hooker from Detroit.

Melantha Fears had spent many lonely nights at home, alone,

while Dacey, back to his usual routine now, roamed the streets of

downtown Asheville looking for action. A business trip, a late-night

meeting at the office for Sultan's tire shop, whatever you want to

call it, and he was fucking whomever he could find. It's a wonder he

didn't end up fucking his own wife. They sometimes worked the

same street but never knew it. Meg Fleming walked down Merrimon

Avenue, with a sense of carelessness, a strong belief that she was a

seasoned hooker, that she really was Meg Fleming, and that she

would take chances with any type of john. Unlimited. There were no

guidelines on the street, no list of rules to follow for screening

potential johns. They ranged from lonely seventy-year-old men to

young boys who could no longer take the peer pressure of being a

virgin. Variety was the spice of life on Merrimon Avenue.

"Ernie and Tiger, you guys up the creek again, gotta stop

trying to fuck cops." Meg laughed, something Melantha wasn't able

to do. She walked back past Sergeant Zubbel and wondered why he

was looking at her so strangely. "It took me a hard pop and two blow jobs to make this money. Guess I'll be airing it out tomorrow night while you gals pay me back." She twisted the black string of fake pearls around her neck, her chest vacant of the gold cross she cherished so much. That was Melantha's. Meg wasn't allowed to wear it. Sergeant Zubbel shook his head in disbelief. *Another crazy.* He thought as she passed.

"We's gonna hav'to get a pimp, if this keps up!" Ernie said.

"We don't need no fucking pimp!" Tiger joined in on the conversation. "We's got each other." The three-woman laughed, as they walked across the empty street, glowing under the sun that was just waking up, soon it would be Dacey stirring, fifteen minutes until seven, time for Meg to get home, quietly slip back through the open bedroom window, where she would slip out of her clothes, and crawl under the freshly laundered satin sheet in order to wake an hour or so later, not knowing where her body had been.

She moved slowly out from beneath the satin beige sheet. She removed the cheap string of black pearls from around her neck and placed them on her dresser top, puzzled about why she was wearing them, puzzled about the pile of clothes on the floor beside the bed, and puzzled about feeling so tired. She looked at her naked body in the dresser mirror and touched the small bruises around the nipples of her breasts, moving her hands slowly down her own body, fondling the lips of her vagina, noticing the soreness that ached from that sacred part of her body. She almost didn't recognize the woman that stood before her. She grabbed a robe from the closet, and quickly walked toward the shower, a hot shower. She would scrub herself, over and over again. Harder and harder each time. This had become a ritualistic part of Melantha Fears' morning. She felt empty, often callous, and unable to love herself or anyone else around her. She dressed in a black turtleneck sweater, matched with a dark wool skirt of black and gray. She fastened the gold chain around her neck, tucking it carefully beneath her conservative attire. The solid gold-cross hung there, between the breasts that had recently been suckled by strangers in the night.

#

It was a hot August morning, even though the end of the month was here. The North Carolina sky had turned to clouds before the clock could reach ten a.m. Melantha smiled when she thought about Dacey, how he was probably up two hours ago, while she slept, heading out the door, his feet in pain, trying to make a living, busting his ass, even on a Sunday. He was the only one working, at least as far as he knew, the only one trying to make the mortgage on another house, this one about fifteen miles from the last. The last home had been foreclosed on, the cost of Dacey's secret life of betting on the horses, or dogs, or sports, or whatever he could find to wager on. He had lost thousands, wiping their savings account clean on several occasions.

Melantha felt surprised when she walked into the living room of the Enka home, where Dacey was sitting in his recliner, the T.V. on, his feet up, eyes half shut.

"What are you doing here?" she asked.

"It looks like it might rain."

"You can't work if it rains? Well, excuse me. How the hell are we supposed to pay the mortgage?" Her dark blue eyes grew even darker. She looked almost evil. Possessed.

"We'll manage." He thought about the game he had money riding on. 1000 dollars. There was no way Detroit would lose their first game of the season. *Maybe I should call and put an extra wager on Detroit.* He thought, ignoring the yapping wife in front of him.

"No, you'll manage!" She looked at him with a frozen stare, and for the first time in months he didn't seem to notice, in fact, he didn't seem to care. "Have you forgotten how easily I can put your ass in jail?"

"I'm tired of your threats, Mel." She could tell he called her that on purpose.

"Maybe that's the problem. Maybe I've been threatening you too much. Maybe it's time I carry through on my so-called threats!"

"Maybe you should. Maybe I'd be happier in jail than with you, in your world. Under your control." The words cut through Melantha like a knife. Jail was no longer a threat to him. There he would be away from her. He would no longer be her puppet. She stood there. Silent. She had nothing but a blank look on her face. She looked lost. Empty. She looked almost dead. Then something Dacey had never experienced before happened. She changed before his very eyes.

"Hey, honey, let's not fight. Make love to me. Make love to me now." Her eyes softened as they peered into his, and she melted before him.

"What kind of trick are you playing on me now, Mel?" He wanted her. He wanted to fuck her over and over again. He had slept on the couch since Enola had left, their bedroom door shut all night, locked, keeping him out.

"I need you." She said it with such desperation. Such sincerity. Such warmth.

"Undress me." He said the words in a demanding tone. He loved to watch her melt, to desire him more than anything, to want to be consumed by him, beg for it, over and over again. Her heavy breathing, her eagerness, and her pleas for his manliness to be inside of her, all the while she was willing to play any game he commanded.

"Dacey, go ahead, hurt me." She unfastened the final button on his trousers and watched the pile of polyester as it fell to the living room floor.

"Bitch!" The impact of his hand stung the left side of her face. He grabbed her uncontrolled body and pulled it close to him, and within less than a minute he had ripped the black and gray skirt off her already sore body, breaking the zipper that had once held it in place. He pushed her body onto the floor and drove her like the seventeen-year-old dead girl had driven her red Trans Am – hard – fast. Bouncing her up and down, pushing into her with an awesome force. Just to hear her scream. Pinching the ends of her nipples, which were already in pain, ignoring her cries to stop, licking the tears that ran down her face.

"Had enough?" He looked at her, hoping the tears would still be there, hoping he had hurt her, as he pulled his penis out of her raw vagina.

She stared up at him and smiled a friendly but unfamiliar grin. "That's only sixty-dollars today, honey." Melantha Fears wasn't there. Dacey didn't know the woman who lay naked on the floor underneath him.

Chapter 9

When I walked out of the free health clinic off Evans Street,

Rex was waiting for me. He wasn't the only one that had followed

me. I noticed the gray van that we had parked next to earlier, from

The Cypress Lake Medical parking lot, again parked, again with a

man inside, who looked away when I glanced in his direction. *Am I*

being paranoid? Am I mistaken? Had he heard I was pregnant when

Rex hugged me in the doctor's office parking lot? Who was he? And then before opening the door of Rex's Gremlin, *I'm losing my mind. It's probably just a coincidence.*

"Our baby will have both parents, Nola." He reached over to kiss me, a look of relief on his face. He knew I hadn't been in the clinic long enough to have any life-changing medical care performed. No abortion – even though I had gone in for the information. "We will show this baby all the love in the world." I looked into his eyes as he spoke. I wanted that, wanted to break the cycle of unloving and uncaring parents. It was up to us to make things change. I knew that.

"I do too." That was all I could say right then. I just wanted the fresh gulf air in my face, windows down, pulling out onto Evans Street, leaving the gray van, still parked. *Who was he waiting for?* I wondered.

The air barely moved, not a wrinkle on the Gulf of Mexico. I felt a bit nauseous and wondered what I would say to Grandpa and Grandma Parrish as we got closer to their house. *What will they think? What about my parents? Everyone will probably think my mom was right all along. The little slut went and got herself pregnant!* I started to tear, as I stared out the window, until I felt Rex's hand take mine.

Homer Parrish was sitting just inside when we pulled up. I could see him, as I stumbled for the words in my brain, before reaching for the door, before feeling Rex's hand on the small on my back. The words poured out, before Homer could even say hello.

"I'm pregnant. Do you mind becoming a great-grandpa?"

"Are you kidding?" That was all he could think of to say, I guess, but I wasn't disappointed as I could see the sparkle in his eyes.

"I'm going to have a baby. Rex and I are going to have a baby. I want you to be happy."

"I am, shocked, but very happy." I noticed he stared at my stomach as I shut the front door behind me, but he didn't notice me watching his eyes.

"Nola, is that what you want? Do you want a baby?" My grandfather always had a very practical side probably the same side that made me walk into a health clinic for a brochure on abortion. They had given me two – one on abortion – one on adoption. I had walked out with both, not realizing I still had them in my hand, where his eyes now looked.

"I'll help you with whatever you guys decide." He stood with his hand on my shoulder. His face had looked lifeless from the years of pain Melantha had caused. He didn't want any more pain for me. He wanted me to be free to make whatever decision I wanted. He was still eyeing the brochures.

"These were given to me by a doctor." I felt Rex take them from my hand, and I heard the sound of ripping behind me. "We've decided to keep the baby."

"I'm going to be a great-grandpa!" I looked into his face, wrinkles seemed to fade, or at least stretch into a smile that was almost the size of Florida. *Was he really happy that his seventeen-year-old granddaughter was going to have a baby sometime in April?* I wondered.

"You're happy?"

"I'm going to spoil that kid rotten!" My grandfather's face suddenly looked ten years younger.

"Great." I felt at ease and was glad someone besides Rex knew I was pregnant. I began to feel nauseous again and hurried past grandma who was standing just a few feet away, her hands over her

mouth, hiding a grin that only great grandmothers get, but I could

tell she was happy too. The cold water felt good against my face. I

braced myself next to the counter and tried not to think about my

parents. I knew that somehow Melantha would cause problems. *But

what could she possibly do to me?* I patted my face with a cool

washcloth. *I'll have to be careful how I tell her.*

I didn't realize at the time that the man in the gray van

already did.

#

Meg Fleming stepped into the downtown motel at precisely one in

the morning, a dump, known for its one-hour guests, and its

revolving door policy. She was wearing leather slacks this time, and

when she walked up to the counter, she waved at the clerk behind the

desk, reached for the key he handed her, and walked down the hall.

She had been there before.

"You've got a real strange one waiting for you Meg." The

clerk flirted after the leather making its way down the hallway,

knowing that her payment for the room would be their usual – a

weekly freebie. "Tall black man."

"Thanks Tim." Dangerous? Did Meg Fleming know what she was doing? The body of Melantha Fears walked toward the dark stranger, but the only personality present was that of Meg. The man stood at the motel doorway, visible when Meg rounded the hallway to room 103. She felt herself getting excited as she thought about fucking the tall black man. She imagined his dick was long and hard. Few words were exchanged, just eye contact. His eyes were dark, almost black like his skin. The voice was tall, about six-three, and rather handsome. He pulled her close, holding her arms tighter than she liked, and she felt herself losing control of the situation. No money was exchanged. She had to regain control. Business.

"What can I do for you, honey?"

"It's what I'm going to do for you." The tall dark voice was authoritative as it locked the deadbolt on 103.

"What do you mean, sweetheart?" She started to feel the grip tighten around her arms. So much pressure was beginning to hurt.

"Whore." He shoved her body down onto the over-used bed. "You do as I say and maybe I'll let you live." He ripped at the leather slacks. "I'll kill you if you scream!" He pulled out a switchblade knife and popped it open. "I'm going to take my time with you. Maybe even more than one time." Melantha suddenly

entered her body. She thought about her mother's funeral and

remembered the smell of fresh red clay being shoveled onto the

casket. Cold-red clay. "Your tit bleeds real fine. Don't move on me,

bitch, or I'll cut deeper and harder. Your nipple is almost off, just

hold still you fucking bitch." He cut circles around the darkened

nipple on her breast, and once again she thought of her mom,

thought about the wasps that had stung her after their nest had been

shredded with the mower, so many wasps, so many stings, over and

over again. *She should still be alive. Why did she have to die?*

Melantha couldn't leave the body being cut. "You need more pain,

bitch? Haven't you had enough yet?" He had the knife in his left

hand now and was hitting her face with his right fist. She remained

quiet. She remained at the cemetery. "Beg me to stop. I should kill

you! Do you want to die, whore? Want me to cut your other nipple

off now?" He waited for an answer. He raised himself off her,

standing like a tower at the end of the mattress, watching blood drip

down her side, the mattress a sponge. He punched her in the

stomach, waiting for her to beg him for her life. He didn't stop

punching her until she was nearly dead. "It's your fault, bitch. I would have stopped, if you'd asked me to." She heard the deadbolt but imagined it was the last shovel of red clay. She felt the pain at the end of her breast, wiping it with her hand, raising it above her swollen face, noticing the color – red. I must be dead too. Red clay.

#

Dacey woke to an eight-a.m. alarm, then rolled off the living room sofa and started dressing for another day of customers wanting expensive tires for nothing, waiting for Melantha to come out of the bedroom and start yelling about something. Or, if he were lucky, maybe he would have a repeat performance of their last sexual encounter. Although, it still bothered him that she had asked for money at the end. *It was her way of being cruel*. He imagined. Still, he wondered why Melantha wasn't out there badgering him yet; she enjoyed her early morning ritual, making him feel small, a failure, a poor excuse for a husband and father, with a smile on her face the entire time. He glanced toward the unopened bedroom door, expecting to see Melantha and wondered why he felt so concerned when she wasn't there. The bedroom was silent.

"Mel?" He spoke loudly, using her shortened name, hoping that the door would open and she would start her bitching. He wanted to hear her voice. "I'm leaving now." He wanted an answer, and he was growing more concerned at the overwhelming silence coming from what used to be his bedroom too, from what he thought was going to be his bedroom again, after the last time they were together, after playing the game she wanted, after coming inside of her. "Is there anything I can bring home? Milk?" He knew she hated milk, knew she would scream at him for even offering, but still no answer. He tried the door handle, which he assumed would be locked, but instead it opened, with his gentle push and cautious entrance, where he expected to see her half asleep. He first noticed a gold cross on her neatly made bed, and he remembered seeing that cross hang from her neck when he pinned her to the living room floor and rode her hard, relentlessly. "Are you in the bathroom?" He suddenly felt very alone, as though he longed to hold her again. Then he opened the master bathroom door, searched the small room with his eyes, and became nervous when he found the room lifeless and still. *Where could she be?* Dacey felt certain something was horribly wrong. He dialed the Asheville Police Station. Sergeant Zubbel, a man in his mid-forties, answered the phone.

"Downtown precinct, Zubbel here."

"I'd like to report" – he searched his mind for the correct wording – "a missing person. My wife, Mrs. – Mrs. Melantha Fears is missing…I don't know what to do. And I'm sure something is wrong. I know she wouldn't leave the house in the middle of the night. I went into her bedroom this morning to check on her, finding it completely straightened like she hadn't slept there at all." Dacey's voice lowered to a whisper and he looked down at the floor from embarrassment even though no one was around. "We don't sleep in the same room anymore."

The sergeant wasn't writing down the information, as he listened to the details being given on the other end of the line, instead he simply listened. He gave a rehearsed reply. "Call back if she is still missing after seventy-two hours."

Dacey stood very still for a long moment as he placed the receiver back in order. His face looked very tired. He had no family to call. Enola and he hadn't spoken in over a year. Easter Humphreys, his mother, didn't want to be bothered with him anymore, having sent a letter several weeks earlier that told him not to worry about April Lynn. *She doesn't need to be raised around such a weak man anyhow.* He remembered her words. *I don't claim you as my son anymore.* He could still remember the knot in his stomach when Melantha read the letter during dinner to him. He had the same knot now. He had no one. He paced slowly, and stopped at the phone once again; then, remembering the lawyer, he started to dial. Melantha had kept his number handy beside the phone, in plain sight, a constant threat to Dacey. He would be able to help. He had connections. And he would do anything for Melantha. Dacey knew they had been together several times. He could smell the expensive cologne on her, *his* cologne, which she wouldn't try to hide. Dacey knew his wife was fucking him. But it didn't matter now, what mattered was finding her. So, he dialed the number carefully and asked for Mr. Grover Starks. He explained it was about Melantha Fears. The secretary patched him directly through to Mr. Starks. Immediately.

"Mr. Starks? It's Dacey Fears." His eyes searched the driveway for her car. Nothing.

"Yes, what can I do for you Mr. Fears?" Grover sounded puzzled to hear directly from Dacey. "How is Melantha?"

"Melantha." Dacey thought for a moment about how ridiculous it was to call in a panic concerning his now thirty-seven-year old wife not being home, at what was pushing 8:30 in the morning. Then he remembered how apparent it was that she hadn't slept there at all. It wasn't like her. She wouldn't sleep somewhere else, not without first advertising it over and over again, trying to make Dacey angry, trying to make him jealous. Dacey knew that simply disappearing wasn't her style. "Yes, yes, I was hoping you'd know where she is."

"I haven't seen Mel since Wednesday. We had lunch at a nice restaurant downtown." He had to rub in the fact that Dacey was just a tire salesman, barely making a living. He hated Dacey. And he would do anything to win Melantha's love. Funny thing is, she didn't want to marry Grover. She couldn't love anyone, no matter how hard she wanted to, but Dacey was the closest she had ever come.

"She's missing. I don't know where she is." God, he hated confiding in Mr. Starks of all people, but he wanted to find Melantha. He wanted to tell her that he could change. He could love her again, the way he used to, the way he wanted to.

"Did she sleep there last night? At home?" Grover had tried to get Melantha to move in with him before, but she didn't want to leave Dacey. She said he couldn't make it without her.

"No. We…" he hesitated to tell him all the details. Why should he tell him that they hadn't been sleeping in the same room? Why shouldn't he let him think of Melantha's warm, naked body beside the one she chose to be with…Dacey? "She wasn't here this morning when the alarm went off."

"Did you call the hospitals?" Grover's mind was racing, wondering where she would be so early. Surely nothing had happened to her.

"No. I didn't think of it. I'll call, right now."

"No, I'll do it; I'll put my secretary to work on it right away." His voice sounded controlling and authoritative. "I'll call you back as soon as I find out something."

"Thanks, Grover. Please do." He thought about how he should probably address him by his last name but remembered that he had addressed Melantha as Mel. She wouldn't like that he thought. *Or was it something she let him do?* He wondered. And then, without saying goodbye, he hung up, as he sat staring at her picture on the coffee table in front of him. Then, he noticed that both kids' photos had been removed from the adjoining picture frames and were filled with a picture of the Cedar View Road house on one side, and a picture of the Enka home on the other. The kids no longer existed, replaced by a house they had been evicted from due to foreclosure and a house that they might soon lose for the same reason – gambling. Dacey had spent many days sneaking off to a local bookie. There wasn't any money for the mortgage that was due in just a few days. None. *But what did it matter now*? He thought, and then began to cry for the second time in his adult life.

Chapter 10

It was almost noon, by the time Rex came over to my grandparents'

house. We had gathered on the back screened-in porch, which was

unusually warm, for a September afternoon. The Florida sun was

hot, and the slight fall breeze was the only thing that kept it from

getting unbearable. I was happy with the reaction I had gotten a few

days earlier from Homer and Barbara. The words played over and

over again in my head. *I'm going to be a great-grandpa!* I hoped the

reaction I got from my parents would be even a fraction as good. I had put off the announcement longer than I thought I would. We had decided today would be the day, so I dialed the Enka residence, no one answered. Instead, there was a rushed recording, an unfamiliar voice, directing callers to leave a message, and emergencies should be directed to the office of Mr. Grover Starks. *What was Melantha up to now?* I wondered. *And, why wasn't she capable of leaving her own voice recording?* And then. *Was Grover Starks the attorney she used to get Dad out of jail?* I quickly announced the name to Grandpa Parrish, who confirmed that was the same attorney. I hesitated before dialing the number, and instead, I chose to hand the phone to Homer. Why not? He knew the attorney from previous conversations and had a knack for handling attorneys. I couldn't read Homer's facial expressions. He kept a poker face throughout the conversation, which only lasted about fifteen minutes.

"That was Mr. Grover Starks, Melantha's attorney. I'm afraid I've got some bad news Nola…your mother is in the Biltmore Hospital. She was…uh…attacked, but she is going to be okay." Rex already had me in his arms, somewhat of a restraint, probably worried about the baby, and somewhat for comfort. There was a look of confusion and sadness on everyone's face, but no tears, more like

puzzlement. *Who would attack Melantha and live to tell about it?*
I'm sure Rex, Barbara, and Homer were all thinking the same thing.
I tried to hide the blank look on my face. *Should I cry?* I knew
everyone was waiting for a reaction to the news about my mother's
attack, but what could I possibly say? I had been mentally abused by
my mother my entire life, and now I had to start making a life on my
own, finally I was just at the point where I felt loved by someone,
and finally I had reasons to live my life to the fullest. I had found
someone who loved me, and I loved him; I wasn't going to feel
guilty for looking out for myself. No more interrogations and
screaming matches – riddled with words like slut and whore. I didn't
give a damn about the person named Melantha Fears. I was finally in
control of my own life and in love, and all I wanted was to be with
Rex and our baby. I glanced at my grandfather with a serious look in
my eyes and held Rex's hand as I began to speak.

"I don't care if she lives or dies, I can't afford to care." But I
knew the words weren't true. I loved my mother. I loved both
Melantha and Dacey Fears.

"Nola, you know you don't mean that. She's your mother,
even if she hasn't been a good one." Barbara Parrish, usually quiet,

piped in. I could tell Homer and Barbara didn't expect the attitude that was coming from me. I also knew her words were right. I had always wanted to get along with her. I would have done anything to have that warm, caring mother-daughter relationship, but not now, it was too late.

"She's only my mother by birth." I wiped a tear that was trying to force its way down my face. "I've got myself to think about now, and Rex, and our baby…" I watched the eyes on Barbara Parrish widen.

"No. You don't want to look back on this and regret it Nola." The voice was still Barbara's. Calm. Insistent.

"I support however you want to handle this." This time the voice was Homer's. Strong. Independent.

"I know you do." I looked into my grandfather's eyes as I spoke. I felt as though he was my real father. He had been there for me more than any other relative. I had a special kind of love for him. It was something real and honest, not like what I had with Melantha and Dacey. I had vowed to myself that I wouldn't settle for less ever again. The happiness I had in my life was something new for me. It was strong, not buttered over like the life I had come from.

"Rex and I, we are going to give this baby a good home." I paused thinking about what this had to do with my mother being in the hospital. "I have to keep myself surrounded by positive people right now. For me, for Rex, and for our child."

"I know." My grandfather understood. He knew that even visiting Melantha could result in tragedy.

"Can I use the phone to call Dixie?" I was already reaching for the phone, already dialing Dixie's number. Positive people. She definitely was one of mine, and I needed her to know…about the baby, and about Melantha.

We talked for nearly forty minutes, talking about Rex, how much I loved him, talking about the baby, and how I was going to love my baby with all my heart, and talking about Melantha, and how Dixie could find out her condition for me. That way I could keep my distance.

#

"I love you." Melantha heard Dacey's voice and felt a squeeze at her hand. She couldn't open her right eye. It was swollen shut. The hospital room was cold and impersonal, just like her life. She opened her left eye to look at Dacey. He was sitting beside her, almost in tears. She stared into his eyes for a long moment, almost wondering who he was, then looked away, toward the white-colored wall. She had been badly beaten and pain emerged from all parts of her body. There was a web of bandages around her chest, and she could barely open her mouth. Her entire face looked like she had been in a boxing match and clearly lost. It was strange, not knowing what had happened, not knowing where she had been.

Dacey let go of her hand, and slowly moved toward the unopened window, and then stopped to turn and look at her. The woman he had been fighting with for over seventeen years was gone. He studied her face, helpless, insecure, and alone. He felt empathy for her. He knew what it was like to lose everything and everyone. At the moment, she looked like she did too.

"What were you doing at the motel? Did you sleep at home last night?" He waited for her to tell him that it was none of his damn business, but she started to cry instead.

"I don't know…I can't remember a motel." She looked at him and tried to fight back the tears, with her hands carefully trying to dry her swollen face. It was obvious that she didn't remember anything about last night, and Dacey couldn't help but notice her confusion.

"Do you remember who attacked you?"

"No – I can't remember." She felt the pain radiate from her face and throb from her breast, where she had been cut and her nipple dismembered like a tree with garden shears. "My breast, it hurts." She tugged at the bandages that covered her, and Dacey quickly calmed her by restraining her arms to her sides.

"The doctor said you probably wouldn't be able to remember much because of shock." He was holding her tighter now, and there was a feeling between them that had been absent for years. It was a strong sense of need, a need to love one another. It was a feeling that had disappeared so long ago, and they had both believed would never return. "I'm glad you're alive, Melantha…I need you in my life…" he waited for rejection; instead, she moved her face closer to his and let him proceed in the delicate operation of kissing her abused face. "Do you need me, Melantha?" He felt his entire life pass before him as he waited for her answer; he looked like his life depended on her reply.

"I need you. You're my man, the only man I've ever been able to truly love." Her pain suddenly relocated, piercing the corners of her heart, as she felt alive and in love for the first time in many years.

"I'm sorry for all the times I've cheated on you. I didn't love any of them." He seemed sincere. "I hope you'll…" her lips stopped him before he could finish speaking.

"Shhh, …it's over." This time she meant it; she was tired of playing games, living alone even when she was with other people, constantly hurting inside.

They fell asleep side-by-side, Dacey holding her gently in the small hospital bed. He didn't even wake when Melantha sat up the following morning, able to move his arm off her stomach, able to dial the number of Grover Starks' office, able to question him about his P.I.'s recent findings, and able to listen as Grover encouraged her to focus on her own health, and then finally revealing his informant's recent discovery. *My daughter is pregnant.* She let the words sink into her head. *Slut. Whore.* She hung up the phone after a rushed goodbye.

Melantha reached for her clothes. Leather pants? *You've got to be kidding?* Confusion sat in again as she heard Dacey stirring behind her. *Whose clothes are these?*

"Melantha?"

She was happy that she at least recognized his voice. "I don't know where my clothes are." She turned to look at him. "They've accidentally given me another patient's."

"Don't worry." He knew those were the clothes the paramedics had delivered with her to the emergency room, knew because he had made it to the hospital in time to watch a nurse label the see-through plastic bag with her initials – MF.

"We need to get you home." He remembered how he had promised her that she would always be the only one for now on, how he would make things better between them, and how he had fallen asleep with her just seven hours earlier, one arm draped over her, protecting her from any further attackers. "I love you, Melantha." He sat up looking at her, watching her confusion, as she tried to slip her legs into the stranger's leather pants.

"I love you too, Dacey."

She stood, pulling them up, noticing they fit perfectly. Then she started to cry. She couldn't stand not remembering anymore. A piece of her life, a glance, would help her understand. She fell into Dacey's arms, a blouse she didn't recognize clutched in her right hand.

"It's okay to cry, Mel. I'll help you get through this." He looked into her wet ocean blue eyes. He wanted to tell her what *he* had found out from Grover Starks, wanted to tell her what the police knew about her repeated presence at the sleazy downtown Asheville motel, but he couldn't. Not yet. Instead, he finished dressing her, finishing putting her into clothing he knew she didn't recognize, and then he gave her every ounce of energy he could, by lifting her to a standing position, making sure she held tight, and helping her to the wheelchair a nurse had parked at the door. "Let's go home." That was all he could say.

Chapter 11

Dixie called as soon as she found out my mother had been released

from the hospital. Discharged. Recovering at home. The information

was helpful, so I didn't worry, didn't wonder about whether she

wasn't going to make a full recovery; although, the information

came about thirty minutes too late, after I had already picked up the

phone at Homer and Barbara Parrish's home, after I had already

become an unwilling participant in Melantha's screaming match,

which vibrated through me and my unborn child.

"You're pregnant Enola!" I heard my mother's voice shouting into the phone, breaking the silence of a September morning in sunny Florida, reminding me that it was time Rex and I set out on our own, away from her, away from her spies. I thought about the gray van I had seen at the doctor's office and again at the free health clinic, thought about how I felt the man was watching me, almost stalking me. Now, I knew. I knew it was Melantha's work. I thought about Billy Joel's song. *Only the good die young.* I tried to see the humor. *Apparently, my mother will live forever.* I thought. Then, like a light switch, or maybe just to take care of the baby, I turned the screaming off. I thought about Rex. I couldn't be more in love. I moved my free hand to my stomach, searching for life, trying to find the heartbeat inside of me, wondering what the baby looked like, and wondering what an eleven or twelve-week embryo thought. *Could it hear its grandmother's screams?* I wondered. I should be happy. But, I felt myself staring into thin air, felt my eyes become motionless. I had enough. Then I hung up the phone and walked away. My life was changing again, rapidly. And, it was time to create an even bigger change. Starting college would have to be put on hold and finding an apartment in the area didn't feel right either. It was too close to Melantha's grasp. It was time to escape.

I spent the rest of the week thinking about my life, taking in the fact that I had hung up the phone on my screaming mother just four days earlier, and reaching for the mail I had seen being stuffed into the Parrish's mailbox earlier that day. I was surprised to see an envelope with my name on it. Enola Fears. Written in bold in lieu of the return address was: *open and enjoy.* I could tell it was my mother's handwriting. Inside there were several photos of a young couple sitting at the beach, arm and arm, close. I read the attached note, short and to the point, before running back inside, before dialing Melantha. She answered right away. I could tell she was smiling. I could hear it in her hello. I had heard it so many times before, when she was about ready to ruin someone's life.

"What the hell are you trying to do mother?" I stared at the photos. Kelsey was holding me close, probably just a week or so before meeting Rex, a secret rendezvous, an agreement to meet just one more time to give a proper good-bye, but just the right amount of time to create conspiracy, which the note manipulatively threatened. *I wonder if Rex will believe it's his?* I read the note over and over again in my mind. I read its determined and controlled tone.

"You should cover your tracks more often, Enola. The detective I hired has been following you for months and had no trouble getting up-close shots of you and Kelsey at the beach." She paused for effect. "You can keep those copies. I'll send Rex his own set, as soon as my detective calls with his mailing address." She paused again. "Can you imagine how it will fill him with doubt? Did you even tell him about Kelsey?" I heard the smile turn into a slight laugh. "For that baby's sake, I hope Rex doesn't doubt you, and suddenly you find yourself alone with no one and a small baby to ruin your life."

"Are you trying to say this baby is Kelsey's? I slid my hand down over my stomach and stared with disbelief into the eyes of Homer Parrish who had started to listen to the conversation. I knew my mother was capable of pulling some cruel stunts on people in the past, the way she lied about people, the way she would get so much pleasure out of causing someone pain. "You know that's not true!"

"Maybe. But I can make Rex doubt you Enola. I can tell him about how close you were to Kelsey, still missing him, even when you came up here to help with your sister while your dad was in jail." She stopped long enough to measure my breathing. Rapid. Stressed. "You didn't think I knew about your little phone call to Kelsey from my home line?" I knew her smile was widening. "That was stupid." She laughed aloud. "All I need to do is show your new boy-toy that it's possible."

I couldn't respond. I simply stood there, hand on my stomach, looking into Homer's face, then hung up the phone, only to pick it up again. Dixie first. Then Rex. Homer watched my every move, studying my posture, my face. He had taken what cash he had and placed it in an envelope before I could get off the phone with Dixie. Four hundred and thirty dollars – enough to leave and get lost. Dixie understood. The conversation with her was brief. *I'll contact you after I turn eighteen, after the baby is born. Don't worry.* I couldn't help but say it over and over in my head while I dialed Rex.

"Hey. Don't come over tonight." I thought about how the gray van or men just like him were everywhere. "Change of plans." I stopped, thinking about how I was going to get him to buy into my plan. "I want a fresh start Rex, in a new place, just the two of us, three of us." I corrected myself quickly, feeling the life kick slightly inside of me. "Will you meet me at the bus station?"

"What?" He reacted like I had lost my mind. "Are you okay?" I heard the worry in his voice. We had been planning on moving, somewhere, but not tonight, not for a couple of months. We needed to save money, get an apartment, steady jobs. Rex had been working at Lundstrom's Jewelers in downtown Fort Myers but hadn't planned to leave so soon. The baby wasn't due until April – plenty of time to save and figure out where we should live.

"I'm okay. I just need you to trust me on this…please."

"Nola, tell me what's going on."

"I will. Just meet me at the Greyhound bus station in Estero, around 7 p.m. tonight." I tried to swallow, my throat dry. "Have someone drop you off." And then, "Don't bring your car." I felt a crackle in my voice, trying to fight back how much I was going to miss my grandfather. He was the only man that had been a father to me. He had already pressed the envelope into my hand as I hung up the phone and stood, still looking into his eyes, which always seemed to comfort me. He knew Melantha had me cornered. He had heard enough of her conversation, her loud bragging, her life-altering threats. I could hide for eleven months, until I was eighteen, giving me a couple of months after the birth of our baby to prove paternity. I would think of a way to nonchalantly get our baby tested, us tested, and to prove that the three of us were family. Then any accusations wouldn't be believed.

"I'll help you pack and drive you to the Greyhound bus station Nola." Homer Parrish hugged me like the father I never had.

#

"Je suis heureux." Melantha could tell he didn't understand. "I am so happy." She propped herself up on one elbow, and Dacey did the same. They had spent the entire night just holding each other, after getting off the phone with Enola, after learning how upset she was about the photos, and after threatening Enola that Rex's address would receive a package soon, an arrangement that Melantha didn't know was about to be foiled. The P.I. was a longtime friend of Grover's, who had started to feel that he had slipped up and started to question himself about Melantha's pleas: send photos, call me directly, get Rex's address, don't bother Grover, just work directly with me, Grover is too busy. He was good at his job, good at following through, but good at being loyal first, so he picked up the phone to inform Grover that Rex's address was available and ready as his client wanted. Grover Starks wasn't happy with her little games. *I have Rex's address, which you won't be supplied with until I figure out what you're up to.* She could still hear the seriousness in Grover's voice when he called. Mad. *My P.I. will not be taking any of your calls in the future.* Still hear his anger. *You deal directly with me – no one else.*

Still Melantha was happy. She would figure out how to manipulate Grover Starks. She enjoyed the challenge. For now, she was happy with her accomplishments. The most recent being that Dacey had been invited back in the room where he belonged – their bedroom.

"I'm glad. I want our relationship to grow stronger." He wasn't sure what she was thinking as he spoke. "I want you to talk to me about anything – even that night."

"I don't want to talk about my injuries!" Her expression was easy to identify now. Anger. Then frustration. "I don't remember what happened anyhow." She could read his face while he listened. "If you know what happened to me Dacey, then tell me."

"I don't want any information that I have to hurt you, Mel."
He liked calling her Mel and wondered why she didn't seem to care anymore. He pushed himself up in the bed and looked at her right in the eyes. "Mel, the motel clerk told your attorney that you had been hooking in his motel for almost ten years under the name of Meg Fleming."

"You disgust me Dacey!" Now, she looked almost hurt.

"I know there's been a mistake. Maybe you just look like her…Meg I mean. And, maybe that's why someone beat you up."

"You're damn right, honey." She faced him with her naked chest, bruised, stitched, although hidden by gauze and surgical tape, in place of where her right nipple used to be. "How much money you got, sugar? I'm selling quick pops and blow jobs and…" he slapped her across her already bruised face, a reaction to the shock he was feeling, and then he looked at her, trying to find his wife somewhere inside of the woman before him.

"Melantha – what has happened to you?"

Smiling, she pushed herself over him. They had just started a new life together – one night: a very short lifetime. Now it was gone: the holding, the laughing, the sharing, and the loving. Gone. She pushed her naked body next to him, and he froze in disbelief, or just horror. He didn't know the woman who had his penis in her hand. He turned to her with a look of fear and confusion. "Who are you? I don't know who you are." He had never been so serious as he spoke.

"Quit kidding around with me sweetheart. You mean you don't recognize me?"

"Melantha?" He searched her eyes for a clue, some proof of her identity, noticing that a small part of her was there. He looked at her for a few minutes, remembering the times they used to spend talking about each other's childhood problems, but he knew those times of sharing were gone. Too much had happened between them. He had cheated on her too many times, and this from a man who had once lived in the name of God and who had once worn the clothes of a conservative Detroit Baptist preacher in training. He wanted the magic of their last day to continue forever but looking into her eyes he knew it was gone. Gone forever. He gently touched the side of her beaten face, as he ran his other hand down her body. "I'll always love you, Melantha." His brown eyes were filling with tears.

"I'm not Melantha! You're just like the others!"

"The others?" He wanted her to finish what she was thinking and carefully coached her forward. "Who are the others?" He tried not to move and waited for her to answer. "What others, Mel?" He watched the tiny bit of sparkle that was left in her beautiful blue eyes die. "Tell me about them." Dacey would understand everything in a minute.

"Oh, honey." Her face took on expressions unfamiliar to the Melantha that Dacey knew. "I can't count them all. It's impossible. Sometimes I'd do five or six a night, sometimes a lot more." She laughed. "Some were fat, some thin, most lonely." She lowered the sheet from her upper body. She was no longer straddling him. Instead she was standing, with one naked-swollen breast exposed, the other still bandaged. "Ernie and Tiger usually did the black ones, except that night." She moved her left hand toward her missing nipple. "He hurt me bad. But hey that's the breaks. That's what Tiger would say when she got beat on, she got cut up some once too. Besides, it was my first bad beating in almost eighteen years. Now that's a record!"

"I'll help you, Mel." Dacey worked hard to fight back the tears. "We'll find the man that beat you."

"I'm not Mel. I'm Meg Fleming from Detroit." She had both arms down at her side now, with her fully exposed naked body standing before him. "I'll be Mel if you want me to, honey." She smiled a wicked smile.

Melantha Fears was gone. She had disappeared with her hidden memories. Memories that would slowly start to surface, but for now, she was Meg Fleming from Detroit, Michigan. A prostitute. A woman with one nipple. A woman who didn't love anyone, including herself. She hovered over his body, that had lowered to the bed, partially out of fear, and partially because of his unbalanced footing, and planted her vagina around his swollen organ.

They had sex; it was the first-time Dacey didn't want it.

Chapter 12

No one would expect Rex and me to go to LA – no one – not

Homer or Barbara Parrish, not Dixie, and not my mother, Melantha.

The two one-way tickets that Homer insisted on buying for us with

his credit card at the Greyhound bus station would throw off

Melantha's scent, and we could hold on to the cash we had, almost

700 hundred dollars with the money Rex had in his wallet and the

430 dollars I had in the envelope, tucked away in a backpack with a

pair of jeans that would soon be too tight around the waist and a couple of clean shirts, an extra bra, and five or six pair of underwear. *We would change directions from another city along the way,* I thought, as I wiped my tears, as the New York bound bus pulled away, and as I watched my grandfather wave at me. New York bound, but not for long.

Rex let me fall asleep on his shoulder until Atlanta, where the bus stopped for a one-hour layover, enough time for people to get off the bus, grab a bite to eat and re-board. I didn't want to talk anyway. I just wanted to close my eyes and put some distance between my memories of the *Kelseys* and *Melanthas* in my life. I was careful not to talk where anyone could hear me when I grabbed Rex's arm and pulled him aside, unnoticed in a corner of the Atlanta Greyhound terminal.

"I know this is a last-minute change, but could we head to California instead? You like…" *I could sell him on the warm weather,* I thought before he interrupted.

"I just want to be with you. Anywhere is fine with me." He smiled his best smile. "It's warmer there. I think we'll like it." I felt like he had read my mind.

"I love you Rex." I thought about how it did make more sense to me. "Thanks for being so understanding." *The weather would be easier to deal with, without much clothing, without knowing if we could find a place to live right away.* My mind was racing. I knew he could see that I was trying to be brave, but he also knew I was worried about the baby, about the future, our future.

"How are you feeling today anyway Nola?" He seemed anxious for the baby's arrival, but he'd have to wait, as I was only twelve weeks pregnant. We had a long way to go. I imagined the baby, its fingers formed, its eye muscles fluttering, and then finally I imagined it was stressed too, probably trying to grab some sleep itself. I was tired, tired of Melantha trying to control my every move, tired of always trying to stay one step ahead. I watched a man waiting in the center of the room, probably for a bus. He looked familiar, but I knew it was probably my paranoia getting the best of me. *Stop,* I thought.

"I'm fine…we're fine." The man behind the counter had just announced loading for the New York bound bus. I took Rex's hand and walked toward the bus, whispering into his ear. "Please don't look behind us." I kissed him on his cheek. "Let's pretend like we're getting back on the bus Rex, the same one we were on, the New York bound bus." I was careful to whisper, wanting to explain, but it wasn't the time. "I'll explain later." I squeezed his hand, and climbed the steps of the Greyhound, and made my way down the aisle, until the dark tinted windows hid us from the outside world. I watched the man exit the middle of the bus station and make his way to the parking lot. Carefully, we exited the New York bus, before it pulled away, and we hid ourselves again, this time inside the terminal. I watched the as the bus pulled away, a gray van followed a couple car lengths behind.

This time we paid cash at the window – for two tickets to LA. That bus was boarding now. I watched a woman hand her duffel bag to the driver who was loading a few things in the carryall underneath. The nametag dangled from her brightly colored red bag, Martha Satchele. *Satchele,* I thought. *That will be my new last name.* I smiled. *Melantha would be proud that I picked a name that sounded French.*

Exhausted, we settled into side-by-side chairs near the back of the bus. My body felt cold as I closed my eyes, my back aching. It was time to get more sleep and put everything else out of my mind. I closed my eyes, trying not to think of anything, except Rex and the baby. I wanted this new life with him. It was exactly three a.m. when the bus pulled out of the Atlanta terminal. Westbound. The vibration and monotonous sound of the large tires humming on I-20 was the last thing I remembered.

#

"Dacey. Is that you?" Melantha spoke as if she had gone blind and could no longer see. She reached for Dacey's hand. She felt the upper part of his arm and tried to hold on for support. As Melantha's face grew closer to his, with the dimly lit room behind it, he could tell why she was acting so strange, noticing the enlarged pupils and dark circles under her eyes.

"Mel, what type of drugs do they have you on?" He gave his wife his free arm for extra support, trying to keep her from falling, as she was determined to stand and not be prisoner to the dimly lit hospital room and its uninviting bed. "Are the drugs for pain, or…" he didn't want to sound like he was accusing her of being crazy as she took notice of the bars on the windows, windows that were placed higher than normal, too high to look out of. With his arms still serving as supports to his wife, he wondered why there were no chairs, and the bed was only a small mattress placed on a frame low to the floor.

"The people here are crazy. They're trying to kill me. Get me out, Dacey."

"Mel, no one's trying to kill you. You had a nervous breakdown. You just need a little help."

"So many men…" she took her left hand off Dacey's arm, and placed it on her neck. "They are waiting for me." Melantha didn't notice the disgust in Dacey's face as she continued to speak. "Where's Ernie and Tiger? Are they trying to get all the action for themselves?" Now she removed her right hand off Dacey, but only long enough to push herself a few steps back, allowing his face to come into focus. "Am I doing you?" She moved closer to him now. "Are you a regular? I feel like I've seen you before." He watched his wife's body move, unfamiliar, as he pushed the call button above the toilet near the front corner of the room. A man in a short white lab coat, stocked with a clipboard and two orderlies appeared.

"I'm Dr. Carroll, a psychiatrist. Can I speak to you in the hall?" He looked at Dacey as he instructed the orderlies to sedate Ms. Fears, and he locked her room as he exited behind the grieving husband. Dacey realized he would never see the real Melantha Fears ever again, and no longer able to contain his emotions, he doubled over in the hall where he used the edge of his shirt to dry his face. He had lost everyone he had ever loved because of one man – Abner Paine – even though he didn't really understand that yet. He tucked his wet shirt-tail back into his polyester slacks, one hand pulling the white leather belt an inch or two outward, to accommodate the invasion, the same belt that he last beat his oldest daughter Enola with. He stood facing the doctor, listening and wondering how he had missed so many signs of mental illness.

"What are you trying to tell me Dr. Carroll?"

"Your wife has had a psychotic breakdown. I believe she suffers from a serious mental illness; she is very unstable in her moods; she thinks she is unworthy; she can't be attached to other people, and she acts out by participating in impulsive behaviors, like prostitution." Dacey felt his heartbreaking, dripping into the already soaked shirt-tail. "I have reason to believe she was sexually abused as a child, which makes her a more likely victim…for rape and other violent crimes." Dr. Carroll put his hand on Dacey's shoulder. "She can't keep a grip on reality. I'm sorry, but I don't want to sugarcoat things for you. She'll probably be unable to live outside of an institution for some time, if ever again."

"Can't she be helped? Given medication?"

"I think we're dealing with borderline personality disorder, which we know very little about at this time, except that it affects mostly women. We're trying mood-stabilizing drugs and other antipsychotic drugs to see how she reacts, but it's too early to determine anything yet. Right now, we just want to keep her safe."

"What do you mean safe? Is she going to hurt herself?"

"The suicide attempt rate is very high with people in her condition. We just want to make sure she doesn't have that opportunity. We might even try hypnosis and psychoanalytic exploration."

"What's psychoanalytic exploration?"

"It's just a fancy term for re-educating one's mind." He tried to give the husband standing before him some hope. Hope, that his wife would one day become healthy But Dacey knew it was probably too late.

"Thanks Dr. Carroll. What can I do to help?" That was all Dacey could think of, all he could offer.

"Well, most patients like your wife need continued psychotherapeutic treatment, because they are constantly facing new symptoms and problems that need worked out. The only thing you can do is visit as often as possible. It might help." *Well, at least, he was honest.* Dacey thought.

"I'll visit as much as possible doctor." He thought about staying in that big Enka house alone, living in a house too big for just one person, and living in a house he couldn't afford. "I'll be moving closer to this area." The doctor gave his sign of approval and hurried off to assist another patient. *Time for me to let the Enka house go.* He continued thinking as he walked down the hallway, through a door that had to be buzzed open, and to the fall air in the Asheville mountains of North Carolina. *I'll get an apartment close to Highland's Hospital.* He got into his old car and turned on to Zillicoa Street. *The house was being foreclosed on anyway.* It was time he faced reality on a lot of things in his life, like losing houses, like losing children, like losing his mother, and like losing his wife.

#

Severe back pain woke me as we were approaching Birmingham, Alabama. The last 140 miles felt good to shut my eyes but feeling good was something that no longer claimed my state of mind. I looked down at my lap just in time to see a pool of blood forming between my legs. Bright red.

"Rex, something's wrong." That was all I got out, when the lady across the aisle stood to offer her assistance. The driver slowed, not only for the light turning red, but he sensed the panic, the same panic I sensed, coming from the woman's voice.

"Driver. I think you should pull over." The woman was a stranger to me, except when I looked into her face. Then I recognized her as the owner of the bright red duffel bag, Martha Satchele, who quickly announced that I needed a hospital. *A hospital? Why?* Rex was fully alert, looking into my face, reading the fact that I was worried, worried about the baby. Martha Satchele was working to calm me, to calm Rex, and to take charge of the decision that I needed an ambulance. I could hear the driver radio for an ambulance, unknown passenger, bleeding, lots of blood, yes, I-20 near Cooper Green. I felt like I was going to pass out between the back pain and blood loss. *Stay focused. Stay calm.* I was trying, right up until the lights of an ambulance parked parallel to the darkened bus windows, right up until men I didn't know lifted me, right up until I felt my body being placed onto a stretcher, and right up until I

heard the ambulance door shut my entire life into a small cramped

area – Rex, two backpacks, and a body that didn't feel like mine.

"Is she going to be okay?" I heard Rex pleading for an

answer from the paramedic who was busy assessing the situation.

"Just let me do my job." Unfriendly. Authoritative. That's the

last thing I remember before passing out, the last thing I remember

before losing a part of me that I would never get back. Never.

Cooper Green Mercy Hospital was right off of Sixth Avenue

South in Birmingham. We were still 2000 miles away from LA, and

another twenty-eight weeks away from having our baby. The latter

of which wouldn't be happening. Instead, I woke to news that

sounded somewhat rehearsed, somewhat cold, and somewhat empty

– like me.

"Your ultrasound confirms that you've had a complete

miscarriage. All tissue has been expelled." The doctor looked at Rex

when he spoke, sometimes glancing at me. "No need to worry.

You're fine." *I'm fine.* I replayed his words in my mind. *I don't feel fine.* Maybe the look on my face redirected his cold words. "I'm sorry for your loss."

Rex and I didn't speak when he walked out. We just hugged as hard as we could, no space between us, except for the emptiness inside of me. It was an emptiness that I had felt so many times before in my life. Gone. Alone. Words couldn't describe the intensity. I wept on Rex's shoulders, until I finally fell back asleep, until an admitting nurse entered the room seeking information. That's the very moment I officially became Nola Satchele. No insurance, no I.D, no address. I would be a cost to the state of Alabama, but I wouldn't be a resident for long. No, it was just a stop, a stop where another part of me would be left behind.

The next morning came early. I was discharged before seven. I could tell I was a priority because of the fact that I had no insurance – a priority to be discharged.

#

Melantha woke up screaming at the top of her lungs, the high-pitched shrieks echoed the hallways and bounced off walls, before Dr. Carroll and a nurse made it to her room. She was mumbling about a woman named Zelda, mumbling about how she needed saved from the fire. Dr. Carroll shook his head at her nonsense before ordering her to be sedated, but the nurse took notice of Melantha's descriptions. Hot. Fire. She needs us. Burning. Nine are dying. Hurry. Nurse Halohand wondered where Melantha had read about the fire at Highland's Hospital, a fire that had taken the lives of nine women thirty years earlier. One of the women was Zelda Fitzgerald, the wife of F. Scott Fitzgerald, a novelist born in the late 1800s, who had died four years before the fire, from alcoholism. *Maybe she read an article about Fitzgerald's work.* Nurse Halohand thought to herself. *Maybe she read The Great Gatsby. That's it.* She thought before imagining Melantha Fears at home reading about Fitzgerald's life and nosing through one of his greatest masterpieces.

Dacey Fears made his way from an apartment he had rented yesterday, first to Chestnut Street, then Broadway Street, and finally Zillicoa. Nurse Halohand buzzed him in the front door, anxious to inquire about Melantha's reading habits. She felt like a detective as he approached.

"Your wife had a rough night, Mr. Fears." She paused allowing him to gain entrance before continuing. "Dreaming about

Fitzgerald's life and a fire that took his widow's life a few years following his own – here – at the hospital."

"She did?" Dacey looked baffled. He didn't know Melantha was so scholarly. He didn't know she had hidden yet another side.

"She was rattling off his wife's name – Zelda." Her voice followed Dacey down the hall, as he lost interest in the conversation and was almost to Melantha's room.

"Mel." He whispered as he entered, the windows so high, the natural light outside hadn't informed the room that morning had arrived, the first one in October.

"Dacey?" Her voice was slurred, also whispering, not because of nature's hidden clock, but more because she was unsure of who was entering, her eyes fighting to un-blur the figure appearing before her. "Is that you? Did you find her?"

"It's me Mel." And "Who?"

She looked at him, puzzled that he didn't know who she was talking about, puzzled that he couldn't hear her screaming, and puzzled that no one was hurrying to help her. Then she answered – "Zelda."

Chapter 13

I moved slowly with Rex's help, getting dressed, talking about the emptiness I felt, talking about Melantha and how she wanted nothing more than to hurt my relationship, and talking about how we could start fresh in LA. I got my point across without talking about Kelsey, without talking about the final goodbyes at the beach, without talking about one last phone call from North Carolina, and without talking about the photos. The crisp Friday October air continued at the breakfast café near the Greyhound bus station in Birmingham –

pancakes with maple syrup, biscuits with white milk gravy, hot chocolate with those little mini-marshmallows, tears, smiles, pain, promises of tomorrow and even laughter. When Rex finally looked at his watch, it was almost noon, with few tables taken, and for a moment, and for the first time ever, I put my past behind me. I realized we were probably being sought after – Melantha would use everyone and everything she had to find us. Melantha would want to find me, before I turned eighteen, before I had a chance to escape all control, and before I had a baby that no longer existed. I knew we had to get to LA, get jobs, to allow us to get on with our lives, to allow us to be safe, and to experience true freedom from Melantha's reach, something I had never had.

We boarded the one o'clock bus continuing to Los Angeles, but it wasn't for at least another two hundred miles, before we heard people chatting, before the bus reached I-40 West, somewhere in the stretch of endless interstate, where we heard whispers about the Los Angeles Farmer's Market and how busy it always was, that we both agreed meant jobs. I was anxious to get there, and I know Rex was too from the way he smiled at me, trying to soothe my emptiness, our emptiness.

It was a long haul to LA, we slept on the bus, only getting off to grab bottled soda and counter-sandwiches, but I felt some relief thinking about the future we could have and tried not to think about the pregnancy that had ended. I thought about how the doctor kept saying it was stress-related, and about how he reassured us we could try again someday. Someday. But now, it was time to start surviving. The Farmer's Market was a collection of almost 200 shops and restaurants, some jobs would be available I felt certain. We hurried from the bus station, walking quickly on foot, an almost two-mile race against the setting sun. The market was open into the evening, the smell of corn beef, the hustle of people with shopping bags, and the laughter of small children running to keep up with their moms and dads. There were lots of help wanted signs, several in retail shops, one in Sabroso's Sandwich Shop, and one in Little John's Candy Store. *We're going to be okay,* I thought as I thought about the last one hundred and eighty dollars stuffed in my backpack.

I had barely finished filling out an application at the candy store, which was a small booth full of different types of fudge and almond bark, when a voice I could never fail to recognize said, "I got it." I looked to the left, and there stood Rex, the man I was in love with, the man I wanted to try and have another child with someday. "I start today," he said. He smiled at the look of relief on my face and went to hug me, but noticed I was standing less than three feet away from the man who might give me the break I needed too. Deserved.

"We'll look over your application and call you when we make a decision." Mr. Johns, the owner of the shop said as he took the completed application from my hand.

"But I think there's something you should know," I explained. "My boyfriend just got a job at Sabroso's Sandwich Shop, and I'm in competition now, so what do you say?"

"I guess you'd like a decision now then." The owner grinned at my tenacity. "I'm afraid I better go ahead and hire you." The man was still grinning at my blue-green eyes. There was a moment of silence between us, an uneasy second where I had thought he had said no. Then – *I'm hired* I thought to myself, *we've both gotten jobs on our first evening in LA; we're going to make it.*

I answered graciously as soon as I realized my mistake, "I can't wait to get started. Would you like me to start tonight?"

Mr. Johns looked at me in amazement. "You're determined. I guess we could use you for a few hours before we close. Grab that apron over there."

"Yes, sir."

"But take a moment to say goodbye to your boyfriend." I wondered if I should have used the word husband earlier, but I didn't want to use it – not until it was true. Besides, I didn't feel like Mr. Johns was judging me. I tried to remember that not all adults did that.

"Thanks," and then after shaking his hand and studying his nametag once again, "Mr. Johns."

Rex hugged me tightly, and even though I could still feel the absence between us, a very special part of us gone, I knew today was a new beginning for both of us. Before we left each other's arms, I looked into Rex's deep brown eyes. I wanted to tell him he didn't have to be on the run with me, that I was the only one running from Melantha, the only one running from my past, that he was free, especially now that there wasn't a child to raise, but I knew from the look on his face that I didn't have to. He wanted me as badly as I wanted him. He wanted a fresh start too, and even though he knew he wasn't bound to me, I could tell he didn't want to go. He needed this fresh start just as much as I did.

"You are so beautiful. I love you." Rex whispered the words to me, yet they sounded so strong, a strength that represented the two of us – together.

"I love you too." I felt the backside of his hands with mine.

"I'll meet you back here when I'm done at Sabroso's." He smiled at me as he hurried off to his sandwich shop a couple rows away. Tonight, we would spend the night in a small motel, one I had seen next to the market, just enough money to rent it for the weekly special I saw on their sign – one hundred and fifty dollars, leaving us enough for cheap food until the week's end. *One day at a time* I thought, as I smiled back.

#

It was a cool November breeze, Melantha surmised, that had made her feel alive again. Melantha had just gotten off the phone with Dacey, who was busy running a small pub, a transaction he made possible by a lucky win, a long shot that finally paid off, a trifecta, enough to buy someone else's business failure, a way to fill the emptiness of having no communication with either daughter or with his mother. It was a way to coexist with a wife who was trying to get back to some sense of normal life. She would make another call, this time to Grover Starks.

"Don't tell me you have no idea where she is." Melantha still had Grover wrapped around her finger. Mr. Starks was a busy man and would hang up on anyone else, but for Melantha, he would listen to her rant and rave on the phone, knowing that there wasn't a judge anywhere that would place a seventeen-year-old high school graduate in a youth facility, especially one that hadn't committed any crimes, but he would listen and act concerned. After all, he still wanted to please her.

"I will do my very best Mel." Grover paused, thinking of the last time they made love, just a few days ago, when Dacey was at the pub late one night, when Melantha had spent her third evening away from Highland's Hospital, when Melantha had decided she needed more than a used-up tire salesman, turned entrepreneur, and more than an occupant of a small one-bedroom apartment two blocks from Zillicoa Street, close to where Melantha had agreed to routine inpatient treatment two days a week, at Highlands.

"Your best better be good enough Grover." Melantha Fears smiled evilly into the phone before saying good-bye and thinking about the next phone call on her agenda, this one to Dixie Nault.

The phone rang just as Dixie was sitting down to dinner. Dixie was going to be eighteen in a few months, a beautiful strawberry blond red-head, just adjusting to her parents' divorce, and just discovering love of her own.

"Hello," Dixie spoke softly into the phone. "No, I don't know where she is." Dixie paused. "But I promise to let you know if I hear from her."

She would never tell Enola's mother even if she did. "It's important we find her." Melantha was thinking about what to say next. "It's a family emergency." Melantha was trying to lay the guilt trip on, stressing the urgency.

The silence between them lasted for what seemed like forever; there was a moment of hesitancy, a review of unspoken promises between friends, and a quick assessment of Melantha's manipulative behavior. "I don't know anything." Dixie wasn't about to tell Melantha that Enola had called, before leaving, before getting on a bus to New York. She could tell by the way Melantha was speaking that she already knew.

"Do you know if she made it to New York safely?" Melantha asked the question point-blank, making sure Dixie was aware that Enola's moves were being tracked.

"No, I haven't heard from her," Dixie was glad it was true. "I'm sure she's okay." Dixie knew that was true also – the Enola May Fears that Dixie knew was brave, smart, and a survivor. She would be fine. *I'm not going to let her mother manipulate my thoughts. I know Enola is okay. I know she'll contact me again someday. She gave me her word.*

The phone call was not what Dixie had needed, not while dealing with the stress of her own parents' divorce. There was a sinister, almost evil tone, a sense of revenge – an air of control in Melantha's voice as she said good-bye to Dixie. "You've been so helpful." Melantha's voice couldn't have been more sarcastic. Melantha hung up the phone before Dixie could think of a response.

#

I felt like Los Angeles was unexpectedly warm for November, but it was too pretty to not enjoy my first day off since arriving in LA, and

Rex had made me promise to meet him for a quick lunch, so I tied a pink ribbon, giving it the job of holding up my long brown ponytail, which I could feel bounce along as I walked toward the Farmer's Market off Third Street to meet Rex, feeling it sway gently in the warm breeze. I looked at the candy store where I had worked late last night, when it was surrounded by people buying boxes of walnut, rocky-road, pecan, and maple fudge as last-minute take home selections. Patty, the assistant manager, who was wearing a large white smock over her slack outfit, was cutting pieces of fudge and white almond bark, but stopped to wave and smile at me – *Nola Satchele* – I thought, as I waved and smiled back.

I couldn't wait to see Rex. He punched out on his time card and then placed it back in the metal rack, tapped Jose, a co-worker, on the shoulder, and moved toward the exit, where I was waiting. I watched the swinging door come to a slow rocking motion behind him. He placed both arms around me, lifting me off the ground and I could tell he noticed the sweet scent of *Wind Song* I had placed on my neck. We walked to a table, to share a corned beef sandwich that he had rolled up in a brown paper bag, but not before I watched him pull out a piece of paper, one he looked like he wanted to give me so badly, one that he announced represented our new life together. He watched my excitement, as I stared at the rental agreement in my hand, our first apartment, a surprise I wasn't expecting for a while, but I knew Rex was good at squirreling away money, especially his tips, and good at surprises.

We hurried through the corned beef sandwich, which made me smile when I realized I had predicted the type from the juicy odor, then ran to the transit system stop with Rex, hand in hand, and boarded a bus to Oxford Street. The five-story brick building on Oxford Street, the place where Rex explained he had handed over 450 dollars earlier that morning, was at least fifteen years old, in an older residential neighborhood, about a half-mile from Wilshire Boulevard, pleasantly surrounded by green shrubbery. He told me that the door to the front of the building stays locked twenty-four hours a day, and each resident is given a key to allow themselves entry through the main door.

"Here is yours." Rex reached in his pocket where he had two sets of keys tucked away. He handed me one set. I watched him unlock the outer door to the building and felt his energy as he quickly took my hand.

Inside the brick building, I noticed an apartment on the first floor with *manager* written on its door, an elevator, a set of stairs, both of which Rex told me led up to all five floors in the building. I could tell the neighborhood was not the most dangerous in all of Los Angeles, but I could tell it wasn't the most desirable either. What it did offer was a chance at a real place together, no more cramped quarters, and a place with a refrigerator and stove. Rex explained that at the corner of Oxford and Wilshire was one of LA's 250 bus stops. He had done his homework. I smiled when he started his history lesson in the elevator, which seemed to move slowly.

"The Los Angeles bus system is a transportation system for all types of people: white, black, Hispanic, Asian, Chinese, Mexican, rapists, murderers, mothers, fathers, druggies, and robbers. It is simply called the transit system by the young, middle-aged, and the elderly." He noticed I was trying not to laugh at his excitement. "The most amazing thing is that it never stops. A bus stops at the corner of Oxford and Wilshire twenty-four minutes after each hour, twenty-four hours a day." He sounded like an announcer.

We got off at the third floor, where the second key on each of our sets was capable of performing its magic – unlocking apartment 333.

"We'll be happier here than in the motel we've been renting," Rex was excited, fumbling with the second key on his set, as he unlocked our apartment door. "It has a stove, frig, and plenty of counter space."

"I've been happy since the day I met you." I meant it. "I love it, and I love you." I looked around, three rooms: kitchen, bathroom, and one large room with a built-in bookshelf and two large windows overlooking the fire escape and back parking lot. "Where do we sleep?" I asked as I inventoried the furniture: two chairs and a small table in the corner of the kitchen, and two more chairs in the living room, one by each window.

"Close your eyes," Rex answered. And then I heard him open the two doors, which I had noticed earlier, which looked like the entrance to a walk-in closet, until he pulled down the bed inside, leading me by my hand to its edge. He put his arms around me and held me tight as I opened my eyes. "I'm going to make love to you Nola Satchele." He did.

Chapter 14

"Quoi? What did you say? What do you mean you're not sure where she is? I thought you had things under control, Grover? And, I assumed you had at least checked to make sure she had re-boarded the New York bound bus after its first stop." Melantha could feel the anger eat at the flesh inside of her, swelling anger. It would be harder to find Enola now that so much time had passed, wasted time that had been spent searching a city that she had never stepped in. The driver was certain he hadn't seen Enola, not on his bus to New

York, not on that day, not ever. No young female matching her description had boarded his bus. He was positive. But the clerk inside told a different story. He remembered seeing a young girl and guy traveling together, remembered them counting out cash for tickets to LA, the most expensive one-ways leaving that evening. And the driver was certain, he remembered her crying out in pain, remembered pulling over and waiting for an ambulance, and remembered cleaning blood off her seat – lots of it. Grover's private investigator followed up, of course, with the paramedics, hospital, a cute nurse, and a very gruff doctor. He knew about the loss of the baby, knew about the miscarriage, and knew that Melantha wasn't going to hold all the cards. Not anymore. He had a few tricks up his sleeve too. He allowed Melantha to listen to his bitter aloofness and then told her he had a client waiting, which he didn't. He thought about the woman he had fallen for, her sass, her wickedness, and then he thought about Enola Fears, a seventeen-year-old female who was trying her best to make it. He wasn't going to be the one to stop her. He wasn't some slip-shot attorney. He had all of his facts straight, especially Enola's eighteenth birthday. The only thing he could do now was slow Melantha's reach without being obvious.

She was way too smart for that. He had two, sometimes three excellent private investigators on his payroll, one of which had been working Melantha's wishes hard, one that never lost anyone, ever. Grover had known this man for years, had known that Melantha tried to catch him in her web, because she was good, and because he had a weakness for a damsel in distress. But, this case would go at his speed, and the sassy woman on the other end of the line would leave Dacey and be his soon.

"Don't worry Mel, we'll find her before Christmas." He thought about his next play. "I've still got my best P.I. on it."

Melantha knew that was true, but she hated racing against the clock. She wanted to find Enola before the baby was due, before the month of April, before she would lose more leverage. "Damn it Grover, don't let me down. This is important to me." For a second, she had forgotten Dacey had just gotten home from his new restaurant business, a small pub, a six-stool bar, a small stage in the back of the pub, with a tiny dance floor that Dacey had made home for three small tables, each covered in a red and white checkered cloth, and each with a red glass candle holder in the center. Melantha adjusted her voice to a whisper, because she didn't want Dacey to hear – and because she could feel herself losing control. Again.

"I won't," Grover promised and then smiled to himself. *She'd freak if she knew the baby didn't make it.* He imagined her reaction. And then he thought – *that's probably what she wants most –* *Enola's baby.* Proving Enola unfit just to watch her die inside would be Melantha's ultimate dream. And still smiling, he asked a question he had asked before, "So, when are you going to marry me?" He knew she would soon. He had thought of an offer that Melantha wouldn't be able to refuse: expensive jewelry, exotic vacations, and luxury cars. Soon.

"Just find her." Grover Starks already had. His P.I. had called earlier, bragging about how the English toffee was the best he had ever eaten, a secret he would keep to himself – for now. He would make his proposal to Melantha soon – his way.

#

I did not have to meet Rex at his new job until four p.m., Ohrbach's Department Store off Wilshire Boulevard. And, after the morning I had spent at my new job, I was glad to have a few hours to myself. I knew from the many times I had been asked if I were tired, that there were dark circles around my blue eyes, circles from long bus drives, circles from searching for a new job closer to our apartment on Oxford, and circles from the constant feeling that I was being followed, watched. I took the bus to Hollywood Boulevard first, watching the people from the bus window stop to examine the sidewalk of stars. *How does a person ever become important enough to have a star with his name engraved on it?* I wondered. For an hour and a half, I rode the bus, first down Hollywood Boulevard, then down Sunset Boulevard, getting off to catch another bus over to Wilshire Boulevard. After two exchanges, and a dollar seventy-five, I arrived at Ohrbach's Department Store.

"Where's the men's department?" I asked the first sales clerk I found. Rex had suggested we change jobs. He didn't dismiss the fact that he felt followed sometimes too.

"Upstairs on your right." The woman answered.

I went up the escalator with a brown paper bag in one hand as the stairs unfolded that dropped me off. Trying to hide my tired eyes, I searched the men's department for Rex. He was not in sight. I noticed a tall, light-skinned black man with green eyes. He had a friendly appearance, and when he turned toward me, I met his name badge with my stare. Smiling. Tony was folding pants, throwing spare hangers into a large cardboard box, laughing and chuckling, and remarking to the familiar voice with quick-witty comebacks. Rex was marking numbers on the inventory list. It had been his jokes making Tony laugh. And I knew how easily Rex could make someone smile, and now that I knew he was there, I felt refreshed and awake.

"Hi Tony, could you tell Rex I'm here?" I shifted the brown paper bag to my other arm. "I'm Enola...Nola Satchele." I hated the fact that I had just called myself Enola. *Maybe he didn't catch it.* I thought.

"If you're here to meet Rex for dinner...I'm afraid I have some bad news. I'll be filling in for Rex today. I wish he didn't have to stay and finish the inventory."

"Don't flatter yourself, Tony," Rex answered from behind a pile of men's slacks. "I'm sure you'll be able to finish this up for me." And then, "Don't try hitting on my girl Tony." He laughed.

"I'm just letting her know she has options." Tony's words were followed with laughter as he turned to properly introduce himself to me. "Hi, I'm Tony. Your boyfriend has been keeping the air light around here, and I can see why he always comes to work in such a good mood. Enola, is it?"

"Nola," and then, "It's nice to meet you."

"You too."

I smiled at Tony, and my thoughts went immediately back to Rex, to all the times he had made me smile. "I brought some nice cold-cut subs for dinner, from the Sunset Deli. I thought – I was thinking it would be nice to eat outside somewhere…if you know of a place." I put my right hand on Rex's shoulder, and he bent to kiss me and placed the inventory sheet he had been holding within Tony's reach.

"Sounds good. If you only knew how hungry I am," Rex smiled, "We've been working all morning on this inventory." He held me close, pressing the brown bag almost flat between us. "I know of a couple of benches outside behind the store. They're facing a small pond."

We spent a lot of time talking, laughing, and discussing our new jobs. Mine was at I-Magnin's, one of the best stores off Wilshire Boulevard. I remember the day I walked in, filled out an application, Nola Satchele, experienced cashier, excellent communication skills. I was hired on the spot. It took some getting

used to, the way the money and transaction slip would shoot upstairs

to the small room where I worked, the way I wouldn't have to deal

with customers, just make change, provide a receipt, and shoot the

small tube back downstairs to the sales associate, a title that sounded

more important than it was. I loved being in the small room with just

two other women, both older than me, and both very friendly.

"I'm staying until nine tonight to get all the inventory done

with Tony." He looked into my eyes, seeing past my tired face, with

a look that I knew meant he wanted to have sex, but he knew it

wasn't the time or the place.

"I'll wait up for you," I answered his sexual urges.

"Good." He answered. "I want you." He said what I knew

was obvious. The sex was great between us, a connection that felt

right every time we were together. "I want us…a future." The

problem was sometimes I just wanted to be held, nothing more.

Nothing.

"I want us too." I looked at him indifferently. I wasn't sure

what he meant, was he referring to the way he knew I couldn't hide

my emotions, to the way I still mourned the loss of our baby, or to the fact that he knew I was afraid Melantha was still trying to mess up my life, and that I had only wanted him to hold me the last time we were alone together?

I blew him a kiss when I boarded the Wilshire bus back to Oxford Street and waved until he was out of sight. I thought about what he had just said, wondering if I had been too frigid toward him lately. For the last two weeks, he had tried to make love to me, as though I should move on, be okay, but I wasn't. I couldn't get my mind off losing the baby…and now recently, Melantha. I wanted him as much as I always did, if I could just get my mind off things that bothered me. He tried to understand, although there were times lately when we went to bed at night without saying much.

Chapter 15

The chart read: relapse due to inadequate follow-up and medication.

In room forty-one Melantha lay silently with her body relaxed after

receiving ten milligrams of haloperidol and a visit from the hospital

therapist on duty. She was back in Highland's Hospital. Dacey,

standing near her, noticed the look of torment on her face, the voices

were talking to her again, muttering sounds that were all too familiar

to her, the humming of a small child, the screams from a woman on

fire, the prompting of fellow prostitutes that were never really there, and the forceful orders from her step-father. She found herself thinking about death and how it would offer her a peaceful silence. It would be like a memory she had of sleeping in her mother's arms, when she was little, before those arms could no longer protect her from Abner Paine.

She searched the corners of her busy mind for Enola's face and listened to the voices within her, wanting the pain to be over, imagining a knife stab Enola, wishing death to the baby that she imagined would be arriving sometime around Easter. She knew, even overwhelmed by medication, that Enola was part of her restless mind. The many **Voices of Fear** ate at her brain, like tiny worms. She thought of the last report she had received from Grover, as she caught a glimpse of Dacey still standing in her tiny hospital room. It was worthless: no idea where Enola was. The months were crumbling away in front of her. November had come and gone. Today, the tenth of December, imaginary voices of control and suggestions took turns stabbing Melantha's soul; and tomorrow, the search for Enola would consume the empty corners of her mind. She closed her eyes to the darkness but still the voices ate at her. *Why didn't you tell Momma?* The young voice kept repeating. Pleading.

Fuck that drunken bastard. The voice with the unsightly overbite was strong and harsh. *Baby, he shoulda been the one to die, you know.* The black voice smiled a warm smile as it spoke. And then loudly, *help me. The fire is burning me.* Zelda screamed. And, *don't make me break your neck like I did your sister's.* The voices were all talking at once – until sleep took over.

In Dr. Carroll's office, hidden in one of the many hallways in the hospital, the next morning, Dacey listened as the doctor reviewed Melantha's charts, actually an almost two-inch file by now. "It might be more serious than we originally thought, besides having an obvious case of borderline personality, she may have a form of multiple personality, possibly developing into schizophrenia. Unlike her recent medical condition, she is showing more symptoms of the disease. In medical terms, we classify it as Vigilambulism." Dr. Carroll looked up at Dacey as he flipped to the most recent page in her file, his hand reaching to scratch the middle of his forehead, a recent habit, and stood up to face him, as Dacey was now standing. He explained in simple terms and made his recommendation without emotion. Dacey thought about the last month with Melantha, how she had been depressed and sometimes violent. He remembered a few days ago, when she threw a glass at him in the pub, in front of customers, smashing it into tiny shards of glass, after getting off the phone with Grover Starks, how she refused to buy April, their youngest daughter, a Christmas gift, at Dacey's suggestion, when they walked around a plaza last weekend, stating that she didn't have two daughters, only one that she needed to find, *now*, and how she would wake in the middle of the night screaming about fire and saving Zelda.

"I suggest continuing the haloperidol and institutionalism so she can get the social support she needs."

"Dr. Carroll, how long will she have to stay?"

"At least a few months." The doctor wanted to make sure Mrs. Fears was able to complete an active rehabilitation program offered at Highlands. He acted as though she would be cured at the end of the program, but Dacey felt he would never have Melantha back again. *She is lost now*. He thought.

Dacey drove home alone to the small apartment he had been living in, shared briefly with Melantha, off Zillicoa Street, not far from his small pub which seemed to be taking off: chili, pizza, soda, and beer. He unlocked the door to the 590-square foot apartment, the television, still on, glowing shades of green and yellow, needing repair, and possibly a new picture tube, in order to work properly. *Is that what Melantha needs too?* He wondered to himself, and almost laughed aloud, a reaction to the stress he was under. He privately thought about his daughters. April, had turned thirteen recently, but was still not accepting his calls, so Dacey would occasionally end up speaking with his mother, who was brief, and anyone could tell by her voice, wanted nothing further to do with the son who had betrayed her. Then he thought about Enola May. She was still seventeen, a stranger and victim of his past. He could hear Melantha screaming into the phone, at Grover Starks, screaming about deadlines and broken promises. He had listened to Melantha rant and rave about their oldest daughter's pregnancy, and the bastard child that would ruin lives, and wipe out civilization, like Enola had for them. He thought about the grandchild he would never know, never meet, never hold, and then he remembered how he had beaten Enola, over and over again, for things that didn't make sense now: letting the biggest bull-frog free from a wax-coated fishing stringer that held the frog prisoner, along with at least seven or eight others, that he was planning on frying up; walking when she should have run; running when she should have walked; talking out of turn; not talking quickly enough when asked a question; having a black friend at school; pleading to help an injured black man who was bleeding on a hidden trail in the mountains; whining about being hit with a baseball in the front yard at the Cedar Hill home; and finally, he thought about how he used that same baseball bat on her left knee cap – until it cracked, until she understood that twelve-year-old girls don't play house with thirteen-year-old uncles. She hadn't deserved the childhood she was dealt, no, admittedly, he knew it was his picture tube and Melantha's picture tube, like the television before him, that had driven him over the edge of no return. He recalled how Melantha would tell him lies about Enola, and later he would discover the truth, but he was too embarrassed to admit he had beaten her for no reason. He watched the television fight to maintain an even shade of green. Then he watched the almost twenty-year-old Zenith fade to blackness before his very eyes. Gone.

#

Two days before Christmas, Grover Starks dropped an envelope in the mail, regretting he hadn't sent it earlier, but almost certain it would be appreciated whenever it arrived. Melantha was under lock and key, he knew, and would stay at Highland's Hospital until at least mid-February, plenty of time to come up with a plan: a chance to think, a chance to remember, to recall, something he had done a lot of since seeing Melantha nearly a year ago, and since receiving recent photos of Enola from his P.I. that still tracked her. It was obvious from the photos that Enola was his blood. According to Melantha Fears, and to the best of her ability to recall, she met Grover Starks in Asheville, North Carolina in 1977, a chance meeting when Melantha followed the lead for a good attorney to get her husband's indiscretions in order, and to get her own life in order. But, Grover Starks knew otherwise; he recognized her immediately when she walked into his downtown office in Asheville. He knew the face, and especially the body, from Detroit. She introduced herself as Melantha Fears. He would spend silent moments looking at her, whenever they were intimate, trying to remember the name of the woman he knew in Detroit, trying to recall the many times he and other law students would party downtown, letting loose from the daily grind of classes at Wayne State University in Detroit, looking for a little "no-strings" action – some much-needed weekend relief from the hustle and bustle of law school. He was normally not the type of man to solicit a prostitute, but when she came in the bar where he and his buddies were hanging out, he couldn't resist the temptation. It wasn't until the photos that his P.I. had recently sent of Enola May Fears, that he was able to piece it all together. First, he remembered her name, Meg Fleming. Then he remembered how he would always look for her, passing up others, even women who were fellow law students, looking for a little relief of their own. Little did he know, he would meet her sixteen years later in Asheville, North Carolina, hunting for representation for her cheating husband, hunting for someone willing to play dirty. She didn't recognize him. She wouldn't. She didn't know she had been Meg Fleming, a prostitute in Detroit; she didn't know she had lived in and out of someone else's life, another life within her own body. Grover, on-the-other-hand, recognized her eyes, the darkest blue-green eyes he had ever seen, the same eyes he had fucked for fifty-dollars years earlier in Detroit, Michigan. Eyes he was never able to forget. When he looked at those eyes standing in his office, he said nothing. It was not his intention to embarrass her, nor was it his intention to bring up a life that she had escaped, but he couldn't leave her alone either. He thought about his last weekend in Detroit, chatting with the bartender, discovering the woman with the dark blue-green eyes had gotten married to a young Baptist preacher, or so the rumors went. But now, staring at the pictures, several up-close shots of Enola May's face, Grover knew she carried a secret into her marriage that belonged to the two of them.

He didn't want Melantha to know Enola's whereabouts. He had given her Birmingham, which was dangerous enough, but he didn't want her to know she had lost the baby, his grandchild he now knew. He had his P.I. retrace the evidence, the paramedics, the hospital, the lab work, the routine blood work, which of course he had tested to confirm what he already knew. He was Enola May's father. It was his job to protect her now. The tables had turned.

That's when Grover decided to make out a check in the amount of five thousand dollars. He would send it to apartment 333, Oxford Apartments, off Oxford Street, in Los Angeles. The note attached would read as follows:

December 23, 1978

Dear Enola,

Your mother doesn't know I'm sending you this check. I'm sending it on my own, as she is back in Highland's Hospital, and she is not going to be released for some time. I want you to have the money for any expenses. Sorry, it is too late to help you celebrate Christmas, but I hope your holidays were happy. Your mother does not know your whereabouts. Don't worry. I will not be informing her. Please use this check to help you and Rex. Let me know if you need more. I've enclosed my business card with my direct line.

Sincerely

Grover Starks

Chapter 16

It was two days after Christmas – December 27, 1978. I had taken

those two days off, now that things had slowed at my new job, just

as Rex had suggested, from my new cashier position at I-Magnin's

Department Store, to think about the past year of my life, since being

shuffled to Florida, since losing contact with my only sister, since

ending things with Kelsey, since falling in love with Rex, since

losing our baby, and since coming to the realization the Melantha

and Dacey were road-hazards that I would have to swerve around for the remainder of my life, or at least theirs. Now, before enjoying my day of relaxation, and before making the decision to unlock the deadbolt to exit apartment 333 on Oxford Street, I took one more look in the bathroom mirror and brushed my hair straight back, long brown hair, wavy with blended sunlit-colored streaks from the California sun.

From the street below, the fire escape looked rusty and unused, leading to the two large picture windows in our apartment. It was smoggy out for late December, warning signs flashed on the side of Wilshire Boulevard where I was walking: Pollution levels exceed limit – stay indoors if possible. It was a sign I had seen before when I walked to my new job on Wilshire. Sometimes I would be out of breath when I arrived at work. Sometimes it was difficult to breathe. I had only been working there for about eight days. I was a cashier, upstairs with two other cashiers in a small room. No customers. Gloria was in her forties I imagined, a woman trying to make it on her own after a bad divorce, wearing bright red fingernail polish, ruby-red lipstick, and sporting bright red hair to match. She wore summer colors in late December, and she put a fresh coat of lipstick on almost every hour it seemed.

I thought about my brief employment there and thought even harder about an incident that had occurred just yesterday, when I noticed the safe in the adjoining room with the door still open, unattended. *Gloria, where's Nita?* I remembered how I asked the question as I reached for another tube of money and a sales slip, which had made its way into the small room via air tube, just like I had seen before at banks. I thought about the thousands of dollars made at the store in just a few minutes it seemed, and how each sale was suctioned up into the tiny room, protecting the people below from any would-be robbers. As I walked along Wilshire, I thought about Gloria's answer. *Nita is picking up the coin order at the bank.* And then. *Sometimes she leaves the safe open accidentally.* I knew Gloria had figured out why I was being so inquisitive. I also knew that Mr. Robertson would have a fit if he knew about Nita's carelessness with the safe door. The safe was about the size of a large executive desk, filled with thousands and thousands of dollars from the sale of fur coats, expensive designer clothing and jewelry that the average American could never afford. The Brink's truck would arrive at three p.m. each day to pick up all the deposits from the proceeding workday. Each morning, the safe was counted, and

recounted, and deposit slips were made out. That's what Gloria
called counting down the safe. Until the Brink's security officers
would arrive it would be full – full of cash – at least eighty to one-
hundred thousand from the afternoon and evening before. There
were two different times that I had walked past the safe, the door
open, both of those times I wondered about what it felt like to touch
all that money. My eyes would glance past the almost empty trays of
rolled coin, toward the back of the safe, toward the stacks of money,
each segregated into marked bands of ones, fives, tens, twenties,
fifties, and one-hundred-dollar bills. It was the bands of fifties and
hundreds, which held my eyes captive longer than they should have.
I would always think about Rex and our future, and it didn't help
that Christmas had been sparse, and it was not going to get easier,
making it together, until I turned eighteen, until I would fall off
Melantha's radar and be able to head back east. I thought about
Gloria and Nita and Mr. Robertson, the manager of the cashier's
office, who had an office down the hall, in another area. To them, I
was Nola Satchele, born in California, my father a well-to-do artist
in San Francisco, who traveled to art shows, and who as a kid I
would often travel with, spending evenings in various towns and

beautiful hotels. My mother, who I called Denise, had died when I was a small child, and so I lived alone with my father, the artist, until meeting a boyfriend who had also come from important parents. *They don't know me…who I really am.* I thought to myself as I fought the smog that walked with me on Wilshire Boulevard. *They would have no way of finding me.* Yesterday, at work, I caught myself having the same thoughts, before Nita shut the thick steel-gray door, spinning the lock.

The smog was too thick for the morning walk I was attempting, so I caught myself making my way back down Wilshire Boulevard and toward the apartment building Rex and I called home. A faded maroon-colored purse that I had found at a thrift shop, and a brown paper bag filled with bread for ducks, that I had planned on feeding at a pond off Wilshire, were all I carried with me as I turned around and picked up speed. Fast. I had noticed a man with a two-piece navy-blue suit following me before, but now I knew he was following me in the opposite direction. As I picked up my pace, so did the navy suit behind me. He was careful not to lose me in the crowd. There was a look about him, which seemed familiar to me, but I didn't want to turn around and stare. He turned the corner onto

Oxford Street, about ten feet behind me. I didn't want to run; besides my chest was hurting ever so slightly from the LA smog. I quickly entered the apartment building on Oxford, making sure the door clicked behind me, happy that Rex had chosen an apartment building with a main entrance door requiring a key to open. I was too afraid to stop and check the mail, too afraid to use the elevator. *What if he got in behind another resident? What if he trapped me in the elevator? What if he tried to rape me?* The questions, like the colors, appeared to bounce up from the carpeted stairs as I ran up the three flights: bright blues, oranges, reds, and greens. *Is he a rapist or one of my mother's spies?* I thought to myself as I ran up the stairs. I was able to watch the man as he tried to enter the building, carefully balancing myself on the fire escape facing Oxford Street, being careful not to let the rust touch my only pair of good jeans, being careful not to make any noise. The man stood at the locked entrance for several minutes. There was a moment when I thought he was going to look up, with his hands cupped above his eyes; blocking out the sun; trying to see what had made the slight clanging sound above him. But then I heard his phone ring, could hear him talking, almost listening to instructions, and then simply watched him walk away.

Gone. I sat still for a moment in the thick December smoggy air,

wondering who had called him. Then I slowly made my way back

down the carpeted stairs to the first floor, where I opened the small

silver mailbox for apartment 333 and found myself barely able to

breathe as I studied the return address on the envelope I found

inside: Mr. Grover Starks, Esquire, 1724 Tunnel Road, Asheville,

North Carolina, 28806. I opened the envelope carefully, slowly, and

with hesitation. Inside I discovered three things: a letter that assured

me that my whereabouts were confidential, a business card with

Grover Starks' direct line, and a check for five thousand dollars

made payable to Nola Satchele. *How did he know where I was? And,*

how did he know to make the check payable to my secret identity

name? Did he know I would be able to cash it easily at my job? And

then, I wondered, *why would Grover Starks help me?* After all, I

reminded myself, I barely knew the man. I hadn't ever seen him in

person. Once, I had seen an advertisement on a billboard, in

Asheville, facing the jailhouse, where I waited with my sister, April,

while my mother was inside collecting what was left of her marriage.

I remember how it caught my eye, the large letters of his name, and

the unfamiliar, but somewhat familiar photo of a man in the

background, dressed in a dark suit, white shirt, red tie, and eyes that looked similar to mine – blue eyes that soothed the worried mind of someone needing legal assistance. What I knew at that moment was that Grover Starks had soothed my worried mind. I would venture back out, into the smog-filled air, walk up Wilshire, this time without worrying about money, and into I-Magnin's Department Store, where Nita would cash my check without question. Five thousand dollars was a lot of money.

#

Spring came early in Asheville. January and February were long cold months. Melantha fought the voices inside her head on a daily basis, without a break, except when heavily sedated, often screaming in the middle of the night about Tiger, Ernie, Jo-Jo, Abner, or Zelda – names the hospital staff had become all too familiar with. Dacey would drop by at least three or four times a week, even though Melantha seldom recognized him, and even though the restaurant required his attention every hour it was open, but it was something he had been ignoring too much lately; instead, he would manage a weekend getaway to the Toledo dog track or a bar where no one would recognize him. Back to his old tricks and old behaviors.

Today, April tenth, he watched Melantha stare out the windows, high and barred, stare at the cardinals perched in the dogwood tree, probably one female and one male. As he got closer to her face, he noticed she wasn't looking at the red birds after all. He said, "I'm sorry you didn't find Enola before her baby was due, Mel, but I'm sure she's doing okay. I'm here to be with you, to help you all I can." And then he thought. *She probably didn't know I overheard her talking about a baby.*

"Grover." Finally, after a few moments of silence, she corrected herself. "Where have you been, Dacey?"

"Mostly working." He lied, ignoring the fact that gambling had taken over his life once again.

"Do you know what day it is?" She glanced at his face as she asked the question, thinking about how she used to love him. It didn't matter anymore. She was trapped inside a mental hospital, trapped inside a world she couldn't escape, and trapped inside a mind filled with voices and thoughts that she knew weren't hers.

"It's the tenth of April, 1979."

"It's 1979?" Melantha suddenly remembered that was the year Enola would turn eighteen.

Dacey studied her expression. "Yes, I was hoping you would be out of here by now." He didn't know she no longer cared about getting out of Highlands; she had given up on that, and that she only cared about finding Enola before she turned eighteen.

"Have you heard from Grover Starks? Has he found Enola? Where's the baby?" Dacey didn't want to think about Enola or his only grandchild. He didn't want to be reminded of his mistakes. *I guess she did know that I knew about the baby.* He thought.

"I'm sure he'd get in touch with you immediately. You know he's trying to locate her. You said that he would find her. Whatever it takes he'll find her. I'm sure she's okay. I know she's smart enough to make it on her own safely. I know she wouldn't do anything stupid. I know she's probably just surviving the best she knows how."

"I don't understand how you can be so calm about the situation Grover." Again, she corrected herself. "Dacey."

"I've spent a lot of time worrying about her. And I can't forget that she's gone, Mel. I can't forget that April is gone too. But, I can't keep living every day feeling upset and ashamed for what I've done and thinking about how you caused a lot of it." He thought about how she had just referred to him as Grover for a second time. He could fill the anger inside of himself. "I can't forget you…what you've made me do through the years. You tore me away from both daughters – hell, my mother. Everything that meant anything to me is gone. What the hell for?" He felt a sense of freedom when he spoke to her, long overdue freedom, finally saying things that needed to be said. And then, he felt a sense of panic, especially when he looked into the eyes that were staring right through him. No blue.

"Get out!" The fiery dark green eyes screamed. Loud.

He looked into her angry eyes. "I didn't mean…mean to explode. I…"

"I hope you burn in hell someday, Dacey." Her tone was evil. "Burn like poor Zelda."

He had lost her again. He turned his back to her pain, to her anger, and walked out of the room.

Chapter 17

It took a long time before I could put pen to paper, maybe I wanted

to wait until I was only days from turning eighteen, wait until I knew

I wasn't going to be grabbed up and returned to Melantha. I had

relived December twenty-seventh over and over again in my mind. I

was lying on the pull-down bed completely naked, scattered with

hundreds, fifties, twenties, tens, fives, and a few one-dollar bills

when Rex walked up to the third floor and opened apartment 333

with his key. The look on his face I remember was one of confusion and joy, the same facial combination I had walking to my job to cash

the check earlier that day. I remember how the letter from Grover

Starks was carefully displayed on the small table between the two

chairs on the opposite side of the room, remember the sound of his

key in the knob and the gentle twist that opened the door, remember

how I whispered *I love you* as Rex stared down at my naked body in

the dimly lit room, naked except for the cash that was scattered over

me, and I thought about my explanation to Rex as he stood there –

baffled. *I got this today – we got this – money from Grover Starks.*

As I started to write, I thought about Rex's face – the same look on

his as I had throughout the evening – the one where I considered not

cashing the check, the one where I thought about returning it, and

finally, the one where I had convinced myself that I deserved it. I

had thought about it so many times over the last seven months. I

didn't understand why Grover Starks had sent the check, but I

surmised that the money wasn't from my parents, no of course it

wasn't, it was probably sent to buy some forgiveness, forgiveness for

fucking my mom, a married woman. At any rate, I felt it was time to

write a letter of thanks because there was something that his money

had given me over the past seven months, something that was

invaluable. It gave me back my identity. It took every day of the past seven months to fight my way back, it took dealing with my past, it took remembering where I came from, not hiding from it. I remembered thinking, staring into Rex's surprised face. *I don't want to hide anymore. I don't want to be Nola Satchele anymore. I wanted to be myself again.* I still think about that moment, about how Rex touched me, the beginning of welcoming back Enola Fears, who would fear no more. We didn't speak much that evening. We made love on five thousand dollars, and Rex broke the silence of the sleeping sun with two questions the next morning, which I can still hear him asking. *Will you marry me Enola? Will you become Enola Narducci?* The answer to both questions was yes. And, now after seven months, after dealing with at least some of my childhood memories that I had tried so hard to lock away, and some too dark to deal with now, I was turning eighteen years old in just six more days – the sixth of August, 1979. We would be getting married on the seventh, the day after, and then flying to Florida to reconnect with Homer and Barbara Parrish, Rex's mother, contact Dixie, and make a new life – a life where I didn't have to hide from anyone – freedom, so now, I begin to write. *July 31, 1979*

Dear Mr. Starks,

I don't know why you sent the check to me, but I wanted to send you a letter of thanks. I'm sorry this letter is so late. I hope you understand my apprehension of communicating, as I'm sure it was your job to find me and bring me back to North Carolina. I write to you now because I am turning eighteen in six days, getting married in seven, and returning to Florida in eight. If you're still working for Melantha, please let her know I had a miscarriage early on, which was very sad, but I'm sure it diverted a legal battle of custody with my mother. I don't know your reasons for keeping my whereabouts secret from my mother, but I do appreciate it more than you can imagine. Your money helped us live comfortably throughout the last seven months with our paychecks, which would have been a struggle alone. Please give my mother my best. I'm sure she is no longer in Highland's Hospital as she was always a fighter. Thank-you Mr. Starks for your help. Maybe someday I'll understand why.

Respectfully,

Enola Fears

#

Grover Starks brushed tears out of his eyes after reading Enola's
letter, before picking up the phone, before returning the last six
unanswered calls where Melantha had called screaming at his
secretary, demanding to speak with him. It was the sixth of August,
1979, Enola May Fear's eighteenth birthday, ironic to say the least –
a day he thought of his daughter because he knew it was her
eighteenth birthday – a day to call Melantha – a day to disclose what
he wanted from her. A nurse put Mr. Starks through to Melantha's
doctor, the one that had been monitoring her the most closely since
she relapsed last November, since spending the holidays at
Highlands, since being in constant lockdown, and since being unable
to leave the hospital on a weekend pass for the last nine months. She
was a prisoner, and Grover was informed that Melantha had suffered
another major relapse, as Dr. Carroll referred to one of her episodes,
during the night, and to expect that she would be somewhat drowsy
when the nurse allowed her to take a call from Grover Starks, all the
while, she was still hearing voices of a small child whispering to her,
instructing her. *Climb fast Mellie.*

　　She listened to Grover speak and describe how one of his
private investigators had finally located Enola in California,

apologizing that legally it was too late to interfere with her adult decisions, and delicately announcing that Enola had lost the baby, a miscarriage. Melantha should have been devastated: about the loss of a human life, about missing the chance to make things right with Enola before her legal adulthood, and about the irreplaceable time they had missed out on as a mother and daughter, but she wasn't. She was pissed that she had lost control: over a baby that could be used as a major bargaining chip, over a daughter that she would have proven unworthy to raise a child, and over the adult decisions that Enola Fears was now free to make on her own.

This is your fault. Alma Paine's voice was screaming at Melantha now. It was 1945. Alma had found Jo-Jo near the far outside corner of the farmhouse, her five-year-old body lying lifeless, at the foot of a four-rung ladder, one Alma had warned her precious girls to stay away from, and one that five-year-old Jo-Jo would climb like a monkey, quickly, to get to the top of the low, but flat tin-covered overhang, one where she would lie on her stomach, both arms dripping back down the ladder, her tiny voice encouraging Melantha to take each rung using a knee, slowly, carefully. *Reach for my hands Mellie. I'll help you.* Melantha could still hear the tiny voice. *Hurry, he's coming.* They would watch the new step-dad silently from the shiny tin, careful not to move as he passed near. Melantha felt protected when she was with Jo-Jo, rooftop whispers about rainbows and dancing dandelions, and princesses that always got away.

Jo-Jo would always make her way back down the ladder first, after hours of magical stories. *Mellie stay there until I help you down. I have to check for the bad man first.* The attempt at hiding worked for months, until the darkest day in October when the sound of autumn leaves could be heard breaking beneath Abner's drunken approach. *Crunch.* Melantha could still hear the leaves announce his arrival, could still feel the ladder being pulled from her reach, purposely, Jo-Jo's small hands knocking it to the ground, flat, out of sight, and out of mind from the drunk that backed her against the hard stucco. *Stay Mellie.* She looked at her sister's blue eyes peering down at her. *Be quiet. I'll keep you safe.*

Melantha remained silent in a world she didn't understand – the sound of a struggle, the smell of whiskey, the simultaneous tearing of her own heart with the lowering of a metal zipper, exposing unfamiliar body parts. Still, she remained silent, even when

Abner Paine put his alcoholic rage inside Jo-Jo's mouth, drowning out her cries, muffling her screams, twisting her neck like the clothes she had watched her mother feed through the metal rollers, hard, until the clothes were lifeless, like Jo-Jo's slender body. Abner Paine could still feel her tiny mouth around his penis when he pulled it out. The sky grew darker at the moment, so it seemed, blocking out all sunlight, Melantha glued to her stomach, staring down at her sister's lifeless body. Abner Paine simply left her there, like a rag doll – no traces of anything, except a broken neck, not in 1945.

Melantha didn't move for hours, the cold tin roof penetrating through her, as she stared down at her sister, watching for life, waiting for the all-clear signal, but it never came. It never would again. The night sky swallowed Melantha, surrounding her in total darkness, and fought to hold her captive on the tin roof, until Melantha heard the sound of her own mother's voice. Then she started to cry, a path of uncontrollable sobbing, like a lighthouse at the edge of a violent sea, a focal spot for Alma's eyes as she approached, her arms extended, pulling Melantha off the low-overhang, stepping over the wooden ladder, comforting her, until her eyes searched the edge of the overgrown flower garden. The sky was

a darker shade of night-gray by that point, a small beam of
moonlight danced near Jo-Jo's head, knocking Alma Paine to her
knees.

At first glance, it looked obvious. Jo-Jo had fallen down the
rickety wooden ladder, unsteady, sending both the ladder and Jo-Jo
to the ground, both lifeless. Both cold. Alma Paine began to scream
in horror. It was those screams that filled the head of now thirty-
eight-year-old Melantha Fears. *You shouldn't have been on the
ladder! Now your sister is dead!* Melantha never climbed the ladder
again. She had nowhere to hide from Abner Paine, the man her
mother counted on for survival, the man who had taken more than
Jo-Jo's life; he had taken Melantha's soul. She would never be the
same. The voice was stern, harsh, growing louder, and
unchallengeable in Melantha's head. She could no longer hear
Grover Starks.

#

My birthday was a day of survival rather than a celebration. I had
made it through my childhood, now I would spend the rest of my life
learning to deal with it. I would start by becoming a wife. My dress
was a crème-laced melt in your mouth floor-length gown that Rex

and I had found at I-Magnin's, a steal for ninety dollars, after a

substantial employee discount that Mr. Robertson had agreed to let

me have, even though my last day was August third, and after Gloria

and Nita graciously pitched in fifty dollars for a wedding gift. Rex,

fitted in a black tux that his friend Tony had arranged, one that

matched his dark features, grinned at me as I stood beside him on the

hotel balcony, the Mara Vista Hotel in El Segundo, rented for two

evenings, starting with my birthday, was near the airport in LA,

where we would spend the second-night making love, our first time

as husband and wife. We didn't have any flowers, except for a strand

of baby's breath in my hair, no music, just the sound of airplanes

making their way overhead to the Los Angeles International Airport,

no family, just the two of us and Reverend Lev, from the yellow

pages, who had agreed to come to the hotel, who had agreed to

provide a marriage license and perform a ceremony for sixty dollars.

Our vows were simple – to love each other always. *Would it be that*

simple? I wondered. The ceremony didn't last long, just long enough

to make it official. The hot August heat could be felt on my shoulder

blades, as Reverend Lev pronounced us husband and wife. I was

officially Enola Narducci. It was the beginning of so many things. I was no longer hiding from anyone. I wasn't sure why, but I sensed that Grover Starks had wanted to protect me since arriving in LA. I hoped that I would never need protection again, from anyone. I looked forward to flying back to Florida. I had explored every inch of Los Angeles since arriving in October. In most ways, I already felt home, alone with Rex for nearly ten months, and having been more and more in love each day. I felt our future would just grow to be stronger from the things we had been through, things most people wouldn't be able to survive together, and I looked forward to returning to Florida, finding jobs, and saving up for a down payment on a small house. I wanted to have children with Rex. I knew I would always feel a loss for the baby I hadn't gotten the chance to know, but I ached to love the baby we could make in the future. We had spent endless hours over the last week, talking about buying a small house somewhere in Southwest Florida, away from the mountains that had smothered me as a child, the mountains that Dacey would beat me in, hidden from his God. All I wanted was a normal life, where I didn't have to be afraid, tricked, lied to, manipulated, beaten, or in hiding. The thought of seeing Rex's face every morning when I opened my eyes made me feel alive, and I knew that we could survive anything now, and I knew I could survive alone if needed, but I didn't want to. I wanted Rex. If there was one thing I had learned living in a city like LA during the last ten months, it was to trust myself. I had lost people from my life that I would never get back. *No one will ever hurt me like that again.* I thought as Rex and I finished the longest kiss I had ever experienced, and as we pulled slightly away from each other, to smile, our future filled with hope and love.

I watched Rex's brown eyes as he stared into mine, and then at Reverend Lev, and then back at me. "Thank-you Reverend Lev." And, I watched money go from Rex's hand into the Reverend's hand, and I watched a stranger that I would never see again leave the small hotel room.

"Nola, what are you thinking?"

"Nothing, just how much I love you." *There are some things I can't share,* I thought as I watched him put the chain on the hotel door, walking back toward me. He had been watching my every move in my crème colored floor-length gown, made up of lace and chiffon, delicately hugging my waist, my breasts begging for attention hidden beneath ruffles of fabric.

He was holding me now. His hands sliding up and down the sides of my body. His fingers were in complete control of every curve. Smoothly. Slowly. He had worked his way to the zipper on the back on my dress and had pulled it down at a steady pace to watch the dress loosen from my shoulders and let go of the waist it had hugged moments before. Rex Narducci picked me up, carrying me over the pile of chiffon and lace on the floor, carefully placing me face up on the bed only steps away so that I could watch him unwrap himself with the same ease. The love between us glowed like a bright nightlight in the dimly lit hotel room. Within minutes he was inside me, rocking me, telling me that he would take care of me, promising me forever. The heat from the evening August air filled the hotel room, the glass sliding door still open, where we had been married on the balcony just thirty-five minutes earlier. We moved our bodies together in sequence, the bed still made beneath me, with Rex's hands reaching for the pillow hiding under the top of the comforter, a pillow that he gave the job of holding me, as he turned me over and directed my legs to bend at the knees. It was obvious that he wasn't done. My body begged him to continue. A siren from the street below broke the silence when Rex plunged his penis back inside of me, this time from behind, and my breasts hung in his hands, which were being caressed and rubbed with a steady even pace. There was a moment when I felt the mattress coils dig into my knees, especially my left knee, the knee-cap Dacey had cracked with a bat, in a rage of anger, to teach me that sex was evil. At first, I thought about readjusting, releasing the pressure on my knees, but then I gave way to the impression of small metal loops that tattooed my skin. Inside of me, I felt an explosion of fire. I moved up a little, resting my stomach on the pillow that had escaped hiding and felt Rex's body melt into mine. He was very still. The hot August air dampened the back of my neck as he spoke.

"I love you." That was all he said, and it was all I needed.

Chapter 18

Grover Starks drove to Highlands before the second week of August

came to an end. He checked in at the desk, which served as a guard

to the unit that held patients, those that needed more attention.

Melantha Fears had been back at Highlands nearly as long as Enola

had been in Los Angeles. "I'm here to see Melantha Fears. There is a

lot of legal business I must take care of with her." Grover handed the

woman his business card, and at her signal he turned right and

headed down the long hallway after being buzzed through a metal door that locked behind him. This had become Melantha's home.

"I'll be about an hour," Mr. Starks announced as the metal door

clicked behind him. "Please see we're not disturbed." He walked

down the hallway quickly and hurried to her room. "Melantha," he

whispered upon entering the room. "It's Grover. Would it be okay if

we talked?"

The blank face suddenly lit up, alive again, and replied, "Est-

il parti? Has he left? I don't think he will ever come back."

"Who?" But Grover knew she was referring to her husband.

He knew about Dacey's last visit, months ago, knew about Dacey's

every move, as he had a P.I. on Dacey too, the man he now knew

had beaten his flesh and blood for years. "Dacey?" He asked just to

fuck with Melantha's head, asked even though he knew it had been

almost four months since Dacey's last visit, since Melantha told him

to get out, since she hoped he would burn in hell. Grover Stark's P.I

had watched Dacey's every move, even flirted with nurse Halohand

to get the inside scoop about the screaming that had ended Dacey's

last visit, had followed Dacey to bars where he would confess about

being a bad father to the bartender, had uncovered a lifelong

gambling addiction to the dog track, horse track, and football (basically anything that moved), and had monitored Dacey's small restaurant, watching business dwindle, watching regular customers switch to a better establishment, newer establishment on the other side of Merrimon Avenue. Dacey was a wretched man. Alone. Even with other people, he was still alone. Even with his old habits of meeting women at bars, he would always be alone. Melantha Fears had made him that way, with her special wand, sentencing him to a life of eternal damnation. She had taken his life from him and a shell of a man was all that remained. Melantha knew he needed her, and the truth is she needed him. Pined for him. Melantha remembered her last words to him. *I hope you burn in hell someday, Dacey.*

"This is not a visit about Dacey. This is about your daughter Enola and her husband Rex, remember?" Melantha did remember. But, *husband?* The word ran through her. She remembered how Enola was eighteen now, remembered how she had screamed at nurse Halohand to allow a calendar to be hung in the small hospital room, remembered how she would cross off the days, using a dull crayon, and finally the day. Too late. *Was she married now?* She wondered.

"Does it matter now?"

She knows I played her, he thought. *She knows I wouldn't have taken more than thirty days to locate her, to locate anyone.* Grover had refused her phone calls over the last couple of months, letting her stew in her juices. He couldn't tell what she was thinking by the look on her face, but he knew she was annoyed with him. She was hard to read. "Enola is safe." *She's probably stewing over the word husband.* He thought and smiled.

"I didn't ask that Grover." Melantha had strength in her voice. Her face was now one Grover Starks had seen before. One that he had always found attractive. "Where is she?"

"Back in Florida."

"I guess your plan worked." Melantha Fears followed his eyes as he bent to kiss her on the cheek. He knew he had lost the woman he had spent his whole life being in love with. She would never become his wife, but she would always be the mother of his only child. "You won."

"Yes," Grover answered. "She is an adult now." Melantha waited for him to play out all his cards. "She and Rex are in Florida, back at Homer and Barbara Parrish's, your biological dad and wife, back with people who love her." He looked into the fiery eyes that had first attracted him in Detroit, eyes that lost the calming blue when they were angry. They were dark green now. "It's over Melantha."

Melantha glared at him. She knew she had lost, but she sensed he wasn't done.

"I had her blood tested from her hospital stay in Birmingham." He watched the dark green fire in her eyes flicker. "We're a match." It burned inside of her. Like Zelda, she was going up in flames. "She's my daughter."

Melantha Fears was screaming at Grover Starks in the darkness of her hospital room. She tried to get control of herself. She had spent the last couple of months taking a new medication to help control the voices inside her head. During the darkness, when she was alone, the voices would speak the loudest and the medication rarely helped them to be quiet. The youngest sounding voice would always whisper, would sometimes cry quietly, and when trying to stop crying, would hum a song Melantha recognized. But there was one voice that would always make Melantha scream out in pain. In the counseling session, Dr. Carroll had surmised that it was probably her stepfather, Abner Paine, so they would spend time talking about how she hated him and how she would never be able to forget the

suffering he had caused her. It was typical according to Dr. Carroll.

But sometimes when Melantha was in control she would think about

the voice that always made her scream, when she could think clearly.

Now wasn't the time. Thinking clearly weren't words that would

describe Melantha's state of mind. Not now. The voices in her head

exploded. They were still there when Grover Starks walked down

the long hallway and out the metal door, leaving the mother of his

adult child. The room was dark, but the visitors remained with

Melantha.

#

September 1979

The white sand was hot, even in September. It was a few hours after

noon as Rex and I walked on Bonita Beach, stopping at the end of a

stretch of nothingness to pull my sandals back off. As I walked, my

feet made prints into the sand, crushing tiny shells into my heels. I

sat down on a wooden bench near a parking lot where we had parked

Homer Parrish's car.

We felt fortunate that Homer didn't mind us borrowing his

car until we got our own. Getting a car was first on the list of things to do. Getting a small place to live was second. Rex brushed the shells loose, my feet tucked up and safely secured in his lap. That's when I noticed a gray van parked near our car. Someone was sitting inside: a man I had seen before. *When will I stop suspecting that I am being hunted?* I watched him as we stood, sandals back on now, and walked toward the parking lot. *Why was he there?* Both front windows were down, on the gray van, the outside faded, with worn tires, that looked like they had traveled coast to coast. Rex hadn't noticed that my eyes were watching the van, hadn't noticed that my hand was pulling him closer. I wanted to get a better look inside the van. Suddenly the gray van's engine turned over, and it pulled forward, slowly, but not to leave the parking lot, only to proceed carefully toward us. *Who was he?* I wondered. It was all I could do to remain calm, not alert Rex who was unsuspecting of everything around him at the moment, but I was done showing my paranoid side to Rex, until the van approached us.

"Excuse me." The man spoke as he slowly came to a stop beside us. "Mr. and Mrs. Narducci?" I recognized him. His face had followed me in Los Angeles. I distinctly remembered. *And the day I found out I was pregnant?* I questioned.

Rex's unsuspecting eyes were now on full alert and stared directly at the man. "Can we help you?"

"I'm sorry to startle you." The voice was calm and polite.

"Yes."

The man handed us a business card – Thomas Smith, Real Estate Agent. "Please call this number at your earliest convenience. Mr. Starks has arranged financial considerations with Mr. Smith for your wedding gift. Mr. Starks would like you to pick out any home in the area that would make you happy."

Rex held out his hand to accept the card. "Why?" It was such an easy question, but I felt like it had an answer that was much more complicated.

"Please contact Mr. Starks if you have any questions." The man paused. "Again, I'm sorry for startling you." We watched the gray van slowly pull away. We stood there looking at each other, both wondering if this was another trick. My private question stayed private. *Why was Grover Starks so interested in my well-being?*

#

When Melantha Fears woke up after weeks of being sedated, it was October, and she was in a different room. Her arms were strapped down to her sides, and she was blurry-eyed from weeks of strong medication. The voice that made her scream was speaking loudly in her head. Nurse Halohand was at her side, unstrapping her arms, announcing a visitor, the first one since Grover Starks had left weeks earlier.

"Melantha, do you recognize my voice?" She was still staring at the ceiling but had allowed her free arms to move her hands to her mouth, where they tried to cover the look of terror on her face. She had been screaming most of the night, and tied down, she hadn't had an opportunity to try and hide her fear. It was only 6:32 a.m. but they let him in to see her. She had been calling out for him. Nurse Halohand had made the call to the restaurant first, but it was out of business, another one of Dacey's failures, and then she remembered hearing him mention the name of the cheap one-bedroom apartment near Highlands, so she made the call. He wasn't prepared for the way she looked. He wasn't sure if it was the result of shock therapy he was seeing, or if it was the almost five months of not visiting her that had sent her over the edge. He felt responsible. She kept her hands over her mouth, trying to block any voices that wanted to escape.

"Melantha? It's Dacey." He watched her eyes after removing her still cupped hands to the sides of her five-foot three-inch frame. Her mouth was propped open. Once again, he spoke to her. "I was wrong to walk out on you. I was wrong to blame you. And I know a lot of our problems have been caused by me. You have tried the best you know how, in the only way you know. But it's – it's hard to fight against you all the time. I just want to love each other. I just want to stop hurting all the time." He was still watching her eyes as he continued. "The women don't mean anything to me, not like you. I know I had no right to hurt you. But I needed to be held by someone, who would hold me without trying to hurt me, when I was shut out of your life. But I never stopped loving you." He was crying now, something he had become used to doing recently. "I've always loved you Mel."

She seemed to stare at the well of tears in his eyes as he bent over her, and she felt the need to speak to him, but she hadn't been able to get control of herself as she realized her mouth would not close.

"I'm sorry." He continued. "And I'll never hurt you again." Dacey collapsed over her, holding her, and listening to her breathing for a long time, until she fell asleep beneath him, his body a protection against the outside world. They stayed that way for almost two hours, until two orderlies entered the room, until Melantha was helped into a wheelchair, and until she was wheeled down the hall to Dr. Carroll's replacement for the next month, while Dr. Carroll and his family were on vacation. His name was Dr. Stevens. He believed Melantha needed daily in-depth counseling sessions. The windows in Dr. Steven's office were closed and bars decorated its view from outside, but Melantha could still see the litter of pine trees from the wheelchair's placement. In the tallest pine, the male cardinal hopped from branch to branch, and in the pine right next to it Melantha could see the faded female do the same. The replacement doctor was a specialist from Raleigh, a person who had worked with Melantha for the last week, a person with years of experience, and a new opinion about the voices, which made Melantha scream. Seated in another chair beside her was Dacey.

"Melantha," the doctor began, "I have reviewed your file from Dr. Carroll. I have worked with others that experienced the same type of trauma, in which they too watched a family member being murdered." *What was the counselor talking about?* Dacey found himself in quiet thoughts. *Melantha watched a family member get murdered? Who?* "The trauma is worsened when you have guilt that you could have done something to prevent it from happening, or that you could have at least turned the person in who committed the terrible act," Dr. Steven's continued. "We have various ways of approaching and working through this situation. We have a lot of work to do to get started. As you start to talk about the incident, please remember it won't be easy." The doctor paused again, but still without emotion. "Some things may be harder to remember than others, some will never be remembered. Details have been buried inside of you for many years…and you were very young."

The doctor paused again, this time shuffling papers, and a list of facts Dacey had never known began to surface. "You were born in 1941. Your parents divorced when you were three, almost four. Your sister, one year older, was named Joanne, and …" He paused for a moment, then turned to a page in the back of the file he was holding. "You screamed during shock treatment that Joanne was murdered…you recalled being just over four years old when it happened…you said your step-father was hurting her…and you said your mother didn't get home to the farmhouse until it was over, and that you were afraid." He flipped the last page over. "You were abused by this step-father before you turned five." He paused. "Until the age of…it doesn't say." The doctor stopped and looked at Melantha. She was still sitting lifeless in the wheelchair, still looking at the cardinals, and still working to block out voices. Dr. Stevens moved his chair, directly in front, obstructing her line of vision, trying desperately to engage her. "Melantha, can you tell me about the last time you remember being forced to have any type of sexual contact with your step-father Abner?"

"I have it every day, several times a day." She looked into the doctor's eyes. "He's always in my head." *Act like you're enjoying yourself, Mel.* She could hear him say.

"Would you rather talk about Joanne's last day?" He tried to redirect the conversation. He tried to get her focused. "Until you face the things that have happened in your past, I cannot help you get better." Dr. Stevens paused again. "Melantha, I need you to think back about Joanne's last day. The day Joanne was hurt…"

When Dacey Fears heard about Melantha's sister, Joanne, he felt chills race through his body. He didn't know about her. He didn't interrupt. Didn't distract her by readjusting in his chair. He just sat silently. Still.

"Jo-Jo wasn't hurt," Melantha almost shouted the words out. "I watched him kill her. Jo-Jo took care of me. She was the lookout. She protected me, so I didn't have to be with the bad man." Melantha stopped for a moment. She thought about one of the many nights she remembered Abner coming into their bedroom at the farmhouse. She thought about how he would hold his hand over Jo-Jo's mouth when he entered her and would threaten to beat the hell out of her the next day if she even looked at him wrong. Then there was the time that Alma's mother, Mel and Jo-Jo's grandma, was sick. Alma spent the night away, leaving Mel and Jo-Jo with Abner, alone at the farmhouse. That night he didn't put his hand over her mouth. That night he let her scream. All the while, Melantha pulled blankets up around her head ashamed to admit she was glad it was Jo-Jo and not herself. Not yet. But it was the second night that Alma was away, a month later, again to help her sick mother, that Jo-Jo fought to protect Mel. Abner tried to touch Melantha that night. He tried to pull the covers off her, but Jo-Jo jumped on his back, and with effort, lured him in her direction, once again. The blanket protected Melantha; it held her small hands that covered her face, hiding from the pain.

"I would like you to tell me about the wooden ladder, Melantha," the doctor spoke softly, "Did Joanne fall off the ladder? Did he push her?" Dr. Stevens was bothered by the fact that Dr. Carroll hadn't pressed harder for more information, noting only that Melantha had watched her sister be murdered near the ladder. *How?* He wondered.

Melantha Fears' hands trembled as she took her eyes off of the pine trees that she had rediscovered behind Dr. Steven's back and looked into the doctor's eyes. Dacey was watching the pain on her face. The now thirty-eight years of life suddenly showed on her. She was every bit of thirty-eight and more. She had aged five years in the last year, and somewhere in there, somewhere while a patient at Highland's, she had turned thirty-eight, unnoticed. Dacey watched her stare through Dr. Steven's body. He felt ashamed that he hadn't helped Melantha more in the past. The screaming inside of her was partly his fault, and he urged her to continue talking with his eyes and touched her hand slightly as she began to speak again. Gently.

"She had tiny red spiders in her eyes," Melantha said, "they looked up at me, after he left her there, after he put his bad parts in her mouth. I stayed quiet like she told me, until Momma came to get me."

The doctor was writing down everything Melantha said and was careful not to interrupt her.

"I heard her bones break."

Dr. Stevens spoke softly. "I need you to go on. I know this is hard for you, but it's the only way…"

"I thought Momma would fix her broken neck."

"Okay."

"I didn't know what else to do. My tummy was cold from the metal, but I kept staring at her red eyes. Red."

"What did you tell your mom?"

The doctor listened to her carefully. Dacey wanted to hug her. But he just rubbed her hand gently.

Almost reluctantly, she said, "I told her she fell because I was afraid of the bad man. I was afraid he would kill me too." Melantha wiped tears off her cheeks, using both hands. "I was afraid…" Melantha Fears said it with shame. "Afraid I would be next."

Dr. Stevens looked through the end of the file to see what other notes he had overlooked. None. He continued to prompt her, "Tell me about the first time your step-dad sexually assaulted you." The doctor listened to Melantha as her voice became softer, talking about how Abner would make her open her mouth too. But she didn't struggle like Jo-Jo. She didn't want her neck bones to break and leave her lifeless. She told about their many times together, whispering as she talked, trying not to wake the voices that were inside of her, humming, chanting, whispering, until she finally gave in to more medication. She shut her eyes. The last thing she said, quietly, to herself, was...*I had to poison him.* She was the only one who heard it.

After listening to Melantha talk for what had only been one hour, Dacey was on the phone to Grover Starks in his law office, and thirty minutes after that he was seated across from his desk explaining he had just learned things that no one had known before. Not Grover, not himself, and not the girls. Dacey was willing to beg Melantha's occasional lover for his help. He wanted Melantha to come home, wanted to help her, wanted to set her free from that place that she was being haunted in day after day. Grover could get the ball rolling if anyone could. Grover did get to work on the situation as soon as Dacey left his office. He picked up the phone the moment Dacey Fears left. It wasn't to help Dacey or Melantha. It was an effort for his daughter. He had to make sure Melantha Fears would *never* get out. His office would pay for the new addition to the hospital, a wing for residential care, an agreement that would secure Melantha's spot at Highland's Hospital indefinitely.

When Dacey drove home from Grover's office to his small one-bedroom apartment, he thought about the woman he would always love – *my sweet Melantha.* She was a woman that had lived through hell – the same hell she had recently sentenced Dacey to.

In the middle of the night, Melantha woke. *Please help me. He broke my bones.* And, then a crackling noise went off in her head and she imagined pieces of her brain exploding around her. Red spiders crawled on her face throughout the night.

Chapter 19

I was confused. *Why did Grover Starks want to help us? What was in it for him?* I waited a few days before calling, not the real estate agent, no my first call was directly to Grover. I thought about the only picture I had ever seen of Grover, a billboard photo that had stared down at me near the jail in Asheville. His features were a lot like my grandmother's in Detroit, Easter Humphreys, my dad's mother, a mother he hadn't seen in such a long time, a mother who was acting as the mother to my sister, a sister I wondered if I would ever see again. Both Easter and Grover had dark features: jet black hair and olive skin. But, I remembered, *the billboard eyes weren't milk chocolate like Easter's.* I dialed, thinking my private thoughts. *They were a non-assuming blue like mine. Just blue.*

"Mr. Starks please," I spoke like I was a client. "Mrs. Narducci calling." The secretary responded quickly, without so much as asking what I needed.

"Hold on, Mrs. Narducci, I'll patch you through to Mr. Starks." No time was wasted.

"Mrs. Narducci." His voice was strong and confident. "I'm so glad my P.I was able to deliver the real estate agent's card. I hope he's been helpful in your search for a first home."

"Who is financing this procedure Mr. Starks?" I kept it business.

"Don't worry, Enola, you don't need to worry about financial arrangements." He paused. "Just pick out something that will make you happy with Rex. *He called me Enola. We're on a first-name basis already?* I wondered if there was anything he didn't know about me.

"Mr. Starks…" But he quickly interrupted.

"G…Grover." He sounded like he wanted to say something else but settled on Grover. "Please call me Grover."

"Grover, I don't understand. Is my mother or father paying for this transaction?"

There was silence for a few moments. And then, "No, your mother does not know anything about this transaction."

"My father?" *I sensed he didn't want to talk about him.*

"Enola, would you be free to meet for lunch next weekend." He clarified immediately. "I have business in Florida next weekend, and I could have a driver take me closer to your area."

"Do we have business to discuss?" *What does he want with me? Is this another one of Melantha's tricks? Why didn't he answer about my father? Did something happen to Dacey and this is a life insurance pay-off?* The questions were shooting off in my head, but then I thought about how I wasn't going to be afraid or hide from anyone. Never.

"It would be nice to discuss a few things Enola." His voice was patient, kind.

"Yes, please get in touch with me when you get here. I would be happy to meet you for lunch." *I'm eighteen and legal. I'm married. I'm not running.*

"That sounds great." He sounded happy. "I will see you Saturday." And then, "Don't worry, I will inform my driver where your grandparents live." *Of course, you will.* I thought.

Two days passed quickly. I got the feeling that Grover's visit to Florida wasn't really for business; I felt he was making the trip to see me. I knew from Melantha's comments, that he was an excellent lawyer, the best advocate anyone could hope for. I just hoped he wasn't on the opposite team. I felt somewhat like a celebrity when the driver in a black Lincoln Town car arrived at Homer and Barbara's house Saturday afternoon. Rex was busy working at a new job in the Edison Mall, a men's clothing store, so it was just me, alone in the Lincoln, shuttled off to a restaurant where the driver said Mr. Starks frequented when in town on business. *Maybe this trip isn't about me. Maybe he does have business in Florida.* And then, I let the thoughts leave my head before arriving at The Veranda in Fort Myers, a place I could tell immediately was way beyond my budget. When I walked in Grover Starks was already sitting near a picture window overlooking the Gulf, sipping ice tea, and looking nervous for a seasoned attorney. He stood to greet me as I approached, and I suddenly felt underdressed in a yellow polyester sundress and black flip-flops.

"Nice to meet you in person Enola." He extended his hand and waited for me to sit before he returned to his seat.

"Nice to meet you too Grover." If he wanted to use first names I guess I was game.

"I wanted to talk to you about your mother." *Here it comes – the old Melantha card. What does she want now?* I wondered.

"I don't see the point." I tried not to sound rude and lowered my voice as the waitress brought me an ice tea, unsweetened. *How does he know I like unsweetened tea? Has he been stalking what I drink too?*

"I just wanted to inform you that I spent an hour on the phone with Dr. Stevens yesterday, discussing your mother's care." He looked directly at me, his eye color an exact match to mine. "Your dad…I mean Dacey…ran out of money to help cover her care. I suspect it's because a restaurant he was running went bankrupt." He paused, long enough to direct the waitress to bring two jumbo shrimp cocktails. "At any rate, I want you to know that I have an arrangement with the hospital, so you don't need to worry." I'm sure my look was one of puzzlement. *Arrangement? And was she going to be there indefinitely?*

"Is my mother unable to leave?"

"She can't live without constant supervision now. She has frequent episodes where she screams for help, and the doctors are concerned she might hurt someone."

"Physically?" *I knew she was the master at hurting people mentally, but physically?*

"Yes, apparently in-depth counseling and treatment have revealed that she is capable of that."

"Has she admitted to killing someone?" I was sorry I asked the question the moment I asked it. I didn't want to know, and I could tell by the look on his face that it wasn't a topic he would ever discuss, even if he knew.

"Both Dr. Carroll and Dr. Stevens agree on one thing, and that is that her condition doesn't allow her to function outside of Highland's Hospital." He was calm and seemed to monitor his words. I felt like he knew a lot more than I wanted to know, so I attempted to redirect, as attorneys would say.

"What are you doing for the hospital?" The waitress sat the large Florida gulf shrimp cocktails down in front of us, and his eyes motioned his approval. I could see he soaked in the question I had just asked but had no intention of answering it, as he was better at redirecting than I was.

"This is going to be hard for you to hear, so I'll just be straight forward." He took a bite out of the jumbo shrimp nearest him, the one begging for attention. "I knew your mother in Detroit, Michigan." He swallowed and for some reason I felt comfortable enough to do the same. "Before you were born."

"You were a couple?" I couldn't think of another way to ask the question respectfully.

"Yes. We saw each other for months." He moved on to the second shrimp. "So, I guess you could say that." And then after swallowing, he stopped, looking at me. "I cared about her very much. I still do."

"I guess she's lucky to have someone that can maneuver her continued care at Highlands." I don't know why, but I sensed he loved her. "Thanks for helping her."

"I'm not doing it for just her, or just me. I'm doing it for you too. You don't need any interference with your adult life." He wiped his face with the red cloth napkin and placed it to the side of his half-eaten shrimp cocktail. "I loved your mother for many years, and I love and care about her daughter...my daughter."

The words almost blew through me. They would have knocked me over had I been standing, but I sat frozen, looking at the eyes that matched mine, moments passing before I was able to speak, after thinking to myself. *He said daughter. He didn't say daughters. He means just me. Does he think I am his daughter?*

"Am...Am I...your daughter?" I asked the question without moving.

"I never knew until your hospital stay in Alabama." He didn't mince words. "I had a lab run our DNA for paternity." He waited to make sure I was okay. Breathing. "Enola, we are father and daughter."

"Are you positive?" I wasn't disappointed. *Why would I be? Dacey had always been a failure for a father.* I was simply shocked. Somehow, sitting there, in silence for a few minutes, staring out at the Gulf of Mexico, allowing his hand to brush mine near the red cloth napkin, I felt relieved. I needed to come from someone normal, someone intelligent, someone that cared about the people he loved. *Was I one of those people?*

Grover Starks sounded like he was in a court of law. He remained calm and made sure he left nothing out. "Enola, I sent you the check in California, because I knew your location. I wanted to make sure you were okay…financially. You mean a lot to me. I could have gone my entire life without knowing, but when my P.I showed me the photos of you and Rex in LA, I knew you were mine. I could tell by the way you stood." He stopped for a moment to gain his composure. "By the way your eyes look." And then, "Your smile."

"I don't know what to say." I was trying not to cry, trying to be as strong and in control as the man across the table. "Is that why you're trying to buy us a house?"

"Yes." He handed me his red cloth napkin for my eyes, even though I had my own. "I want to do whatever I can for you and your future."

"I don't need money. I…" He interrupted me before I could finish, even though I didn't know what I was going to say.

"I have lots of money Enola. But, it's not about the money." He reached out to touch my other free hand, the one free of cloth napkins, the one whose job it wasn't to collect tears. "It's about family. I've never had a family. No one. I've always been alone."

"Me too." He knew Melantha and Dacey enough to know what I was talking about. I have been alone since the day I was born. Suddenly, it all made sense. I was always missing a connection with Dacey Fears, the man who beat me. *Did he suspect I wasn't his?* I wondered but didn't feel like asking.

For now, I would just enjoy the moment.

Chapter 20

The voices kept talking; sometimes Melantha could hear her name

being called. *Mellie.* Softly. She knew it was Jo-Jo. She could see

her dead sister playing in a field of wildflowers, the white dress

gently blowing, a future hand-me-down, because it had become too

short for Jo-Jo, but one that would never be worn by its recipient –

instead, Melantha would neatly fold it, placing it under her pillow,

the same pillow that held her head when Abner Paine would violate

her small body. Afterward, she would dry her tears on the ruffled front, smelling Jo-Jo's scent, and listening to her dead sister's whispers. *The coast is clear now Mellie. The bad man is done.* Now, Melantha would talk about the tiny white dress, how she took it to the farmhouse, the night before Abner died, a visit no one knew about. Dr. Stevens sat across from her, waiting for the voices to stop, waiting for the last dose of medication to take effect, and waiting for Melantha to discuss her last visit with Abner Paine. More than two years had passed since that visit. A lot had happened since then. Enola had left with Rex, miscarried, and married; April had moved to Michigan where Easter Humphreys had taken over as her new mother. Melantha's role as matriarch had disappeared.

In Alma Paine's large fan-back wicker chair, in the corner of the living room, facing the garden, where there was no sign of life, where visions were overgrown with weeds, and where the wooden ladder had once propped against the low tin overhang, Melantha sat quietly, waiting for him. She knew he was outside checking the cornfield; she had noticed him deep in work, when she had first parked her Toyota, unannounced, when she first noticed the field of wildflowers, dancing in the overgrown grass, camouflaging her sister Jo-Jo, who she could see dancing in the gentle breeze. She watched her run toward the ladder and thought about sounding her car's horn to warn her that he was approaching from behind. Instead, she watched her become a small spot. *Why did she go down the ladder before the coast was clear?* Melantha's medicine was not helping her as much as Dr. Stevens had hoped. The voices were everywhere around her. Melantha continued to stare at the white dress, which seemed to float in the air above Dr. Stevens. *No, No, No.* Melantha closed her eyes and began to hum a song. Dr. Carroll pulled up a chair on the other side of Melantha, part of a procedure allowing the patient to feed off the questions of both doctors. He had returned from his family vacation, several weeks after much-needed rest, several weeks after being away from the crazies. He was now in the middle of hell – Melantha's imaginary world. The closed eyes did not acknowledge his return, but she turned her head in his direction as he started to speak, slowly.

"Melantha, It's Dr. Carroll. I'm back to assist with your case."

Melantha Fears' eyes didn't open, but she continued to permit her head to face his direction. She had recently had another room change at Highland's Hospital, this room had one window, very small, and was covered with thick cast iron bars. It was a room reserved for suicidal behavior. There was no phone or clock, and the only end table had been padded on all its corners.

Dacey Fears had stopped by earlier that morning to check on her, but she was unresponsive. He reminded her that he would take her home soon to his apartment where they could go swimming in the community pool. "I love you, Mel." He said to the lifeless face before leaving, a face that made him feel that he would always swim alone. Dr. Stevens and Dr. Carroll had both informed him that there was no release date in sight. Twenty minutes later he was back in his car, devastated by the emptiness around him and wishing he could make her nightmares end. His forehead wrinkled into three wide lines, and his dark brown eyes, almost as lifeless as Melantha's solid now-green ones, had the same fear and worry pooled in them that had been there several times before. *How can I survive without her? Why can't she function just for me?* Dacey Fears felt empty and alone. *I don't know how to help her.* Dacey's thoughts ate at him as he drove to his tiny apartment.

The small solo window made the world look cold outside, colder than the already dropping November temperatures, and the rubber trimmed end-table next to the mattress on the floor reminded her she was locked away from the rest of the world. She started to hum again, even though her eyes were now open, now looking at the two doctors in her room, one in a chair beside her mattress, the other seated below the window. She rocked herself slowly, back and forth on the mattress, like a small child, her knees close to her face. A voice of a teenage girl filled the silent air. The room reminded her of her dorm, the one she never spoke about. The one she lived in when arriving in Detroit to finish high school – a southern Baptist teenager in a Catholic world, but Alma Paine thought it would be okay since the head nun was French. The nuns with long black cloaks snapped at her in a French language she did not yet understand. The Savior's Boarding School would teach her how to act properly, and stepfathers wouldn't be accused of immoral acts. The mother she would always love did not agree to send her away but felt forced to, after one December evening of accusations and finger-pointing. The nuns were singing in her mind as she mouthed their words.

Melantha's gentle words filled the hallway at Highland's Hospital. The doctors sat still. Listening. She sounded like an angel as she sang:

Réveillez-vous,

il est temps

de laver les cernes rouge foncé

de vos yeux.

"Can you tell me what you said in English?" Dr. Stevens asked.

"Yes." Melantha answered. "Wake-up, it is time, to wash the dark red covers from your eyes."

A second of silence passed between the three of them. She had her hands folded in her lap, unaware she was sitting Indian style and unaware she had sung the song so beautifully. Dr. Carroll began to write on his clipboard, descriptive and suggestive, a thirty-eight-year-old woman sat still beside him. A teenage life had passed in front of her, and the sister she knew as a child would disappear again, for now, leaving her alone with the doctors.

It was 1959 when Melantha left the security of Savior's Boarding School in Detroit. She was only eighteen years old. She missed her mother but refused to go home while Abner Paine was still there. Instead, she would become a familiar part of the streets in Detroit, doing what she knew how to, doing what she had been taught to, until Dacey and his church saved her. It was short-lived. And, now, being saved was not something anyone felt was possible.

Melantha thought about her mother's only visit in the two years she was at Savior's Boarding School in Detroit. It was a two-day drive from the farmhouse nestled in the mountains of Asheville, North Carolina to Detroit. Hard driving. She could still see her mother's face. It was hard to see the bruises right away. Melantha noticed them when the light by the front entrance to the boarding school hit her mother's face like Abner's fist – the reflections of black, blue, and purple were pooled around her left eye and jaw. Melantha had never seen her mother like that before. She cried at the bruises and hoped it hadn't happened more than once, but she knew it probably had.

"My step-father beat my mother." She said to Dr. Carroll who was still writing on the clipboard. "Because of me. She found out the truth." Alma Paine had questioned him about the accusations one night when he was drinking, one of his many nights. *Why didn't she make him leave then honey? Why didn't she come get you?* The voice was Tiger's. Melantha was drifting in and out of her different worlds. She watched Tiger, strolling in her tight dress, waiting for the next john.

Abner Paine would drink the evenings away, his back propped against the wooden ladder, the same ladder Jo-Jo had scurried down to her death. Alma thought about bringing Melantha home, but she realized she was safer right where she was, away from him, away from his immoral advances, hidden in the safety of the French-speaking nuns.

"She found out he had been sexually molesting me, that he had raped me since I was four years old." Melantha looked at Dr. Stevens now, and then she went into deep thought, thinking about all of the nights he would come in her room to rape her, in the same room he used to rape Jo-Jo in and the way it made her feel cold and empty like the outside wind. Abner had taken everything away from her: Jo-Jo, her mother, and her soul. Every time he raped her.

After Melantha married Dacey, she tried again to save her mother. Alma Paine tried to leave him, but he would threaten to kill her. Serious threats. The smell of alcohol would penetrate her mother's nightgown, night after night. Melantha never gave up on trying to take Alma away from him, for years, but it would always end the same. She would always refuse to leave him. Melantha would confront him, but then he would beat her mother as punishment as soon as he got the chance. She couldn't protect her twenty-four hours a day, nor could she pry her away from him. It was a war Melantha couldn't fight; it was her mother's fight, and one she wasn't winning. The man who had raped both of her daughters, and as Melantha kept secret until after her mother's death, had killed Jo-Jo, was now the man who had grown to be old and permanent in Alma's life.

"He killed Jo-Jo. I didn't stop him." Then thinking back. "I watched him hurt her in the darkness. I would pull the covers over my face. I would hide." Both doctors sat still and listened.

"You were only three, maybe four, when that first started happening." Dr. Stevens tried to calm the hysterical tone in Melantha's voice.

"I should have stopped him." She sounded mad at herself. "I shouldn't have waited so long to stop him. I heard him coming in the back door to the farmhouse when I went there the night he died." Melantha's voice was very controlled. "I sat still in my mother's wicker fan-back chair. I looked down in my lap to see what my hands were doing. One was holding the dress – Jo-Jo's white dress, my thumb played with the ruffled-front, trying to feel Jo-Jo's heartbeat." Melantha paused for a moment. Remembering. "My other hand was still clenched shut. That's when I knew he had to die."

"What happened next Melantha?" Dr. Carroll was taking notes while Dr. Stevens asked the questions.

"All he cared about was his stupid cornfield. Nothing else. He didn't care that he had raped his two step-daughters, didn't care that he had twisted the life out of Jo-Jo, and he didn't care that he had lost his wife, the one he had beaten for years." Melantha looked at Dr. Stevens. "He only cared about the stupid cornfield. He thought the world was coming to an end when he found stink bugs eating his stupid corn." She took a deep breath. "He was so happy to get his hands on a bag of monosodium methylarsonate, thinking that would protect his stupid corn." Melantha wasn't emotional, only factual. "But it didn't. The stink bugs had thick skin and were impermeable to his attack, like I should have been." She laughed out loud. Uncontrollably. "I wish I was a stink bug."

Dr. Carroll was jotting down words; Dr. Stevens encouraged Melantha to continue.

"I knew he wouldn't be able to refuse me." She smiled. "I consoled him when he walked in the living room, almost frightened by my appearance, as I remained sitting in the wicker chair." She smiled more. "I offered him a drink. Told him we needed to put the past behind us." *What a fucking asshole.* Melantha remembered thinking it. "I saw the bag of barely used monosodium methylarsonate sitting by the counter, sitting within reach of his recently opened bottle of whiskey." She thought of the stinkbugs. *Try penetrating me with your poison now asshole.* "He didn't notice the powder in his whiskey. I poured so much." She smiled again. "Then I offered him another…and another…each filled with more of the poison." She looked at the small window in the room now, its wrought-iron bars keeping her in, keeping her prisoner. But she felt free for the first time in a long time. "It was too easy. He drank it down like water. The entire bottle of whiskey, one glass at a time, each filled with the poison." Her laughter grew. "He complained he didn't feel well, so I offered to help him to the bedroom, so he could lie down." *The asshole thought I might suck his dick, like I had done so many times before,* Melantha recalled. "I placed Jo-Jo's little white dress in his hand." Melantha smiled. "I watched him choke on his vomit as he looked at it. I listened to him drown, his lungs filling with his spew, his hands trembling as he held the white dress, and then he was gone." She looked relaxed. "I waited until I heard his final breath, then I went into the kitchen, stood at the sink and slowly washed his glass." *I'm not sure I turned off the water.* Melantha looked happy. *I think I left it running, dripping, overflowing – like the voices in my head.*

Chapter 21

December 15, 1979 –

I felt the warmth on my face as I dug my feet into the small strip of

beach in Clearwater, Florida. Pier 60 was a stone's throw away. I

knew from the way Rex looked at me that I had a permanent smile

on my face. We had spent the last month searching for a place, a

place we could call home, and a place Grover Starks, my father,

could call his wedding gift. We finally found a place in Pasco

County about two and a half hours north of Homer and Barbara

Parrish. Waiting for Thomas Smith, the real estate agent to seal the deal on a three-bedroom home in the Gardens of Beacon Square off U.S. 19, we walked on the beach. It was the perfect starter home, which was all we wanted. It wasn't my style to take advantage of Grover. I had a hard time calling him my dad, but I liked the idea. The agent knew we were hanging out in Clearwater, waiting for his office to tie up loose ends, waiting until we drove into New Port Richey to meet him at the house that would hopefully be ours. It was just after four in the afternoon when we pulled up. The realtor was waiting in the driveway.

"You're all set Mr. and Mrs. Narducci." He handed us a set of keys as we got out of a used station wagon to greet him. It was old but ran well. A step up from the Gremlin that Rex left with his mother.

"Thanks, so much, Mr. Smith." Rex and I said it just about at the same time.

"Don't thank me. Mr. Starks was a pleasure to work with." I suspected Grover hadn't needed financing. I was sure it was a cash deal without haggling on the price. "Here's a letter from him that he wanted me to give you." The letter was quickly handed to me, leaving us standing there with one set of keys, one letter, and two smiles.

Dear Enola and Rex,

I hope your marriage is long and happy. I'm sorry I can't be there to admire your smiles, but I have a large case pending this week. It means a lot to me to be part of your family. I look forward to seeing you for Christmas dinner. Thanks for sending an invitation to my office Enola.

Grover Starks (Dad)

I read the letter several times. I thought about how I had sent a picture of the house and its buyer information sheet to Grover's office along with an invitation to Christmas dinner if we took ownership in time. *I wonder if he'd come to Florida just to eat with us.* I recalled thinking as I dropped the invitation in the mailbox. I stared at the parenthesis for what seemed like forever. *(Dad)…He's my dad.* I thought, smiling, and following Rex into our new home.

The next week flew by leaving only three days until Christmas Day. We had a phone put in right away. One of the first people I called was the man who called himself my father, assuring him we would pick him up at the Tampa International Airport, only to discover that he wanted to drive. *It's only a twelve-hour drive.* I remembered him saying. And then, *I love you.* I thought about the only people who had ever said that to me before: Homer Parrish, Barbara Parrish, and Rex. That was it. Homer and Barbara weren't going to be able to come until the New Year, as they were celebrating Christmas in Hawaii, a dream of my grandmother's. So, it would just be the three of us – Grover, Rex, and Me. I thought about my response. *I love you too.* I knew he was still a stranger, still someone I would spend years getting to know, but I wanted to have him in my life, and I wanted him to know that I cared.

Christmas Eve came quickly. I spoke with Grover early that morning; he had just left Asheville and was on his way. I imagined the mountains as he described them, rolling peaks, bends, and twists of white cotton, a sign that winter had set in and was displaying its newest painting – a blanket of snow. I had so much I wanted to share with him when he got here; I had registered for classes at the community college which would start in January; I had landed a job as an editor with a local construction magazine that simply needed a good writer and someone willing to pick up the phone and interview companies about safety or other construction concerns; and I had gotten a hold of my friend Dixie Nault, perfect timing as she wanted me to be her maid of honor in her wedding just one week away. *I'm getting married Nola.* I remembered Dixie shouting the words into the phone. *It's just my mom, dad, and brother attending.* I remember the excitement in her voice. *I was hoping I'd hear from you. Please be my maid of honor.* I thought about her excitement, imagined seeing Asheville for the first time in a long time, thought about how it would feel to see Dixie and the love of her life – Ryan Durant, and then I thought about my mother. *Maybe I should try to make amends. Maybe I should drop by Highlands to see her when I go to Dixie's wedding.* And then, *maybe Grover will let me ride back with him to Asheville.* I continued thinking as I made sure the Christmas day menu was perfect: Ham with pineapple rings and cherries, mashed potatoes, green bean casserole, dinner rolls, pork flavored gravy, an apple pie with vanilla bean ice cream, and a bright red candle that I had already placed in the center of the table. It was simple I suppose but would be the first family dinner I was hosting in our new home. *My biological father was coming to my home.* Rex spent the day making sure the outside was welcoming: a quick cut of the grass which hadn't grown much over the last two weeks, a quick collection of broken palm bark, and the putting together of a new patio table and chair set that had been delivered boxed from Home Depot – a surprise delivery from Homer and Barbara Parrish. *Dixie Durant.* I thought. *DD.* I liked her new name. *She always lucked out with the names.* I thought.

My thoughts were interrupted by a loud ringing sound that I hadn't grown accustomed to. The *ding-a-ling* of a cheap kitchen wall phone filled the room, as did the smell of apple pie, which I had baking in the oven. It was a gruff but friendly voice I recognized. Grover Stark's P.I. – the same one that had tracked us to California and back, the same one that had followed my life around in his gray van.

Grover's car hit a patch of ice and went over the side of a mountain off I-26. He didn't make it. That's all I remember hearing before hitting my knees in the cinnamon filled room.

Chapter 22

Meg Fleming lived in a boarding house off Jefferson, since turning

eighteen, since being released from Savior's Boarding School, since

refusing to go home to North Carolina where her mother was being

beaten, back to the mountains that hid her abuser in North Carolina.

She had a small Christmas tree in her room, one she had displayed to

remind her that the season was approaching – still too early, still

only November, still a reminder that she lived in a fantasy world.

Small, red, cheap stockings replaced the absence of ornaments, each with the name of a different john, but each a regular. She had a Bill, Sam, Owen, Alan, and a fifth stocking that served as the star hung the highest. Accordingly, she saw Bill on Monday night, Sam on Tuesday night, Owen on Wednesday night, Alan on Thursday night, and Friday nights were always reserved for the man on the highest stocking – Grover Starks.

Meg rarely stood on the street corner in those days, the bitter cold and wind forced her to conduct her business from the inside, and she felt safer collecting regular johns. They ranged in age from twenty to seventy. Bill, or Billy as she called him, was the youngest, a community college student, who liked kinky sex. Sam was black, married, two kids, and bored. Owen was approaching seventy-one and his wife had died two years earlier from cancer. He rarely was able to perform but enjoyed and was willing to pay for Meg's company. Alan was a drunk, a loner, and smelled of whiskey, reminding Meg of Abner Paine. And, then there was Grover. Grover talked about how he could take her away from all this, about how he cared about her, and about how he could start a life with her.

Melantha was constantly fighting the voices inside her mind. Tiger and Ernie would talk to her throughout the day and night at

Highland's Hospital. *Honey, you've got to get out there and make more money.* Tiger would say. Melantha would often talk back to her.

"It's cold now Tiger. Too cold to be standing on the street corner." Melantha imagined Tiger standing beside her when she spoke. She was white, dirty white trash, as most would call her, with long fried dirty blond hair, and an overbite. The only reason she was as good in the business as she was, Melantha imagined, was because she was good at sucking dick. Tigertooth got her name from her clients, a street name that became part of her in Meg Fleming's mind.

Ernie, Ernestine, was the smart one, the one always thinking ahead, trying to recognize when a situation was too dangerous, or just didn't feel quite right. Meg relied on Ernie. Ernie wasn't happy when Meg disappeared in the middle of the night, standing in dangerous areas, soliciting men that weren't regulars. Ernie would tell Meg to go home, back to her boarding house, back to safety. *You need to get yourself home Meg.* Melantha could hear the black voice say. *You need to stop this and get home.* And Meg would return to her boarding house each morning, unaware of the night's activities that had proceeded. Sometimes she would hear the voice of Jo-Jo in her head. She would hear others too. She could keep the voices quiet sometimes. It was the middle of December in 1960 when the voices became bad, shouting, blaming. It was then when Melantha tried to come back, overtaking Meg Fleming, and pleading for someone to help her. Anyone. It was Tiger who told Meg to walk into the church.

"God can help you find peace with yourself!" He shouted the words from the pulpit that Sunday afternoon, and she listened. Then she saw the warmth in his brown eyes, and her desire to touch him became stronger.

"Excuse me, Pastor Fears, I need to talk to you privately."

"Of course, but I…I'm afraid I don't recall your name." Dacey Fears was a young man, twenty years old, aspiring to be a real pastor someday, but felt pleased when the members of the small Detroit church addressed him with such an honorary title.

Melantha batted her dark green, barely blue eyes, and smiled. "I'm sorry. How rude of me. I'm Melantha Paine. I've been coming here for the last two Sundays, and I'm quite taken by your sermons." He had forgotten he was a man of God when he looked at her. He didn't know what she wanted to talk to him about and didn't care; he just wanted to be alone with her.

The church was always empty on Sundays by two in the afternoon, offering her a chance to follow him to the bible study room. He would tell the church secretary she could go home to her family, and he would watch her lock the front of the church on her way out. They would be alone and undisturbed until the six-p.m. church social. He had sensed she would want to be with him for several hours.

"I hope this isn't an inconvenience." She routinely watched his broad shoulders as she followed him into the small room. She felt the warmth inside of him through his smile as he spoke.

"No, Mrs. Paine. I'd be glad to help you if I could." He paused studying her face. "I'm glad you came to me for advice." He guessed she was having problems with a new marriage and wanted counseling from a man of God.

"Please call me Melantha. And, it's Miss." Then she stopped for a few seconds thinking about her last name. She had been born Melantha Parrish, but it was a name short-lived, when she was three years old, she had taken, no, was legally given, the name of her abuser – Paine. *I hate that name.* She thought. And then she thought, *I wonder if the good pastor wants me as badly as I want him.* But, she only smiled.

"I see…Melantha. What can I help you with today?" He felt like he knew her already.

"I want to get to know you." She watched his face and was happy when she could see that he didn't flinch at her suggestive words, didn't try to direct them another way, and only waited to see what she was going to do next.

"You're looking for friendship?" His question sounded so awkward, but he didn't know what else to say. She had completely derailed his religious way of thinking.

"Is that okay?" She looked into his brown eyes, evaluating him, and wondering if he was catching on to what she wanted.

"It's …" Before he could finish, she stepped forward and her lips targeted his. He didn't fight or resist.

"I'm sorry." For a brief moment, she wondered if she had misread him. She had thought there was a look in his eyes, one of desire, one of lust…like she had seen so many times in the eyes of her johns. *Am I wrong?* Melantha wondered.

"No, please, don't stop." The brown eyes didn't care about God now. They only cared about Melantha.

#

I felt like the chance I had been given to reinvent myself had slid off the side of that mountain with Grover Starks. I would always be a *Fear*; that's who I was. I could change my name a million times, but I would never escape it. I was Enola May Fears, although the ID I had shown to board the plane simply read Enola M. Narducci. Rex offered to go with me several times, but I needed time *alone*. Ironic I guess. Eating the ham with pineapple rings and cherries, the mashed potatoes, and the green bean casserole, wasn't as much fun, just the two of us, words weren't exchanged, only the flicker of the red candle swayed in the small dining room in our new home. Everything else was still. I boarded the plane at Tampa International Airport two days after Christmas, still silent, kissing Rex goodbye, leaving him to fend for himself in our new home with lots of leftovers. I told him I would be home by New Year's Eve.

Grover Starks' P.I. picked me up at the airport; he didn't have to, but he insisted. He wanted to inform me about Grover's final arrangements. Grover's funeral was on the twenty-eighth and

Dixie's wedding was on the twenty-ninth. He insisted on putting me up in a hotel off Merrimon Avenue, a central location for the funeral, the wedding, and my mother's hospital. He said that's what my father would have wanted. *My father.* I thought about life and how cruel it can be. Maybe I was meant to be a *Fear* I thought because *Fear drives you and makes you brave.* I remembered reading that from a fortune cookie one time in LA, remembered how Rex and I laughed about how it was meant to be my fortune – my path.

The P.I. dropped me off at the front of the hotel, insisted on carrying my one suitcase for me, and hugged me after signing at the front desk on Mr. Starks' business account – an account the hotel had set up for his office to put up clients that had flown in from out of town. *Was that what I was now?* I wondered, but quickly stopped when I heard the gruff voice instruct the desk manager.

"Make sure Mrs. Narducci gets whatever she needs. This is Mr. Starks' daughter. His office will see to her expenses." And then, "Please make sure she has a driver at her disposal." Suddenly I felt important again. *Daughter.* Then the burly man hugged me and told me he would see me at the funeral in the morning. Tomorrow.

I would try to get some sleep I was exhausted inside but unable to relax on the outside. I tried to think happy thoughts as I fought the darkness. *Dixie is getting married. Dixie Durant. That's a nice name. She always gets the nice names.* I thought again, and I laughed at the darkness before dozing off, finally.

Morning came early. The December twenty-eighth air was cold. I imagined my mother at Highland's, only five or six miles down the road. I wondered what she'd think about Grover Starks' death, wondered if she knew he was my biological father, and if she did, I wondered how long she had known. I planted myself in the backseat of a shuttle van, used to transport all the patrons to and from the hotel, but noticed I was the only passenger. The driver didn't ask me where I was going; instead, he greeted me full of knowledge.

"Good morning Mrs. Narducci. The funeral home is only about a fifteen-minute drive." He looked at me in his rearview mirror. "Please let me know if there's anything you need." *I need a decent set of living parents.* I thought, but then I remembered what I had learned about Grover Starks in the short time I had known him.

He was strong – emotionally strong. That's how I would try to be over the next few days. That's who I would be forever.

"Thank you, sir." That was all I could say.

Besides Grover's secretary, his two closest private detectives, and a couple of other attorneys, there was no one else at the funeral. He had always had a private life. I was his only family. His secretary hugged me and told me he talked about me often. And, the burly man who had tracked me from North Carolina to Florida, to Birmingham, to LA, and back to Florida, hugged me and presented me with two things – a large sealed manila envelope, and his name.

"Please call me if you ever need me Enola." He wiped a tear from his eye. "I've been a close friend of your fathers for years and would help you any way you needed me to." He put out his hand. "Just look up Dwayne Summons under private investigator in Asheville." I noticed how honest his eyes were, as I tried not to cry, tried to be strong.

Funny thing about funerals is they don't last long. An entire man's life can be summed up in a matter of minutes and dirt hides him forever. Gone.

I spent the evening hiding in the hotel room, beneath blankets I didn't know, hiding from my past, hiding from my future, until the phone rang in my room.

"I miss you. Are you okay?" It was Rex.

"I'm okay." And then the information I knew he wanted. "The funeral was sad, like all funerals I guess."

"Were there a lot of people there?" I thought about how many people would be at my funeral. *Maybe six: Rex Narducci, Homer Parrish, Barbara Parrish, Dixie Durant, Ryan Durant, and maybe Dwayne Summons, my new P.I. friend.*

"No only a few." Then I thought about the envelope, removing the edge of the blanket that blocked its view from the bed, still lying across the room on the table by the television that sat black and silent.

"Okay, well get some sleep." He knew I wasn't much for talking – not now. "Have a good time at Dixie's wedding tomorrow.

"I love you too." I was already standing to get the envelope. "I will."

I turned on the light closest to the television and sat down to open the envelope that Dwayne Summons had handed me at the funeral. I dumped the contents on the round table. Inside there were four things: a key to a safety deposit box with the bank address attached, the results of a DNA test proving Grover was my father, a deed to a piece of property in Roswell, New Mexico, and a five by seven photo of my mother. I recognized her eyes, the way they used to be, with more-blue in them. Her hair was longer, almost jet black, and wavy. Her skin looked milky and smooth. She was beautiful.

I thought about the key. Tomorrow I would go to Dixie's wedding, but I would have the driver stop me at the bank on the way. I went to sleep that night dreaming about Roswell. *Why Roswell?* I knew nothing about it. I imagined desert and hot days in my dreams. *Why would he own property in Roswell? Why did he want me to have it?*

Meg's shoulder-length jet black hair felt cold in the January wind as she stood on the corner of Jefferson and Rivard, supplying little protection to her ears, but complimenting her dark olive eyes that glowed in the cold of the new year as she spoke with the familiar face in the black, obviously new, 1961 Cadillac. She almost turned away when the car pulled alongside her, preferring to see one of her regulars, but then realized it was Grover. Instantly she became his, talking differently, and walking differently. She had become Meg Fleming and was happy to get into Grover's new car, someplace warm, someplace out of the unforgiving January weather. She noticed his watch, a Rolex, and his suit pants – Versace. He had recently graduated law school and had gotten in with a promising firm in downtown Detroit. He was muscular, medium build, very attractive, and not the type of man who needed a prostitute, who needed to pay for sex. She was more than that to him though. He had been seeing her for nearly three months. Tonight, he was celebrating winning his first case. He wanted her for the entire night. He desired her.

Meg, you need to go home. Melantha heard Ernie's voice. *You're married now remember?* But Ernie wasn't there. No black woman was directing her, trying to keep her safe.

Honey, don't miss this opportunity child. You can make up some story tomorrow, about how you didn't feel well, about how you checked into a cheap motel to rest and fell asleep. Tigertooth was urging her to go. *Dacey will believe anything you say, honey.*

Melantha knew that was true. She had tested him before – many times.

The MGM Grand off Third Street in Detroit was high class. Grover Starks didn't stop at the front desk; instead, he only nodded to the hotel connoisseur, before ushering Meg Fleming to the elevator, escorting his desire to his room on the seventh floor. Few words were exchanged when he closed the door behind them, his hands quickly traveling on the highest parts of her shoulders, and his blue eyes slowly undressing her, dropping her baby-blue cotton dress to the floor, the same cotton dress she had worn to church earlier that day. He reached for every part of her. He wanted her. He would spend two hours touching her, caressing her, and melting on top of her, before plunging inside of her, over and over again. There was so much he didn't know about her, which made her so much more intriguing. He didn't know she had recently married a man she barely knew, didn't know she already had a life growing inside of her, and didn't know the life inside of her would always be proof of their time together.

Chapter 23

I left the hotel early the next morning in time to get to the bank
before the wedding. I instructed the driver I would be just a few
minutes, made my way inside, and looked for the nearest available
banking representative.

"Hi, I'm Enola Narducci." I wasn't used to my name yet. I
had heard it a hundred times by now, but it still didn't feel like mine.
Not yet. "I'd like to get into this safety deposit box." The

representative took the key from my hand, noticing it had the bank address attached, underneath the numbers 1-1-3-7.

"I'll just need to see some I.D." She was already walking toward her desk where she had the bank vault cards organized into a metal filing drawer nearby. She pulled out the signature card for box 1137. "Oh yes, Ms. Narducci." Now, I had heard it over a hundred times. "Mr. Starks added you on two weeks ago when he was last in." She put a signature card in front of me. "Just sign here."

We went in the safety deposit vault together, but she left me alone after pulling out box 1137. I wondered what was in the box, opened it slowly, and then closed it as fast as I could. I knew there were at least fifty, one-hundred-dollar bills in the box. *That's five thousand dollars.* I thought. I paused, long enough to get my composure, and long enough to open back the lid removing three separate one-hundred-dollar bills. Two bills were for me, and one for the Durant-Nault wedding. *I can't believe I didn't think to get DD a gift. Things have been very stressful lately.* And then, *thanks Grover*, no, *thanks Dad.* I remembered.

The driver was smoking a cigarette when I walked outside. He opened the door and waited for me to get in. I handed him one of the one-hundred-dollar bills. "You deserve it for putting up with me."

"Wow, thanks so much." I could tell by the way he responded that I was his new best friend. "Let's get you to your friend's wedding." I stared out the window, the December twenty-ninth sky looked cold. It looked like rain.

The driver told me he would be on standby. I wasn't sure what that meant, but I liked how important a one-hundred-dollar bill made me feel. I walked into the small church. A woman I didn't know greeted me. She asked me my name and checked a list she was holding. "This way," she said.

I walked down the hallway and into a back room where I could hear Dixie's voice. When I opened the door, she moved away from her mother who was busy styling her hair, almost tripped over the bottom of her white satin gown and fell into my arms. "I've missed you so much Nola."

"I've missed you too." We stood there hugging, almost crying over lost time together. The white satin dress made her natural strawberry red hair pop, which had grown longer since the last time I had seen it. I was there just in enough time to say hello to her mother which I hadn't seen in years, help give my opinion on the hairstyle, and talk about the love of her life – Ryan Durant. The wedding started promptly at ten a.m.

Dixie walked like an angel. Each of her steps gracefully illustrated with the cello, violin, and oboe music that Dixie had explained they were lucky to find on tape. Dixie's father walked her down the church aisle, before taking his assigned seat by his ex-wife and Dixie's adult brother. I stood on the other side of Dixie as she quickly instructed me. Rehearsal is not required when seven people are at your wedding: bride, groom, bride's father, bride's mother, bride's older brother, bride's best friend, and the minister. *I'm impressed that Dixie's parents are friends after their divorce.* I thought about Melantha and Dacey. They would never be able to be in the same room again.

The vows were simple and Dixie's mother smiled lovingly when Dixie and Ryan were pronounced husband and wife I noticed. I thought about Dacey and Melantha again. *They would have never been supportive of me.* Then I thought about Grover. Sadness hit me. *I wish I could have more time with him.* Then the tears started to fall. I'm sure Dixie imagined they were for her. But, they weren't. They were for me. I wanted a father in my life, a mother who would help me through pregnancies, and a family that would be my safe place to fall. I didn't have that anymore. I guess I never did. Homer and Barbara Parrish were getting older and had done enough for me already. I would have to face life on my own. I thought of Rex. *I wish he were here.* I didn't realize how much I needed him. I wiped the tears from my face and smiled at Dixie. *Things happen for a reason.* That was all I could think of to calm myself down.

The reception didn't last long, long enough for Ryan to dance the first dance with his bride, long enough for seven people to have a taste of a cheesecake that Dixie's mom had made from scratch, eight including the lady who had been guarding the door, and who had now made her way inside, and long enough for me to meet Ryan and quickly realize what Dixie saw in him: kind, humble, down to earth. It was almost time for Dixie and Ryan to head off in Ryan's decorated Chevy truck. I handed Dixie a church envelope I had taken from the pew. Inside I had stuck the one-hundred-dollar bill and a note on a piece of church stationery that I had discreetly asked the door woman to get for me, a last-minute plea on my way to the restroom where I thought about what to say. The note was simple.

Dixie,

Thanks for being my friend when no one else thought I mattered. Congratulations on your wedding. I hope you and Ryan have true happiness together.

Love,

Nola.

I watched my childhood friend drive away into adulthood, someplace I felt I had been since I was born into this world. I thought about how Melantha was locked in a room. The hospital was only another fifteen minutes away. It was early in the day still. Noon. I waved to my driver who was on *standby* across the church parking lot. *I like what standby means.* I thought to myself as I walked toward the hotel shuttle for one. The rain I had predicted started to come down from the December sky. Cold rain.

"Where to Mrs. Narducci?" The driver asked, but my lips changed my plan. I didn't want to ruin a perfectly good wedding.

"The hotel sir." *Tomorrow is another day.* I thought.

#

Dacey Fears made his way in the rain to Highland's Hospital after five p.m. He found Melantha in her assigned room lying on the bed, facing the door, and staring into the darkness. The only light in the room was the occasional flash from lightning outside the small window, and the only sound he could hear was the boom of mountain thunder. Deep.

"I'm here, Mel." His voice fought for attention with the last echo of thunder. Melantha heard it even though the voices in her head and the constant sound of December wind fought for position.

"Don't turn on the light, Dacey. Just come here and lay beside me." She paused, long enough for Dacey to be glad she recognized his voice and remembered his name, and long enough for him to realize that she wasn't overly medicated at the moment, a rare thing lately. "Hold me."

It was something Dacey wanted to do, something he missed doing, a loving moment with the woman who had shared almost nineteen years of his life with him. He thought about the first time they had met – in the church. That first meeting made him want to hold her in an uncontrollable rush, frantic lust, which when acted out, resulted in hours alone in the Bible study room, hours of hot sex, boundaries ignored and orgasmic sweat. He wanted to be inside her, but he didn't know when the *birthday nurse* would be making her next rounds. He thought about the gathering at the nurses' station, around Nurse Halohand's office birthday cake, and thought about how he might have enough time. She hummed lightly now, trying to soothe the Asheville mountain wind. Her hands were cold, and her legs were shaking, slightly. Slowly, he inched his way into the small hospital bed, placing his body as close to hers as possible. She quit shaking moments after he was near her. She felt warmer when Dacey touched her, as he caressed her arms, rubbing her hands inside of his, and then she stopped the humming and lay silent. She had been lying there, in the dark, alone, for hours and was enjoying the warmth and companionship that his body offered her. She looked at him through the flash of light, but Dacey couldn't tell her condition. The flash of light was too brief only lighting her face for a second. She kissed upward into the side of his face and moved her fingers down his knit shirt. She pried at the belt buckle he wore and unfastened it with one hand. Something she was a pro at. Then she grabbed the hardness she found ready for her and laughed.

At last, Melantha's body began to grow cold again, her body highlighted during the last strike of lightning just outside, sending a glow through the still-dark room. She stood, her hospital gown wrinkled about her hips, in the glare in front of him. "I don't know how to love anyone," Melantha admitted. "I don't know how to fix myself. I only know how to hurt."

"You can learn how to love Mel." Dacey wanted to calm her before she got upset.

"I don't want to." Melantha said it with certainty like she knew she had a choice but had decided to choose the announced option.

Dacey knew she had been broken, was broken, and would be broken forever. There was no changing who she was. He was just as helpless as she was.

"What do you want me to do, Mel?"

She glared at him in the darkness. "You can't do anything."

Dacey stood and walked toward her, the hospital gown still wrinkled at her waist, inviting him to move closer. He wondered if he could take her before Nurse Halohand would walk away from her cake, away from colleagues she had worked with for years.

Melantha's body seemed to be inviting his manhood, as she stood in the crinkled gown, thighs illuminated during the last lightning flash. His thoughts were organizing but suddenly came to a halt when Nurse Halohand entered the room, a promised piece of cake for Melantha in one hand – one she would have to eat with her fingers, reminding Melantha that even plastic utensils weren't allowed in Melantha's wing. The nurse sat the cake on the rubber padded end table, along with two other items that the doctor had instructed her to leave, at the end of her shift, a shift she wanted to end so she could get home to spend some portion of her birthday with her own family. She was there to escort Melantha to Dr. Stevens' office. Dacey Fears would have to leave and come back tomorrow morning to visit. The scheduled session was about Melantha's to-do list, a technique the doctor used to get his patients focused on the future. He needed to evaluate her alone this time, needed to note her progress on his chart, and needed to access his patient's mental state.

A pad of paper was placed in front of her on the round table in his office, offering her a chance to write down her thoughts. Melantha thought it was funny that Dr. Stevens only allowed crayons. She felt like a child holding it in her hand, and for a brief moment she thought about watching Jo-Jo hold crayons, thought about the pictures she would bring to life, and thought about the white dress that had seen Jo-Jo's last breath. *He deserved to die.* Melantha thought.

Dr. Stevens had given the crayon to Melantha as an experiment, to bring out her feelings, a blue crayon, to signify new beginnings. Dr. Stevens loved to use the information he would gather at in-services and from other doctors. It was the first session Dacey had not been allowed to sit in on, another request from the doctor.

The doctor instructed quietly, "And now, Melantha, I would like you to write down things that are *new* for you – something you plan to do or recently accomplished. It is important to list as many things as you can. It will help us figure out what your goals are and what makes you feel *new*."

"Good things I've done or plan to do?" Melantha asked and then laughed like she had earlier with Dacey.

Dr. Stevens leaned toward her. "I know this is difficult. But we need to focus on goals." He paused. "This session is about bringing a sense of rebirth to your life."

The pad of paper looked up at Melantha Fears. *Tell him.* The blue crayon said to Melantha. Then she heard Tiger's voice. *Tell the fucker what's up.*

Yeah girl, you know about rebirth. It was Ernie, the black voice trying to encourage her. *Brag. Write it down.*

She looked at the blue crayon, imagining it was a knife, then after only a brief moment of thought, she wrote. GROVER. In a moment, she would add a few more words and then place the pad of paper face down on the table, signaling that Dr. Stevens could look.

Dr. Stevens looked at Melantha, acknowledging her invitation to read what she had written, "Surely you have more new goals or new accomplishments than that." He paused long enough to study the coldness in her dark, now green eyes. "We'll have to think up more things you want to do or have done that make you feel alive."

Melantha watched his eyes as he turned over the pad of paper and began reading what she had written. Underneath Grover's name it simply said: CUT BRAKES.

"Melantha, did you do something to Mr. Starks' car?" The doctor looked like a bolt of lightning had worked its way in the window and struck him head-on. He knew Grover Starks personally, knew he was one of the largest contributors to the hospital, and knew he was the reason Melantha would receive care for as long as needed. He also knew an unfamiliar face had recently visited Melantha, posing as a new P.I. from Grover Starks' office, showing I.D. from out of state. *Michigan?* He tried to remember.

"I hired someone to cut them," Melantha spoke without emotion. "He hid my daughter from me." Five minutes later, Dr. Stevens had two orderlies remove Melantha, and take her back to her room, before calling the police.

Nurse Halohand had already gone home, already left a small piece of birthday cake near the bed in Melantha's room, and already left a pad of paper with a red crayon, as Dr. Stevens and she had discussed earlier, before Melantha released new information, before Dr. Stevens found out that Grover Starks had slid off the side of a mountain with Melantha's help, off I-26, to his death, and before Sergeant Wayne Zubbel agreed to reopen the investigation. Now Sergeant Zubbel had agreed to reopen two cases with Melantha Fears being the primary suspect in each: Abner Paine and Grover Starks.

Chapter 24

You're alone again, Ernie was saying. *Why don't you write down how you feel?* Melantha tried not to respond to Ernie. And then, *Dr. Stevens left you a red crayon this time.* Tigertooth's persuasive voice piped in. *Dr. Stevens will read it in the morning when he gets here, baby.* Again, Melantha tried not to respond. She simply reached for the pad of paper and the red crayon that guarded it. *Just write down how you feel.* Melantha responded this time. Loudly.

"Why can't I have my own fucking lamp?" Melantha was shouting now at the hall light that shined just outside the locked door.

You'll cut yourself with a piece of the light bulb, girl. Tigertooth was sitting beside her now. Melantha could see her even though the one small window didn't offer any help. Darkness had set in outside. Melantha Fears wrote with the red crayon on the blank pad of paper. She could hear several voices inside of her and wished she could keep them clear and separate. They were getting jumbled together. First Ernie, calm and reasonable, then Tigertooth, loud and bold, and then Jo-Jo, screaming and pleading, and then Zelda, begging for someone to save her. *Write down whatever you want Mel.* It sounded like Dacey. Or was it Grover? Melantha continued writing on the paper in front of her, a lot more. Then she turned her attention to the cake, fingering the white frosting that stuck to the tiny saucer. *Suck it hard.* It was that fucking bastard, Abner Paine. She looked at the pad in her lap and smiled when she noticed the words she had written were now covered with dark chocolate crumbs. *They can blow those off to read it.* Tigertooth spoke loudly and laughed in Melantha's head. *Heaven knows we've blown off enough things, baby girl.*

The light outside flickered causing a momentary second of blackness. Melantha could feel her right hand, the one that held the red crayon, slide into the saucer. In a burst of anger, Melantha threw the saucer across the room into the darkness. She could see its lifeless broken body scattered into three or four pieces when the hallway light came back on. She put the pad down, now covered in red words, dark chocolate cake, and snow-white frosting, and traveled across the small room to rescue the saucer. She felt the sharp ends of the biggest piece slice at her frosted covered fingertips in the darkest part of the room. She pressed the sharpest edge of the saucer into the skin that covered her left wrist and moved it back and forth until she could feel her fingers floating in blood. *They'll read it. Please don't worry,* said Jo-Jo. *Tomorrow they will read it Mellie.* Jo-Jo's voice was the last sound Melantha Fears would ever hear.

Then she saw Dacey helping Enola blow out the candles on her first birthday cake on Lorman Street – chocolate with white frosting, before closing her eyes permanently.

#

I got up early to make it to Highland's Hospital. I wanted to get a flight out and back to Rex as soon as possible. I missed him, his smell, his laugh, the way he touched me. I couldn't change the life I was dealt, but I could make myself better. Stronger. I missed having Grover in my life even though we hadn't had the chance to get to know each other. I missed my sister even though she and I were worlds apart in every way. I missed the parents I never had. And, I missed the life I always wanted. All I could do now was pick up the pieces and do the best that I could. I wanted to have children with Rex, wanted to visit Homer and Barbara Parrish when they got back from Hawaii, and wanted to start college in January.

My driver called up to my room when he arrived on shift. I was happy to see that my one-hundred-dollar bill was still paying off. I did a last-minute sweep of what I needed. Three things: my I.D., a folded-up copy of the results from DNA Diagnostics Incorporated that I had the hotel run off for me, and my room key.

"Good morning, Mrs. Narducci." I think I was beginning to like the sound of that.

"Good morning." I smiled. "Highland's Hospital please." It was nice having a driver who knew the best way to get everywhere.

"Yes, ma'am." He had a southern twang that sounded sort of cute. I tried not to smile again, but I couldn't help it. Living in Detroit while my language skills were forming, and then recently in Florida and Los Angeles had cured my southern bell accent. Rarely did I slip up unless I was hanging out with Dixie, then watch out. *I wonder if Mr. and Mrs. Durant were enjoying their honeymoon.* I was still thinking when we pulled up to Highland's, until I saw Dacey Fears heading in the front door. *You can't afford to be afraid of him anymore.* I thought it was time to get everything out in the open. No more hiding. I didn't slow my pace and opened the main entrance, just as Dacey was being seated.

"Enola, I thought you might be in town." He looked at me. Dead on. "I heard your friend was getting married." I wondered how he would know that.

"Yes. Her father walked her down the aisle. It was very nice." I got in the best dig I could and was careful not to back down from his eye contact, until I noticed the nurse staring at us, whispering into the phone, and mouthing my mother's name. That's when we were both escorted down the hallway to Dr. Stevens' office. Inside, and already seated, were the following people: Dr.

Stevens, Dr. Carroll, and one uniformed police officer. They were all seated around the table in Dr. Stevens' office, with two empty chairs being brought in behind us, quickly.

"Have a seat Mr. Fears." Dr. Stevens directed. "And, your daughter." He pointed to the other chair. I thought about correcting him – *Grover's Daughter.* I thought. But, decided to let it go. I would show Melantha and Dacey the DNA Diagnostics results together. Perfect.

"Is Melantha finally being released?" Dacey questioned the table, not any particular person.

"No." Two members at the table responded.

"I'm afraid we have some bad news for you both," said the officer. Name tag: Sergeant Zubbel. The doctors remained quiet. "Mrs. Fears was found dead during the five a.m. rounds by Nurse Halohand." Dacey's expression went from expecting to shock. Total shock. I sat without emotion. Strong.

"I'm sorry to inform you that she took her own life." Dr. Carroll was speaking now – firmly but gently.

"You said she took her own life?" Dacey looked baffled.

"She used the rim of a saucer." I felt sorry for Dacey Fears at that moment. I knew, however dysfunctional he was, however dysfunctional she was, and however dysfunctional I was fighting against, that they loved each other. I couldn't help it. I put my hand on his, the same hand that had beaten me.

"The nurse meant to change out the saucer but forgot, Mr. Fears." Dr. Stevens added. "She cared about Melantha and was extremely upset when she found out Mrs. Fears used a broken piece of the saucer to cut her wrist."

"Of course, our office will determine if there should be any charges filed against the nurse." I could tell by his dismissive tone that his office wouldn't be pursuing the hospital or the nurse. Sergeant Zubbel then excused himself from the office leaving Dacey and myself alone with the two doctors. I felt like he knew something he wasn't saying.

"Nurse Halohand found a note." Dr. Carroll handed Dacey Fears a sealed envelope. "Normally we don't release things like this. But, the sergeant said he won't be needing it." *Why did the sergeant seem somewhat stone-faced about my mother's suicide? Was that just part of the job?* I removed my hand from Dacey's. *Was this where he would play hardball?* I thought, remembering I had tried to show him a moment of kindness. *Would he share the note with me? I wondered* as we both stood.

"I'm truly sorry for your loss." Dr. Stevens was standing now, his hand extended, first to Dacey, and then to me.

"You did the best you could, Dr. Stevens." And then Dacey looked at Dr. Carroll. "Thank you both for your help." He continued and then waited for me to stand before walking out. Together.

He fondled the edge of the envelope on our way to the parking lot, looking at me, and then looking back at the envelope. He handed the envelope to me. *Why?* I wondered. Was this *his* act of kindness? He turned to face me. "I'm sorry Enola." He cried. I stood there, unable to move, noticing my standby driver across the parking lot, and then signaling him to go ahead without me, leaving me alone with Dacey Fears the man who had beaten me for years, shown me his dark perversions, broken my knee cap, shown me that hatred is a necessary part of existence, and taught me to trust no one. And then, without hesitation, I spoke to the man that hadn't known how to be a father, but I spoke to him with kindness.

"Let's go somewhere for coffee and read the letter together."
I thought about the other letter folded in my pocket – The one from
DNA Diagnostics Incorporated. I had read it over and over again in
the hotel. *The relationship probability is 99.9957%.* But I didn't
mention it; instead, I allowed him to drive me to a small coffee shop
near my hotel.

We ordered coffee without blaming, without insulting, and
without criticizing, just crème and sugar. I placed the sealed
envelope in the middle of the table.

"Are you sure you want me to open it?" I asked him.

"Yes." He took a long drink of his coffee after adding one
crème and three sugars.

"Okay." I tore open the envelope, business size, with the
Highland Hospital name and address in the upper right, typed in
black print, a professional presentation for the suicide victim's
family. "Do you want me to read it?" I noticed food crumbs were
falling into my lap, bits of what looked like chocolate crumbs and a
tiny dot of white frosting. *Had she eaten cake?* I wondered.

"Yes." He was trying not to cry again. Sipping slowly.

I took a big gulp of mine before beginning. Two crèmes. No sugar. Then I started to read, slowly, all the while choking back tears for the mother I had lost and for the mother I had never had. It was written in thick red crayon:

THIS CRAYON MAKES BRIGHT RED MARKS LIKE THE BROKEN VESSELS IN JO-JO'S EYES. SHE WON'T WAKE UP NO MATTER HOW MANY TIMES I SING THE FRENCH SONG TO HER. THE BAD MAN TWISTED HER NECK. HARD. MAKING HER BRAIN EXPLODE INTO HER EYES.

Neither one of us spoke, but we knew, knew about Jo-Jo, the sister who had died at the hands of Abner Paine, and we understood, the absence of God, when living in darkness, an emptiness that is passed from one generation to another. We could see it in each other's eyes, the pool of sorrow and fear, and the struggle to survive. *We can't choose our parents. We can't choose whether to be born. We just are. We exist. We breathe. We survive. We do the best we can.* I took another long sip of my coffee, removing my hand from my pocket, letting go of the hidden secret that had slid off I-26 to its death, and placed that hand on the top of the table, on top of his once again.

"I forgive you Dad." That was all I could say, and I could tell that was all he needed.

We sat for almost an hour. Few words were exchanged, but a lot was said.

Chapter 25

Sometimes life is just about closure. Dacey Fears and Enola

Narducci arrived at the Morris Funeral Home around the same time

– ten forty-five a.m. the following morning, enough time for Enola

to have her driver stop at the bank, enough time to remove all of the

cash from the safety deposit box, enough time for Enola to meet with

the director of the funeral home. Two thousand dollars – that's how

much it cost in 1979 to have an overnight rush cremation and a small

spur of the moment service. *There's something ironic about having*

Grover pay for the entire thing, Enola thought as she handed the cash to the director, thanking him for putting something together so quickly. There was a sign-in area when they entered. Two signatures: Dacey Fears and Enola Narducci. That's all Melantha Fear's life was worth. Dacey had tried calling Easter Humphreys. She hung up on him when she heard his voice. There were no others. Just Dacey and Enola. Dacey smiled at Enola. They hadn't healed a lifetime of wounds, but the look on both of their faces, matched the looks they shared at the coffee shop – just for today we will be civil. Dacey sat in the front pew facing a bouquet of red roses, Melantha's favorite, and Enola sat in the front pew nearest the podium. Behind the podium, on a waist-high cloth-covered table sat Melantha Fears. She was housed in a medium-sized, silver urn. Dacey didn't look at the urn. He couldn't. Not yet. Enola sat facing straight ahead, staring at the silver-colored urn that held her mother. Reverend Hays walked to the podium at eleven o'clock sharp.

"We are gathered here today to pay our respects to Melantha Fears. She was a beloved mother, wife, and daughter." He paused. "She only got to spend thirty-eight years on this earth, but she will get to spend forever in eternity." He paused again. "She touched so many lives in her short time on this earth but will forever be remembered." He looked at the two adult faces, one and then the other. One cried. One sat emotionless. "Let's all bow our heads and follow along in prayer for Melantha Fears." Reverend Hays who knew nothing about Melantha, continued as he read from the following script:

Melantha's death represents a death inside each of you

No one else will have the same effect on your soul

Her death is an end to one part of your life story

God will guide you as you remember Melantha's life

God will show you a way to continue your own life

And God will keep Melantha free from her pain and suffering

We ask you for all of this in Jesus' name

"Amen." Reverend Hays opened his eyes.

"Amen," Enola whispered the word even though she questioned its worth.

Dacey stood. It would be his job to decide where the voices would rest in peace, scattering the ashes from the urn, releasing a lifetime of pain. Enola wanted no part of that. She simply wanted to walk away from this part of her life. Closure.

Enola stood facing Dacey who had both hands wrapped around Melantha. "I'm going back to Florida." She avoided a full hug, but got close to him, close enough to see the sorrow in his brown eyes, and close enough to feel the cold from the metal urn. Bitter cold.

"Thank you for paying for this Enola." The director had informed Dacey when he collected the urn. "I'll pay you back."

"Don't worry." She wanted to tell him that Grover paid, but she didn't want to hurt the man that stood broken before her. She just turned and walked away without saying anything else.

#

I packed as soon as I got to the hotel. It was the thirtieth of December, a hard time to get a flight out, but I had twenty-seven hundred dollars in the zipper compartment of my jacket, enough to figure out a way home, enough to take a gamble and stake out Delta's outgoing flights. I missed Rex, our first house, and my new life. I had attended two funerals and a wedding in the last three days. Exhaustion set in by the time I talked my way on to a flight. I had never flown first class before, the only thing they had available. Four hundred dollars later I was being given a wet hot cloth for my face and hands, a choice of chicken or beef with asparagus, and a blanket.

I didn't realize how exhausted I was, placing my chair back, after

devouring a piece of chicken and four spears of asparagus. I felt the

edge of a folded paper in my outer jacket pocket. I took it out,

unfolding it, unfolding my life, my past, part of me I would never get

to know first-hand. I reclined my seat and read it word for word:

DNA Diagnostics Incorporated

Atlanta, Georgia 30301

Results for lab #17894-6

Dear Mr. Starks:

Our lab performed a paternity DNA test, per your court order, on the

following blood samples: 12.A collected from Nola Satchele, aka

Enola Fears and sent from Cooper Green Mercy Hospital in

Birmingham, Alabama and 116.B collected from Grover Starks and

sent from Mission Hospital in Asheville, North Carolina. Based on

our DNA test results, the alleged FATHER Grover Starks – 116.B is

the biological FATHER of the CHILD Nola Satchel, aka Enola

Fears – 12.A because they share the same genetic code. The

relationship probability is 99.9957%. If you have any further

questions, please don't hesitate to contact me.

Sincerely,

Tim Burton

DNA Analyst

I refolded it. *Does it matter? I've never belonged anywhere. Do other people feel this way?* I wondered. *Do other people feel alone?* I tucked it back inside my pocket, this time in the zipped pocket on the inside of my jacket, next to the twenty-three hundred dollars I had left, zipped away. *Is that what has happened to me?* I wanted to cry but was too exhausted. *Have the first eighteen years of my life been zipped away?* I pulled the blanket up around my face and slept until the plane landed.

Eighteen Years Later

Chapter 26

I spent eighteen years of my life trying to outrun dysfunction, and I

spent the next eighteen years of my life trying to prove I had. I

couldn't have been more wrong. I woke up screaming in the

darkness. LOUD. Even in my conscious state I could still feel the

pain, my t-shirt and panties both soaked with sweat, and even with

my eyes verifying that there was nothing there, I still felt like something had been on me, pulling at my flesh, taking small nibbles of my skin, trying to get inside of my thirty-six-year-old body.

Rex and I celebrated our eighteenth wedding anniversary on the seventh of August, 1997. Two months later, he walked in from a business trip, said hello to our two children: Mitch, a couple of weeks away from turning eight, and Allie, just over two, and made two major announcements.

"I don't think I've ever loved you." He looked at me without emotion. "I want a divorce."

"Rex, what happened in New Orleans?" *Was there someone else? Another woman?* I could hardly breathe, much less control my thoughts. *We've loved each other since the day we met in our high school gym.* I looked at him, trying not to cry, to crumble. *Strong.* That's what my biological father would do. I thought of Grover Starks. I could use him now, but he had slid, no, was pushed, off the side of a mountain to his death, something I had learned Melantha was responsible for, and something that I felt was now happening to me. Rex was pushing me out of his life. Eighteen years of loving someone so much it hurt. Gone. *How can one person do so much damage?* I thought, but only briefly, remembering where I had come from, remembering my mother. *Melantha Fears could destroy a person's life without much planning.* I remembered the call I got from Sergeant Zubbel about a year into our marriage. *Your biological father's brake line was tampered with. I have arrested the man Melantha hired.*

"You've never loved me?" I could barely get the words out. The Rex Narducci I had known for the last eighteen years adored me, would fight for me, and at times I believed would die for me. We waited ten years before we tried to have another baby, we worked our way through college, each getting a degree, Rex in Public Administration, mine in teaching, and had just moved to a bigger house in Lake Padgett Estates, not far from where we started eighteen years ago. I had just begun my seventh year of teaching at Land O' Lakes High School. Rex was running a small college in Tampa. We had two beautiful children. Healthy children. We went to the malls as a family, beach, zoo, theme parks, and holidays were a big deal.

"No. I don't love you." Rex's brown eyes spoke with little emotion standing in front of me. The twenty-first day of October in 1997, that's the date my heart broke inside my chest, exploding into nothingness, yet I didn't die. I felt empty standing in front of the man I had shared eighteen years of marriage with, and I didn't recognize the man I had kissed good-bye just five days earlier at the Tampa International Airport, three kisses: one from me, one from Mitch, and one from Allie.

"Did you have an affair while you were on business in New Orleans?" I could feel myself ask the question in slow motion.

"Don't be stupid Enola. There's no one else."

"Then I don't understand, Rex. What's going on?"

"It's a missing connection, I guess."

"Connection?"

"Yes. We've never really connected. We are very different."

"We are different in a lot of ways." I agreed with him on that one. Rex had grown to believe that life was too short for forever. I could tell by the way he dressed, drove, talked, and even looked at people we passed in the mall – quick and impersonal. He believed in pleasing himself in the moment. And, he especially believed in never getting caught.

"Something is missing," said Rex Narducci, the thirty-eight-year-old man who had married me the day after I turned eighteen in

Los Angeles, California. "I've never really been happy. I always tried to be and loving you was one of the ways I tried. But, it's not working anymore."

I looked at him. Rex Narducci was empty inside. All signs of life had left his brown eyes. I remembered that look from the past. Melantha and Dacey both had the same look.

"Rex, what are you saying?" I tried to catch my breath. "Do you want a divorce?" Silence grew in his empty brown eyes, eyes that were searching for a way to respond to me.

"Yes." He didn't look directly at me when he let the cold word escape his mouth. I tried to keep my footing, tried not to let my soul flow out of my eyes and down my cheeks. Instead, I simply watched him turn around, walk his empty shell of a body into *our* master bedroom, retrieve *his* pillow and a blanket, and head for Mitch's room.

"I just want to get some sleep," he informed me before shutting Mitch's door and locking it, locking out more than eighteen years of history together. *Didn't he remember how much we loved each other? We had two kids together. We had a life together – just the four of us.* I stopped my mind from wandering. I'm a mother. My priority could be heard calling me from Allie's room, where Mitch had taken his two-year-old sister, had hidden her from the loveless-air he had sensed in the living room.

"Mom, what's going on?" He looked at me when I walked into Allie's room. "Is Dad mad at us?" How do you explain to a boy that's not quite eight, that his dad has decided to duck out of his responsibilities? Is there a correct way?

"Dad needs some time to himself." I felt bad for Mitch, his toys, his clothes, and his life had been taken away by shutting one door, Rex now locked in Mitch's room, where he planned on sleeping. I remembered what it felt like to lose everything around that age. "Let's go to the store and buy you a new set of pajamas." That's all I could think of to say. *Are things replaceable? Are people replaceable?* I didn't see it coming. We laughed together as a family every day. We told each other we loved each other all the time. And now, after a business trip, that's all taken away? *What changed?* I questioned myself.

I gathered Allie's diaper bag, her sip-cup filled with juice, her unawareness to what big changes were in our future, and Mitch's hand. We didn't drive far, but I felt a world away from my life, as we searched Kmart for Toy Story pajamas and a coloring book for each with new crayons. One day at a time. That was all I knew how to do. Strong.

The next six or seven days were spent just going through the motions. Rex didn't want to discuss anything except moving out, so I focused on just that – finding a small apartment near his job in Tampa, helping him select one stainless steel cooking pot, deciding which Corelle dinner plate was leaving, feeling bad for the other cooking pots and Corelle plates that would never be part of a full-set again, a blanket, sheets, his clothes, shoes, and cosmetics. I didn't have any relatives to leave the kids with on moving day, just one week after he had returned from the business trip, a trip that had taken more than his input on how to set-up and run a small college. It was a Saturday when the kids and I followed Rex, he in his car, and the kids and me in mine, both full of Rex's life, only part of which he would carry up the stairs to his new one-bedroom apartment. At first, the kids thought it was fun, Mitch helped carry items up the cement stairs leading to his dad's new home, Allie sat on the carpeted floor, pulling items from boxes, and redecorating the empty-space that surrounded all of us. It wasn't until we had carried up the last box of Rex's life, that first, Mitch realized that his dad

wasn't coming home, and then Allie started to cry, calling his name

on the way to our vehicle for three. It was done. Officially separated.

I didn't know what else to do except keep breathing. I told Rex I

didn't want to file for divorce right away, reminding him that

eighteen years was worth more than that, at least six months, maybe

a year. I felt like he wanted it over – now.

#

Enola May Narducci sorted through what was left of her life:

missing bed-sheets, segregated dishes, missing cookware, empty

hangers, and empty drawers. Everything was reorganized, dispersed,

and spread out to accommodate the empty spots, except for some

empty spots that couldn't be filled. Not now. The days were spent

hustling Mitch off to Lake Myrtle Elementary, dropping off Allie at

Primary Training Daycare, teaching English and work-study classes

to twelfth graders at Land O' Lakes High School, picking

Mitch up from the after-school Place-Program, picking Allie up from

daycare, cooking dinner, doing homework, reading stories, playing

with the dog, shuffling papers, and sorting through pieces of her life after the kids had gone to bed. Enola kept the routine going, kept life going. Breathe.

It wasn't until Rex had been gone for almost six months that Enola came across the manila envelope that Dwayne Summons, the burly private investigator that worked for her biological father, had given her. It was the same envelope she had dumped out in the hotel before heading back to Florida, the one with a photo of Melantha, a deed to a piece of property in Roswell, New Mexico, and the original report of DNA results proving Grover was Enola's biological father. The fourth thing, the safety deposit box key, had been left at the bank eighteen years ago, when Enola cleared its contexts – money spent on a tip for the shuttle driver, Dixie's wedding gift, her own mother's cremation and funeral costs, and a plane ride home. The rest of the money disappeared like the love Rex once had for Enola. Not a trace of either one could be seen. *Just think of happy times. Strong times.* Enola thought to herself and then smiled thinking about the first-class flight home from Asheville eighteen years back. She had flown with Rex and both kids just last year to Asheville, North Carolina to visit Dixie and Ryan Durant. They didn't have any kids, but they were happy, working, raising two lab puppies, and spending time on the weekends at the lake or with extended family.

Enola was envious of the way they always seemed to hold it

together. They reminded her of Barbara and Homer Parrish, both of

which had died of old age over the last ten years, but still having one

thing in common with the Durants – being able to hold it together.

Enola wondered why Rex no longer wanted to hold it together.

Nothing major had happened between them. Nothing. She took a

moment, touching the deed to a piece of unknown land in Roswell.

Wondering. Thinking. Why would Grover Starks have property

there? Was it just a piece of desert? Dusty? Dry? Nothingness? And

then, she thought about Dwayne Summons. *Was he still a private*

investigator? Enola walked to the computer in the living room and

turned it on. Search: Dwayne Summons, Private Investigator, in

Asheville. Within minutes, his office address appeared. Beneath was

a phone number. Enola dialed, not thinking about the time, almost

nine o'clock at night.

"Hello. Summons here." Enola could still hear the burly,

deep-throated man she once met."

"Is this Dwayne Summons?" She asked then realized the

time. "I'm sorry. I didn't realize I was calling so late."

"Don't worry, pretty lady." He had taken on more of a southern drawl since the last time Enola remembered speaking with him. "How can I help you?"

"I'm Enola…Narducci." She hesitated, not even wanting to say the last name. "Do you remember me?"

"Are you kidding?" He sounded surprised. "I can't forget my best friend's daughter." He missed Grover Starks every day. "How's it going?" And then, "Everything okay?"

"I…I don't want to burden you, just your opinion please." Enola felt uncomfortable telling him how her life had turned out. First the good – two great kids, a teacher, a nice house, but then the bad – a husband who went on a business trip, came home, and moved out. He listened, making her feel glad she dialed the number and making her glad she was listening to her instincts.

Dwayne Summons needed to get out of North Carolina for a few weeks anyhow. A little R & R would do him good. He had a way of making Enola's comfort level return, without making her ask, without making *it* be her suggestion. "Don't worry Enola. I'll be down in a few days." He copied her phone number off his caller I.D., all he needed to trace her address, find out which school she taught in, hell, he could even trace Mitch's school and Allie's daycare.

"You don't need to say anything more."

Enola liked the way he didn't make her ask. She suspected Rex was having an affair, but she didn't have to say the words, not to Dwayne Summons. He would uncover Rex's secrets.

Chapter 27

Being married to Rex Narducci, I always thought was an improvement over my childhood. He never hit me. Never. He hit walls. We never lived anywhere during our eighteen-year marriage where there weren't patched reminders that kept me walking on eggshells. CAREFUL. Still, I couldn't imagine being anyone else. I had been a Narducci for eighteen years. Now, I was lying in the darkness, still, and soon to be nameless.

Rex wasn't dead on the outside, but on the inside, he was. I could see it in his eyes. He was no longer there. The kids had only seen him five times in eight months since he had moved out. He was too busy at his job and too busy with his new life. I still hadn't filed the divorce papers. *Why wait any longer?* I wondered. I thought about his five visits. The first was Halloween. Allie was dressed as a witch, and Mitch as a bad-ass pirate. They ran through the neighborhood, Allie slowly and carefully with her not quite two-and-a-half-year-old legs, and Mitch with his still only seven-year-old ones. Rex and I walked about six paces behind, unable to do anything but small talk. *How's your job? How's your apartment?* I still remember asking those questions out loud. And, I still remember his responses, both cold and short. *How's your girlfriend?* That's when I remember his answer being the longest. I imagined eggshells breaking beneath my feet as he answered. His answer was hostile and condescending.

"I don't have a girlfriend." He looked at me with pure hatred, in the October dark street, filled with masked children. I knew he was *one* of them. "You always blow things out of proportion."

I took a deep breath. I didn't care about broken pieces of eggshell anymore. Not now. "I hired a private detective Rex." I watched his step slow. "I have photos of you and a girl." I chose my words carefully. She was a *girl*. Dwayne Summons didn't leave a stone unturned. Within one week after flying down to Tampa, he knew exactly why Rex was leaving – another woman. He knew exactly who she was. She was the eighteen-year-old receptionist at the college in Tampa where Rex had been working as the director, the same receptionist that accompanied him to New Orleans that October, a receptionist that was twenty years younger than him. "Your receptionist is only eighteen years old Rex. She was just being born when we were getting married!" BROKEN SHELLS. "Don't you think it's pretty low to leave a wife and two children for an eighteen-year-old girl?" CRUSH. "Does it make you feel younger?" I thought of Dacey, his perversions. *Had I married another Dacey?*

I watched Rex walk away, back to *our* driveway, *my* driveway, get in *his* car, and drive away. I spent the next hour walking through the neighborhood, smiling at Allie in her black witch dress with purple trim and black hat to match. Smiling, laughing, and holding the hand of her pirate brother, she cautiously walked door after door, not knowing what was on the other side.

Mitch would protect her from any evil spirit that answered. That's

how I had always felt about Rex. I felt he was there to protect me,

take my hand, and lead the way. Now I was standing alone. I

remembered the feeling.

A second visit came on Mitch's eighth birthday, about a

week before Thanksgiving. I felt like I was the only parent. I

attended Mitch's soccer games alone, attended Allie's ballet

rehearsals alone, fed them alone, dressed Allie alone, and seemed to

love them alone. Not until Rex finally returned my call, did I know

whether I would be orchestrating Mitch's birthday party at Laser Tag

in Tampa alone. Rex showed up on time, a new basketball in hand,

and participated by wearing a vest and hiding in the dark, shooting

innocent faces. I wondered how easy it would be for him to lose

control. I most certainly didn't know the man hiding in the dark with

a laser gun. His face glowed yellow from the light of his weapon.

Was he crashing and burning like my mother did? Should I save

him? Could I? I didn't think saving him was worth the risk of losing

the kids or myself. I shot at him in the dark, hitting the red target on

his chest, and then ducked behind a barricade to hide my identity.

Rex's third visit with the children was on Thanksgiving. He called the evening before, inquiring about what I was doing with *the* kids, not *our* kids, just simply – *the* kids. I told him I was taking them to Busch Gardens for the day.

"Can I meet you and the kids there?" I knew he wouldn't stay long by the way he asked the question, again, *the* kids.

"Yes. That will be fine." Polite. The only thing I had left to give him.

I turned the ringer up loud on my cell phone and placed it in my pocket on Thanksgiving.

After two hours of watching the gorillas, and petting the goats just outside the nursery where they kept the newborn babies, I heard the phone ring. "I'll just meet you at *the* house tonight, okay?" I thought about how it used to be *our* house.

"Okay. We'll be home by six p.m." I didn't tell the kids. Maybe it was best if we just enjoyed the day, and maybe it was best they didn't get their hopes up. Animals, cotton candy, and water rides seemed to be enough to distract them from the fact that their dad had stopped being someone they could count on. He did swing by the house around seven that evening – long enough to tuck Allie in her crib that I had recently transformed into a bed by disassembling the side railings and long enough to sit with Mitch in the living room and talk about his favorite animal at Busch Gardens.

"The tiger," Mitch said it with certainty.

"Really? Why the tiger?" Rex asked the eight-year-old who was in his lap.

"Is has stripes that it uses to scare its prey and it jumps real high and fast." He sounded knowledgeable.

"Yes, I can see why you like it." He hugged Mitch, and headed out the door, barely glancing in my direction. I imagined Rex as a tiger: jumping out of a marriage, quickly moving on with his life, and all the while, carefully disguised by stripes I had never noticed before.

On Christmas Day, Rex came over to watch Mitch and Allie open gifts. We had managed to discuss what they wanted on the phone, in enough time for me to go out and get the items, and in enough time for Rex to write out a check for half. I felt sad that we had become *that* type of family. Just write a check: a new Brat's doll for Allie and a hot pink plastic convertible car, a Game-Boy for

Mitch with a Mario Brother's game. Half totaled seventy-two dollars and sixty-eight cents.

The fifth visit was Easter, a time that we were used to coloring eggs as a family. It still was, only the family was smaller. I helped Allie color two eggs: one purple, and one bright pink. She was in charge of the stickers. Her small hands placed a bunny sticker on the purple egg and a vibrant yellow duck on the second. Mitch had the other ten eggs colored by the time she was done. I had already stuffed a dozen plastic eggs with candy and coins. Twenty-four eggs. All of a sudden, I realized I was the one who would hide them. I did. I hid some in tall grass, some along the fence line, some in trees, and some on the other side of a small plastic pool, one under the grill, and one inside the grill. The kids jumped to their feet when Rex arrived, pulling him toward the backyard – anxious for him to watch them find eggs. They found them all. I noticed a few that Mitch would come to, but when he realized they were too easily discovered he would step around them and urge Allie to check that area. I saw a kindness in him that was fresh and untainted. I hoped it would always stay. I knew how cruel the world was, and I wanted to protect him, protect the both of them. Forever.

#

Enola May Narducci filed for divorce on the third of June, 1998.

Ironically it was the date of Melantha Fear's birthday. She would

have been fifty-seven. *I hope that you are happy Mom.* Enola

thought as she handed the paperwork to the attorney's secretary, a

firm familiar with family law, a woman attorney who would make

sure Enola got sole custody of the children, an experienced attorney

who would make sure Enola received a fair amount of child support,

the house, and her choice of holidays with the kids, a referral from

Dwayne Summons.

The divorce was final four months later, October 5, 1998,

almost a year to the exact day since Rex's two big announcements. *I

don't think I've ever loved you.* Enola remembered. And, *I want a

divorce.* She held her head high walking from the Pasco County

Courthouse to her car. Rex would miss moments that could never be

made up: soccer games, ballet recitals, school award ceremonies,

teeth falling out, teeth growing in, scraped knees, training wheels

coming off, candles being blown out, bad dreams, first kisses, prom

dress shopping, laughter, sadness, and questions about life and love.

Rex had made a decision that he would always carry with him, a

decision to be an occasional weekend dad, a once in a while fill-in.
He had set into motion a butterfly effect for the Narducci family.
The new family of three, led by Enola May Starks, would decide
where to live, what schools to go to, what books to read, whether to
have cereal for dinner, official bedtimes, what television shows are
considered appropriate, and what age a teenager had to be to stay out
past ten p.m. *Was this the way it was supposed to be?* Enola
wondered, as the warm October sun caressed her face, as she drove
home to Mitch and Allie, home to *their* house, to the kids who were
instructing their first babysitter on the ins and outs of making frozen
popsicles: cherry for Allie, and grape for Mitch.

Suddenly Enola felt afraid for the first time since marrying
Rex. She realized she was solely responsible for two young lives.
They had no one else. Every decision that Enola made would affect
them. *Kids pay for their parents' mistakes.* She felt the thought burn
into her flesh. She knew better than anyone that it was true. There
was no time to stop the damage that had been done by DNA, by
adult choices, or by society. The only thing Enola could do for her
children would be to teach them to survive, to stand on their own.
Strong. She thought of Grover Starks, her real father, as she gripped

the steering wheel, turning it into Lake Padgett Estates. He would want her to teach his grandchildren how to survive. He wouldn't want her to interfere with their individual paths in life, just teach them the skills needed to best survive those paths.

Enola May Starks pulled into the driveway on Forest View Drive. She turned off the car and sat looking at the large newly constructed house with vaulted ceilings and a pricey mortgage payment in front of her. It wasn't who she was, and it wasn't who she wanted the children to be. They didn't need material items to be happy; they needed love, patience, and guidance. Enola got out of the car and walked to the door, placing her key inside the lock to her life, noticing the sound of feet running, jumping, and carrying bodies that were giggling in excitement. The room was filled with happiness and joy. The darkness couldn't be seen through dark red tongues and purple-stained lips.

Tomorrow she would call Dwayne Summons for four reasons: to thank him again for his investigative work, to reiterate how much she loved having him over for dinner with the kids when he was down, to brag about the attorney he referred her to, and to ask one more favor.

Chapter 28

I held the deed in my left hand before I dialed the phone. I gave a long glance over the page before me, relatively clean, but the white paper was now yellowish from years of being tucked away. I wondered who Grover Starks was. I didn't know anything about him, except that he had never been married, and I was his only biological child. *How old was he?* I wondered, but imagined he was around forty when he died. *What a short life.* I thought about how I had recently turned thirty-seven. *Who's going to take care of the kids if something happens to me?* I wondered if Dixie and Ryan Durant would step in. I needed them too. There was a horrible feeling of being the sole caretaker for two young lives, especially those with no grandparents and a dad that couldn't be counted on. Life was unfair sometimes. I read the deed trying to take my mind off things before dialing Dwayne Summons, before making a plea for closure, before asking if there was some way he could reveal a piece of my genetic make-up through Grover Starks, just a glance into the past to figure out what type of man I came from. I knew he was emotionally strong, but everything else was a mystery. I looked at the paper in my hand, yellowed by time, but holding secrets of my past, some of which I would never learn, because the answers I needed were dead and buried. I looked at the deed, reading it carefully, word for word. It read:

Title Deed

Title Number: 118762

Approximate area: One and one-third acre

This is to certify that Grover Starks or his surviving heir is now registered as the sole proprietor of the plot of land commencing at the southeast corner of the Pecos River of section 30, township 24 south, Chaves County, New Mexico, go 112 degrees west for a distance of 889 feet, then run north a distance of 403 feet, and continue west 256 feet, and then east a distance of 227 feet, then south a distance of 256 feet to the beginning point.

Signed by county clerk

Peter Mosey

Chaves District Land

This twentieth day of May 1951

I dialed the phone. "Dwayne Summons please," my father's blue eyes spoke into the phone.

"Enola, is that you?" He had an ear for detective work.

"I want to thank you again for helping me figure out what happened to my marriage." I was glad I was talking on the phone. I knew the look of regret could still be seen on my face, a look I tried to hide from him, at the dinner with Mitch and Allie, the dinner where truth was revealed minutes before settling at the table, while Mitch and Allie played in the center of what used to be a *family* living room.

"No problem, Enola," he answered, knowing I would have rather not ended a long-term marriage – one I had hoped would last forever.

"You hooked me up with a great attorney too. She crossed all her T's and dotted all her I's." I was very happy with how smoothly it went. I knew I would feel the tiny sting of empty space inside me for a while, but I also knew it could have been made worse. I had heard of divorces that took years, filled with mud-slinging, bitter trials, and endless meetings. I guess I should be glad to just get on with my life.

"I thought she'd make a great match for you. She knew your dad for years. And, I think she helped him out on a few cases where one of the opposing clients moved to Florida." He paused. "I still miss your father."

"I don't mean to burden you." I tried to think of what I wanted to say. "But, I miss him too." I paused. "Especially now with everything that has happened." I knew he understood what I meant.

"He was a great man Enola." His voice left no room for question. "I wish you would have gotten to know him better."

"I do too." I wondered how I could – now. "Is there any way I could learn about him?" I tried to be more specific. "I don't even know his date of birth, where he was born, if he had good parents." I looked down at the deed still in my hand. "And, did you know one of the items in that envelope was a deed to a piece of land in Roswell, New Mexico?"

"I'll admit I looked through the manila envelope before giving it to you." He laughed innocently. "P.I. habit." His speech was full of questions. "I don't know why he had a piece of land in New Mexico. I knew Grover from Detroit. He never mentioned living anywhere else." He spoke into the phone with an inquisitive tone. "I don't remember if either one of us ever discussed anything about our childhoods." He sounded disappointed. "I think sometimes you can know someone for twenty years and not know them at all."

I thought about how true that last statement was. I thought I knew Rex's character inside and out. I thought he would die for me. I would have argued with anyone about his loyalty, his passion for life, and his ability to survive any situation. None of those things were part of his soul. He wouldn't save me from a burning building. He had proved that loyalty had no meaning in his life. And, his passion for life couldn't be seen in his brown eyes anymore. He had lost his passion, and with it his survival would become harder.

"I agree with you there." I tried not to laugh about Rex. This wasn't about him. It was about me, and the biological father that I hadn't gotten a chance to know. I wanted that chance before it was too late, before his best friend was too old to go digging around for information.

"Do you want me to dig up what I can on your father?" He paused. "Maybe even on the deed?" He was good at not making me ask directly.

"I could use your help." I thought about how he once had a twenty-year friendship with my dad, Grover Starks. "I know you're invested in this and will find out everything you possibly can."

"Fax me a copy of the deed and give me a couple of months. Okay?" He paused.

"Thanks Dwayne." I hoped it was okay to call him by his first name.

"I don't mind." I could tell he didn't. "There are some parts of him I want to know more about too, some parts I shouldn't have ignored for twenty years."

"I'll fax it to you tomorrow." I thought about how people don't ever really know someone. "I appreciate you."

"You're family to me." He meant it.

"Thanks Dwayne. So are you." I meant it too.

#

November and December passed quickly. Mitch turned nine that November, his blue eyes seemed to sparkle even on the darkest days. He played soccer several times a week at the Collier Recreational Center in Land O'Lakes, Florida, had a few close friends that would sometimes sleep over, adored his dog that had become old somewhere in the middle of a divorce, a long-haired golden Collie named Lady, was in the middle of fourth grade at Lake Myrtle Elementary School, smiled often, guarded his baby sister with his life, drew characters that he created from his imagination, and would crack up at *South Park*.

Allie was a happy three-and-a-half-year-old little girl with brown hair and chocolate eyes. She was still in pre-school, would suck her thumb constantly, laugh at her brother's wit and charm, help build forts in the living room, curl up with Enola on the couch to read children's poetry, and made imaginary entrees from her plastic kitchen set, which seemed to take up a large part of the living room.

Enola adored them both. She couldn't imagine life without them, their smiles, and their laughter. They were the two people in life that kept Enola going, kept her breathing each day, and gave her a reason to be strong in her career and as a mom. Enola May Starks, a name she was happy had become legal at the time of the divorce, a name she chose to represent her strength and past, was thirty-seven, and had just started dating on the weekends, when the kids would visit their dad and his now third wife.

Wife two, the eighteen-year-old, didn't last very long. Drug problems and cheating soon surrounded Rex Narducci. Enola wondered if he missed their marriage, if he missed the stability that they had made their way of life, although, if he did, he didn't let on. Being friendly wasn't his forte. He avoided eye contact, spoke directly to the children, and gave Enola the cold shoulder whenever possible. He'd cancel weekends here and there, leaving Enola with the kids sometimes for months without a break, but she never seemed to mind. They were her whole life.

She didn't need more. She lived off their smiles and laughter. She'd sit on the couch drinking imaginary cups of tea from Allie's green plastic cups and listening to Mitch talk about the characters he had drawn. Sometimes she felt like she lived in a world with just them – no one else.

That's when the phone rang. A new year, a new beginning, and now a piece of her past that would help her make some connection to the name she had chosen.

"Hello." She recognized the area code, but knew it wasn't Dixie's number, as she chatted with Dixie and Ryan Durant weekly, and had their number memorized.

"Hey Enola. It's Dwayne Summons." The voice was friendly and full of life. "I've found out a lot of information." He paused. "Do you have time to sit and chat?"

"Yes, Dwayne." She was excited to hear whatever he had uncovered, a glimpse into her biological father's past, and a glimpse into herself.

"Grover was born in Roswell in 1936. His father was a lawyer in Detroit, Michigan just after the turn of the century, but died just before his only child was born in 1936, so Grover's mother moved to Roswell to be with her only living relative – her father, a lieutenant in the Roswell Fire Station, and to give birth to her son. Grover Howard Starks." He paused allowing Enola to soak it all in.

"So, he never knew his father?" She thought about how much they needed each other. "Did his mother ever remarry?" She thought about Grover, growing up in Roswell, New Mexico in the late thirties and forties, without a dad, without a brother or sister, living with his mom and grandfather.

"No, she never remarried." He read from his notes. "His mother's father didn't live very long either." He calculated numbers in his head. "He died when Grover was eleven, 1947, at the age of fifty-seven, the same year the Roswell UFO incident occurred, leaving his daughter and grandson to fend for themselves on a piece of land." He thought about the deed, wondered when he would be receiving the information he had sent for from the Chaves County Clerk's Office.

"What was the Roswell UFO incident about?" She had only heard a few people in her lifetime mention it, one being her high school science teacher, but that was over twenty years ago, before falling in love with Rex's brown eyes.

"There was a top-secret airbase in Roswell, New Mexico. It was referred to as Area 51." Dwayne had always been interested in extraterrestrial life, so he knew most of the details by heart. "About seventy-five miles away from Roswell a flying disc crashed. The army covered it up by saying it was a weather balloon, but I've always thought differently. I've seen documentaries where people say they were threatened to remain silent."

"Wow, my dad lived through some hard times." Enola thought about Roswell, its secrets, her own mother's secrets, and Rex's secrets. *The world is full of secrets.* She supposed. "His mother must have been a strong woman. Maybe that's where he got his strength."

"I think so. She only lived to be forty-one, a short life, and a lot of hard times." He looked at the paper he was holding, trying to make sure he had told Enola everything he had discovered – so far.

"Dwayne, I needed this information. It helps me get through my own life, having just a glimpse of where I came from." She thought about Grover, only eighteen when his mother died, like herself. Alone. "How did he end up back in Detroit?"

"After his mother died, he went back to Detroit." He was anxious to get more information about the deed. "I imagine the deed is for the property where his mom raised him." And then, "I'll let you know as soon as I get the information from the Chaves County Clerk's office. But, for now, I'll mail you a copy of everything we discussed."

"I can't tell you how much I appreciate you." She thought about how he'd always been a phone call away. "I'm glad we're family."

"Me too." They hung up the phone, but somehow Enola still felt a connection.

Chapter 29

The silence of a March night was broken when I woke up at one a.m. I woke up to my own screams, worried that the kids had heard, and grateful when I became alert enough to realize they hadn't. I vividly remember something that appeared to be tiny winged insects biting chunks of my stomach away. Crunch. Bright blues, light greens, dark greens, and even a violet one. I hurriedly stood up in the darkness, brushing the neon glows from my skin, imagining them still on me, even as I struggled to find the light switch. There was nothing there.

Only my imagination and thoughts that had run wild had woken me. I knew I was struggling with the balance between being a good mom and having a life for myself. I was spending some time dating, but unsure that I wanted anyone in my life around the kids. *Should I just be alone?* I wondered. *Should I wait until the kids are grown?* I thought about another call I had made to Dwayne Summons in Asheville. Sometimes we just talked on the phone about the kids. We had been calling each other for no reason – except to share life's ups and downs. I'd fill him in on Mitch's soccer game and Allie's fight at pre-school over a doll. She always won.

He shared the name of a woman he had been dating. He said I would like her, and that I'd have to bring the kids and come up around the holidays for a visit, to meet her, and to visit Dixie and Ryan. I agreed. I shared the name of a man I had seen three or four times in Florida. Probably a mistake. I had forgotten I was talking to a private investigator.

I didn't expect Uncle Dwayne, at least that's what the kids now called him on the phone, to investigate the man I had seen occasionally in Florida, run his background information, but he insisted. *Better safe than sorry.* I remembered him saying. A week after our last phone call, and a night after I dreamed of being attacked by insects, the phone rang. Dwayne Summons. Private Investigator. Family uncle.

"I've got a lot of information for you Enola." He sounded happy – happy he was so good at his job – happy that nothing escaped his eye, especially at his age.

"You do?" I was happy to hear from him. He had just celebrated his sixty-third birthday, the same age that Grover would have been if he were still alive. "What kind of information?"

"Well…first, let me say thanks for the birthday card from you and the kids. I can't believe you sent one that says Happy Birthday Uncle." He laughed. "I was so happy when I opened it."

"You're welcome." I thought about his burly laugh. "The kids love you and want to see you." I paused. "I love you too."

"I love you guys." He sounded like a father, even though he had never been one. "How's Dwight, the man you've been seeing?"

"Is that what you're calling about Mr. Detective?" I smiled into the phone. "Did you find out some dirt on my Mr. Wonderful?"

"He was arrested in Maine for OUI when he was in his twenties and for a DUI in South Carolina when he was thirty." *Red Flag.* I thought.

"I guess it doesn't make a difference whether it starts with an "O" or with a "D" it's still drunk driving." He could tell I was disappointed.

"Enola, it doesn't mean anything." He was trying to reassure me. "Just keep your eyes open." He paused. "He hasn't had any other arrests."

"I don't need an alcoholic." I thought about how I felt when I was with him. Warm. Alive. "I hope that's not what I found."

"Keep your eyes open." He did sound like a father. "Just be careful."

"Okay…Dad." I laughed.

"I love you Enola…like a daughter." He said it with emotion. "Okay, now on to other news." He paused. "I finally got the deed information from Roswell."

"Hey, that's great!" I wanted to hear what he had found out. *Was it the property that Grover had grown up on for his entire childhood?* I wondered. "Let's hear it."

"It's a little over an acre and a third. It is mostly desert but has a lot of wildlife on it and a spring-fed creek loaded with fish." His voice went up when he said the word *fish*. "Bass." He looked at the report, which he had waited long enough for. "That entire area is loaded with deer and wild ducks." He sounded excited.

"I take it you've got an outdocrsy side to you." I smiled into the phone. "It does sound beautiful."

"It sounds like the perfect spot to build on." He announced. "It reminds me that I need to slow things down a bit myself and start thinking about hanging things up."

"Are you thinking about retirement?" I asked.

"I am reminded each day that I'm getting older." He whispered into the phone. "I think it's time I finally live out my days with someone special."

I knew he was referring to the woman he had been dating, the one he had mentioned during several phone conversations over the last couple of months, someone special he had met at the courthouse in Asheville. She was from Kentucky, a newly divorced woman in the research department at the courthouse in Asheville, a sixty-year-old face that made him feel alive. I could hear the sparkle in his voice whenever he said her name. *Margaret.*

"I think you deserve to retire and be happy." I thought about my own life. I was alone now, raising two kids, and the only man who had made me smile in over a year was Dwight Leary.

"She has family in Kentucky." He sounded like they had discussed the possibility of a future together. "I've wondered how it would be to live somewhere else." He paused. "I've been in Asheville for about forty years now."

"Don't leave town without staying in touch," I said it into the phone.

"You'll be the first to know." I could hear voices in the background. More clients.

"Thanks Dwayne." I knew he had to go. "Thanks for researching everything for me." I pictured the spring-fed creek and ducks floating on the top.

"I'll send you follow-up copies." He sounded like he was in a hurry. "Love you."

"I love you too."

#

The Asheville police called Enola May Starks to close out a murder investigation during the first of April 1999; they called to ask about a Mr. Dwayne Summons who was shot to death by a man that he had been hired to investigate. Enola was the last person he spoke with on the phone according to police records. They just wanted to ask her a few questions, wanted to know if she heard arguing between the man who had entered his office, as they were hanging up the phone, and wanted to know if Dwayne Summons had any idea his life was about to end. Enola was in shock when she got the call. *How much more can I possibly take?* She spent the night crying, crying about Dwayne's dreams of retiring, crying for the love of his life that would no longer have him, and wondering if the man who had tried so hard to help her was at peace. *Did Margaret, the woman he loved, know about me?* Enola wondered. *Did Dwayne have a funeral?* She thought about how she never received the last hardcopy of information he had promised to send, now only details of a spring-fed creek, bass, and deer danced in her head. All traces of Dwayne Summons were gone. Enola didn't have the time or the means to drive to Roswell, New Mexico from Pasco County, Florida. She had two kids to raise and a life to get on with. Connecting to her past was something she would have to put on hold. The kids were young – too young to stop life and focus on putting pieces of her past together. She thought about Dwight Leary, how he had asked to move in, how he had told her he loved her, and how the kids would laugh when he was around. It was time to get serious about raising children. They needed her. She wouldn't maneuver around Dwight's offer to get serious anymore.

A few days passed before Enola May Starks called Dwight on the phone, before she could make her fingers dial, afraid of decisions, and afraid of not making them.

"Hi Dwight." She had known him for almost six months now, since the divorce was final, since allowing herself to date. "How's the restaurant coming?" She knew he had been working extra hours installing the glass windows for a new restaurant in the Brandon area.

"Hey darling." He rarely called her by her name. *Darling.* Enola remembered. "We just finished this morning."

"So, where's your next job?" Enola thought about how they sometimes did glasswork in Brandon, sometimes in Tampa, and sometimes closer to Pasco County where Enola and the kids lived.

"It's off of Livingston Avenue…a new convenience store."

He wanted to see her. It had been a week, but he felt like she wasn't that interested, remembering that the last time he saw her all she talked about was the property in Roswell and how it was loaded with all kinds of wildlife, redirecting his conversation about moving in together.

"That's only about twenty minutes from Lake Padgett Estates, where I live." He knew that but wasn't going to bring it up.

"I guess you're right." That's all he wanted to say.

"Would you like to stay with me while you're doing that job?" She realized the offer sounded temporary, and she tried to correct her mistake. "And, all future jobs?"

"Darling, you mean it?" She didn't know what she meant. She just knew that chasing rainbows and trying to find the pot of gold to make up for her past, wasn't what she was supposed to be doing right now.

"Yes." She eliminated the hesitation she knew was in her voice. "I want you to live with me."

"Help me move in tomorrow?" He sounded excited. "Okay?"

She thought about how tomorrow, was only a few hours away.

Nervousness set in.

"Yes." That's all she could say without being obvious.

Dwight Todd Leary moved in on the tenth of April 1999.

Nibble.

Chapter 30

Dwight lived with us for ten months. Ten months of no child support

from Rex, ten months of canceled weekends with the kids, ten

months of foreclosure notices, and ten months of just trying to

survive. Marrying Dwight seemed like the logical thing to do. The

kids needed a father. I needed a husband. And, we needed stability: a

new home with a more affordable mortgage and a routine where two

parents got to watch Mitch play his new passion of JV football and

Allie grow into a kindergartner. We got married on February 14,

2000. We drove to Asheville, North Carolina, where Dixie and Ryan

welcomed Dwight like they had known him for years, where my

mother had taken her own life, where Dacey had beaten me and

broken my knee cap, where my biological father had tumbled off a

mountain to his death with the help of my mother, and where

Dwayne Summons, the world's best private investigator, was

murdered in his own office. Asheville. The mountains held secrets.

We got married in the Durant's living room. Mitch, now ten,

walked me from the bedroom to the living room, arm and arm, his

ten-year-old body dressed in a pair of black dress pants, a black

dress shirt and a bright red tie. He smiled the entire way, smiled at

the way I was trying to start over, almost thanking me for my

courage to lead, to pick up the pieces. Allie walked a few steps

ahead of us, constantly looking back, trying not to drop the basket of

red rose petals that she dipped her small hands in, hands that would

turn five in another four months, removing just enough to scatter a

path, showing me the way to the front of the living room, near the

fireplace, near a notary, near Dixie, near Ryan, and near Dwight.

Dwight smiled at me as I walked closer to him, smiled at Allie for

the job well done, and smiled at Mitch for giving his mother a chance at another marriage. Allie became nervous as we turned to stop at the front of the room, grabbing the hand of Dixie, fidgeting in her tiny white tights and dark red velvet dress trimmed in lace and a white-collar. She looked at me, unsure of what was about to happen, but trusting that I knew what I was doing. *I hope she's right.* I remembered thinking.

I was wearing a dress I had purchased at Dillard's, the length flirted with my knees, the ivory-colored long sleeves hugged my arms, and the bodice worked up from a flowing river of chiffon into an intricate pattern of white beads. I didn't have baby's breath in my hair this time; instead, I wore a small simple bridal veil that matched my shoes. I looked at Dwight, still smiling, his outfit matching Mitch's, watched how he looked at me, and could see how he wanted a new start to his life too. He had worked hard to find a permanent job running heavy equipment with the county, great hours, steady pay, nothing to get rich off of, but a good job for someone with a family. *Family.* I thought about how that was the one thing I had tried my entire life to have. It had been a challenge to find it since the day I was born, and I knew from experience that it was even more of a challenge to keep.

"We are gathered here today to bring together a family." The notary read from a sheet of paper that I had given him. "We present two loving adults, Dwight Todd Leary and Enola May Starks, to join hands and become husband and wife."

I stared into Dwight's blue eyes, much lighter and brighter than mine. I wondered if I was making the right choice. I felt myself doubting, but I stopped quickly as the notary continued to read.

"Dwight, do you promise to love Enola and to take her as your wife?"

"I do." He smiled.

"Enola, do you promise to love Dwight and to take him as your husband?"

"I do." My smile could be heard and seen.

"At this time, I would like to ask Dwight, Enola, Mitch, and Allie to join hands." Dixie and Ryan helped the kids to form a small circle with us. "By notarizing the marriage license and witnessing this event, I now pronounce you husband and wife." I realized how some of the biggest moments in one's life can take the least amount of time, how some things are just a formality, how we only needed to sign in front of a notary to become husband and wife, and how ceremonies are just for our mental notebooks. *Closure.* I thought about how much that word had come to mean to me in my life.

We left the Durant home after a small reception in their dining room, after the cutting of a small wedding cake, my first one, and after testing who would be able to gently feed a piece of cake to the other, without smearing, without coloring outside of the lines. Dwight went first, a small piece of white cake with red and white frosting in his hand, gently sliding it into my mouth, and finally kissing me on the nose. Then it was my turn, holding a somewhat bigger piece, covered mostly with white frosting, minus most of the red trim, my hand carried it to his mouth, but slid over his lower chin and suspecting lips as they grew closer. Everyone laughed. Allie let her defensive uncertainties go, and joined in, giggling at her step-dad's messy appearance.

We left the kids with Dixie and Ryan for two evenings, making our way to Chimney Rock, to spend our first night in a log cabin bed and breakfast that Patrick Swayze had once stayed in. We checked in as husband and wife, spent the night making love, deep in the western mountains of North Carolina, surrounded by nature, singing creek beds, deer, raccoon, opossums, and trails that had been explored by visitors and locals, leading up to the highest point in the area – Chimney Rock.

The next morning, we climbed the hardest trail to the top. Dwight pulled me up over rocks and peaks; together we balanced and wiggled our way through obscured paths. I suddenly felt I had made the right choice, trusting my gut I fell in love with him deeper than I had ever allowed myself to go before.

#

Enola May Starks-Leary felt she had reestablished some of the missing balance in her life. Somewhat. She spent the next four years of her life, reconstructing holiday traditions, doing family-of-four activities, moving to a more affordable house in Spring Hill, teaching high school, and just being a mom. Breathe. Strong.

Enola loved the holidays, a chance to give the kids things they could carry into their future: coloring Easter Eggs, Fourth of July fireworks, October pumpkin patches, Thanksgiving turkeys stuffed with Enola's crème of chicken bread stuffing, and picking out and cutting down just the right tree for Christmas at a tree farm in Dade City. The weekends that Enola and Dwight had the kids were spent fishing, at the beach, in a boat, camping on an island near

Anclote, at the zoo, rummaging through flea markets, or at a theme park.

They had settled into a brand new three-bedroom mobile home on a big piece of property in Spring Hill, with a fireplace, all new appliances, and a big wooden porch that Dwight built by hand. He seemed to fix everything that broke and mend everything that needed mending. He came home at the same time every day, kissed Enola every morning, and made love to her every night. He helped Mitch work on an old go-cart he had picked up at a garage sale, taught Allie to ride a bike, and built a chicken coop for a pet duck that Allie had to have. He loved being a part of something he had never had. His dad died of alcoholism when he was only a teenager, and he never felt that he fit in anywhere. Enola knew that feeling more than anyone. There were things about him that Enola liked; two things were his attention to detail and his ability to bounce back.

Enola had been married to Rex for eighteen years, nineteen including the year of separation, and had known him even longer, and never once in all that time, did he ask about the shape of her nose or the protruding bone from her left kneecap. Dwight noticed everything. He knew Enola's father had taken a baseball bat to her kneecap, knew because he asked about the shape of her knee, and knew because he was the first one she would share the truth with. He also noticed her nose, ever so slightly bent, hardly noticeable, but a centimeter off, and a secret reminder that she had once hit the car window after a sudden stop when she was about ten years old, a deliberate punishment for not wearing a seatbelt after being told to do so. Dwight noticed the little things in life: Enola's favorite flower, a daisy; Enola's favorite ice cream, butter pecan; and the song she would always turn up the loudest on the car radio, *You're my best friend* by Tim McGraw. He loved to go shopping, to the movies, travel, explore, hike, and do family activities. Enola felt lucky to have him, until four years into the marriage, then everything seemed to come to a screeching halt. Everything.

It was the second time since they had been together that Dwight didn't come home. The first time, about two years earlier, Enola worked through it with him, sympathized with him, and assisted him in getting help. Dwight started attending AA meetings a couple of times each week, gave up the occasional beer at a Mexican restaurant, and conceded to the fact that he was a binge drinker like his father, and would die like his father of an early death if he didn't turn things around. Meetings helped. Until he stopped going, until trying to be normal became too much stress for him, and then he got his third DUI, an overnight stay in jail, and lost his driver's license. Shortly after that, his job found out, and he was let go. He needed a driver's license to run their heavy equipment. He felt empty, spinning out of control, and left one evening in his truck, one he had no license to drive, leaving two kids at home alone, while Enola was attending a play with a few coworkers, a rare outing, probably the first in over a year. A Broadway play in Tampa at the convention center turned out to be the opening act for a second divorce.

"I'm on my way home," Enola spoke into her cell phone from the back of a coworker's Ford Expedition carrying a total of six women. She was surprised that Mitch had answered the phone, instead of Dwight, but figured he was building something in the shed out back.

"Okay Mom," Mitch answered. "Don't worry. I'm taking care of Allie."

"What do you mean?" She sounded confused. "Where's Dwight?" The kids sometimes called him Dad Dwight. He seemed to like it.

"He left in his truck to get something from Home Depot about three hours ago, but he hasn't returned." Mitch was turning sixteen in one month, still very protective of his sister, and not one to panic too often. Allie had just turned ten years old, adored her brother, and was now at the age where she took notice of everything. Even Allie knew something was wrong.

"Mitch, thank-you." Enola looked at the clock inside the car where she was a passenger. It was nearly eleven at night. *Home Depot had been closed for two hours.* She thought. *He's drinking.* She knew it was going to be a long night. "I'm being dropped off at my car soon and will be home in about forty minutes." Enola could hear Allie crying in the background, crying because life was getting ready to change. Again.

Chapter 31

I woke up in the middle of the night feeling like pieces of my life

were being nibbled at. I studied the bedroom clock enough to realize

I had only been laying down for about an hour. Before that, I had

been on the phone with police verifying that Dwight hadn't been in

an accident, had driven up and down Hudson Avenue searching the

route to Home Depot, Mitch riding shotgun, and Allie sleeping in the

backseat of my car, finally content that not all adults leave her. Now,

I sat up to the sound of a key entering the back door. Nibble.

I struggled to make it to the light switch by the master bathroom. I could smell the strong odor of whiskey ripping at my insides. The man I had grown to depend on entered the bedroom in someone else's body, his hands grabbing for the edge of the bed, and his weight settling into it. I could feel something inside of me, ripping at the flesh lining my lungs, as I struggled to breathe. Everything came to a slow. All of my feelings of fear and distrust filled the room. He was in no position to talk, unable to move, passing out, leaving me standing alone in the dark. It was that moment that I knew. It would be a forever battle living with Dwight Leary. *Is this what I want the kids to learn is acceptable?* I wondered.

The next couple of weeks were hard. We talked about everything: how he no longer wanted to hold it together, how he no longer wanted to go to AA meetings, and how he didn't want to pretend he was someone he wasn't. He wanted his old life back in Maine: wanted the small town he grew up in, wanted the familiarity of knowing everyone, wanted to be like his brothers who, he added, were functional alcoholics, wanted to spend time around his widowed mother who had recently opened her home to a man released after serving ten years in prison on a child molestation charge, and wanted to spend the remainder of his days in a city that was built around a few small bars, a gas station, and a post office. He wanted his life back, the one he had spent the last four years of our marriage trying to escape.

It was a Saturday when I drove him to the bus station in Tampa off Cass Street. He reached over, kissing me good-bye on my cheek, thanking me for handling the divorce paperwork, and wishing me the best. I cried all the way home, collapsing on the shag carpet in the living room when I entered the mobile home, allowing my face to bury its sadness in the welcoming shade of beige, for what seemed like hours, until I was unable to cry anymore. I sat up when I realized it was Sunday, realized I had a sixteen-year-old and ten-year-old that still needed me. I couldn't give them the white picket fence scenario. I couldn't give them a two-parent household. I had tried and failed, like my legs that refused to let me stand, still folded at the knees, still holding me in an upright sitting position, the majority of my weight still unable to move, a prisoner from the moment I was born, part of a plan that would destroy lives by decisions. *Was I cursed from the moment I was born? Was there some overpowering authority that had made me responsible*

for the devastation that had surrounded me? Was it my fault that I

was conceived out of wedlock? Was it my fault that my mother

committed suicide? Was it my existence that made her kill Grover? I

screamed at God. *Did I deserve to be beaten? Am I not capable of*

having anyone love me?

"Fuck you God!" The thunder in my voice shook the mobile

home it seemed. "I don't believe in you!" The tears poured down my

face. "You've never helped me!" I could barely breathe. I laid back

down, this time face up, looking at the ceiling, shouting at whatever

entity hid behind it. "Why am I alone?" I screamed at the ceiling.

"Why are you punishing me?" Nothing answered back. I felt the pain

in my stomach. Nibble. Swallow. There seemed to be bits of me

disappearing while I was still alive. I moved my hands down to my

stomach, feeling the tiny fluttering movements inside. I couldn't

move. I found it harder to breathe. I turned my head slightly toward

the back-dining room windows and was able to catch a glance of the

eight-a.m. sun over the top of the shed. If it got up each morning so

could I, then I sat up, wiped the tears from my face using my already

soaked shirt, directed my legs to push me into a standing position, and turned to face the sun directly at my face. I could feel the warmth of its rays coming through the back windowpanes, could feel Grover Starks' presence. *Strong.* I walked toward the window. I pictured Grover and Dwayne Summons in some magical land together. I touched the windowpane with my hand, sticky from my tears. It felt extra cool and crisp for a January morning. I knew what I had to do. Baby steps: take a shower, get dressed, get in the car, pick up the kids – from Rex and wife number three at four p.m. – bring them home, explain why Dad Dwight no longer lives with us, feed them dinner, talk about their weekend at their father's, and help get them ready for school. I took a deep breath. I wondered what damage I had done to the kids. *Why did I get married so soon?* I wondered. *Why didn't I listen to Dwayne Summons' warning about someone having two DUIs? Why wasn't I more honest to myself when Dwight got his third DUI?* I took a real deep breath and turned on the shower, stepping in, allowing the water to wash off all my mistakes, letting the hot water kill any demons that I felt had surrounded me. I stood underneath the water until it ran cold, until the hot water heater had exhausted itself, and until I promised myself that crying had to stop. Today I would wear my favorite pair of jeans

and a soft pullover V-neck that reminded me how good comfort felt.
I brushed my long medium brown hair back into a ponytail, noticing
the mahogany that my stylist at the Allure Hair Salon added in for
me a couple weeks earlier. I put on my blue studded earrings to
match my eyes, and I wore a necklace that showed off a *Mom*
pendant that the kids had picked out two Christmases ago. I looked
in the mirror, trying to forgive myself for any mistakes I had made,
trying to forgive myself for not being perfect, and trying to figure
out how to make another transition okay for the kids. At least this
time, I was living in a more affordable place, a mortgage I could pay
on my own, a lawn I could mow on my own, a safe haven for me and
the children. *At least the deed's in my name.* I thought, smiling at
Dwayne Summons' suggestion. *I listened to you on that one.* I
looked up at the sky that I had cursed at earlier when I thought the
words. *I hope you are up there, God. I need your help.* I thought the
words that I couldn't say aloud. I grabbed my purse, cell-phone, and
keys, and then made sure the door to the Narducci-Starks' home was
locked behind me. It was time to treat myself to my favorite drink:
unsweet green iced tea from Starbucks. I had to make sure I was
recharged before picking up the kids, had to make sure I could

handle Rex's cold habit of getting up when he saw my car pull in his driveway only to unlock the door and disappear into another room. His goal over the last five years had become avoidance, something he did quite well. *At least he was good at something.* I thought, and then quickly wondered if God, if he were there, appreciated sarcasm.

After going through the drive-up, I drove slowly on the Veteran's Expressway, sipping my green ice tea, wondering how to approach things with the kids. I knew they both liked Dwight, maybe even loved him, but I didn't know how they would react to the way he had left, simply disappearing, without so much as a good-bye. Gone. I pulled into Rex's driveway, saw him get up to unlock the front door before I could even exit my car, and watched him disappear from sight. Jessica, his third wife, said hello as I entered, calling Mitch and Allie, the smaller of which ran and hugged me immediately. I felt they both loved their dad, but I also felt that they didn't trust him. I was surrounded by stories about television and the community park playground as we got in the car. Mitch couldn't wait to tell me about how he watched Allie, saving her from a neighborhood bully.

"At the park?" I asked.

"Yes, the kid thought he was going to pick on her." He laughed.

"Where was your dad?" I wondered if Rex spent any time with them when they visited.

"He stayed home with Jessica," Allie announced from the backseat.

"What did the kid do?" I questioned.

"He told her to get off the slide," Mitch announced. "He said it was his slide and that she needed a permit to go on it."

"What did you do?" I asked Mitch's sixteen-year-old very protective side.

"I simply informed him that the entire playground was *our* playground. And that he was no longer welcomed there." He smiled a cocky smile.

"He went for that?" I asked

"Mitch was going to stab him!" Allie informed me from the backseat, not noticing Mitch's facial expression to keep that detail secret.

"Mitch, did you bring your pocketknife with you?" I asked in a serious tone.

"I always carry it with me, Mom." I knew he did. I knew he slept with a pocketknife in his room, under his pillow. *What was he afraid of?* I wondered. *Had life already filled him with distrust?* I thought about the days he used to smile and laugh and trust everyone. *Were those days gone?* I wondered. *Did the sins of his father take his innocence? Did I?*

We had almost reached home before anyone noticed Dwight's absence or at least spoke of it.

"Where's Dad Dwight?" Allie's ten-and-a-half-year-old body asked.

"He's gone back to Maine for a while." I had a hard time lying to the kids. I thought about the time Allie asked about Santa Claus. She was six. *Does he sneak in here at night Mommy?* I remembered the question like it was yesterday. Only it had been over four years. *No, Allie, the parents put the presents under the tree now, because Santa couldn't do it all.* I thought about how it was a half-truth, sort of like going to Maine for a while. Half-truth.

"Are you guys getting a divorce?" Mitch asked without beating around the bush. I knew they both had caught on to the fact that Dwight was having a problem with alcohol, having a problem

attending AA meetings, and having a problem coming home.

I looked in the rearview mirror to see what effect the question

had on Allie. She looked out the window, trying to spot her pet duck

as we pulled in the yard. "Yes." I didn't elaborate. I didn't know

what else to say.

Allie opened the car door the moment I shut off the engine,

laughing at the duck, instructing it to get out of its water dish, and

reaching for the garden hose to fill it up again. *Maybe she's not

paying attention to the conversation.* I thought.

"You deserve better, Mom," Mitch announced. "We're fine

on our own." He looked at me. "We don't need him." I looked at

him, my eyes fighting tears, reached for his shoulders and pulled him

close. *Maybe you gave me things I didn't notice.* I thought as I

looked at the sky.

"Mommy, look, the duck is so happy I gave her extra water.

She's swimming!" I thought about how the duck was alone but

happy, happy to have the kids, and happy just to have water. I was

glad she was paying so much attention to the duck, glad she wasn't

part of the conversation that was occurring with Mitch.

"That duck loves you Allie." I looked at her dark brown eyes, full of fascination, and full of life. I thought about how resilient kids are – the bravest people in the world.

"I know Mommy." She looked over at Mitch. "So, does my brother." Then she looked at me. "And, so do you." She reached in her pocket pulling out a piece of paper. Unfolding it, she looked at me and smiled. "Gvgeyui." *Ga-gay-u-ee.* She said it perfectly.

I started to cry, remembering I had told her the story about two weeks ago, about my grandmother, about how my sister and she always said it, and about how no one ever said it to me.

Mitch smiled. "I helped Allie look it up on the internet at Dad's…so she could practice saying it."

"Gvgeyui," I said it to both sets of eyes. And then I said it to the sky.

THE END

Sherie L. Howard began keeping journals at the age of ten. Her first published work did not appear until the age of twenty-four, and included a smorgasbord of topics, everything from opportunities to travel aboard, to workplace safety. Sherie earned a BS in English Language Arts from the University of Central Florida and M.Ed. from National-Louis University, both of which she used to teach college writing classes and high school English. Sherie has traveled throughout all of the USA's lower forty-eight states, and visited South America, Mexico, Canada, Spain, France, Italy and North Africa. As an autobiographical fiction writer, Sherie takes readers on her travels, while skillfully weaving in pertinent and useful topics that have relevance in people's lives – mental illness, addiction, infidelity, physical abuse, sexual abuse, criminal homicide, parent-child relationships, adult relationships, and emotional, physical, and spiritual battles that people face during different stages of personal growth. **Sherie L. Howard** currently lives in Washington state with her dog Miles. *Voices of Fear* is her first novel in a series.

www.ingramcontent.com/pod-product-compliance
Lightning Source LLC
Chambersburg PA
CBHW061313170626
46817CB00001B/171